Books by Genella DeGrey

Single Titles

A Touch of Destiny
Whisked Away
Cat and Mouse
Unmasked
Joust of Hearts
The Trouser Game

I0542488

The Trouser Game

ISBN # 978-1-78686-169-6

©Copyright Genella DeGrey 2017

Cover Art by Posh Gosh ©Copyright 2017

Interior text design by Claire Siemaszkiewicz

Totally Bound Publishing

Published in 2017 by Totally Bound Publishing, Think Tank, Ruston Way, Lincoln, LN6 7FL, United Kingdom.

THE TROUSER GAME

GENELLA DEGREY

Dedication

Dedication: To every woman (including myself) who has made a mistake (or came close to it) whether for honor, duty or just plain stubbornness.
The head and the heart should work together, not one exclusive of the other.
Special acknowledgment:
To Emma Thompson for her brilliant and boundless talents. She is an inspiration to any woman whose goal it is to entertain.

Chapter One

St. Helens, England
Summer 1895

"Aren't you going to welcome me home, Miles?" Jillian Kelley, having just arrived from university in the United States, addressed the man whom she'd been intrigued with throughout her youth.

He stood at the opposite end of her mother's formal parlor, unblinking. He was as handsome as Jillian remembered, with his light characteristics and sky-blue eyes—perhaps his facial features had grown a little more mature, but she didn't mind. She and Miles would grow old together and outward appearances would mean nothing with a love as strong as theirs would be.

Standing here with him now, she felt the familiar stirrings in her breast of the unrequited love she'd harbored for him for over half of her twenty-three years. She supposed, if she was pressed, her former determination to win him could be considered an obsession when viewed in a harsher light.

However, none of that mattered now. The status of their association was indubitably about to change.

A reticent smile, he obviously intended for her alone, caused soft creases beneath his eyes. "I—" Almost imperceptibly, he shook his head. "I am in awe," he offered in an unusually enigmatic greeting.

Granted, Jillian was wearing trousers.

She had denied her mother's request that she change into a proper gown in which to receive her guest, but had thought nothing of it at the time.

Mrs. Kelley now sat in her chair wringing her hands, either in disappointment or anger or a combination of the two. It would have taken a psychology scholar to pinpoint the exact reason.

Since no one had made an effort to initiate conversation, Jillian took the task on herself. "How have you been occupying yourself, Miles?"

"Er." He glanced at her mother and continued, "Reading, mostly. Visiting my father's tenants."

"Reading?" Now, here was a promising occupation. "Novels?"

Miles took a breath before he spoke as if mulling over his answer. "No. The Classics."

"Oh." An uncomfortable silence fell upon the threesome, the second in the minute and a half or so since Jillian had stepped into the room.

She felt everyone jump as she broke through the nonexistent din. "If you are so inclined, I've brought back some entertaining books and a few fabulous plays to read, as well. Have you heard of Oscar Wilde?"

She could have sworn she saw Mile's eyes widen momentarily. "Wilde is — not read in the finer circles."

"Why, because he's a homosexual?"

Moving with much more agility than Jillian thought possible, her mother shot to her feet. "That will be all the time we have for a visit today, Mr. Bassett. Perhaps you could dine with us tomorrow evening?"

"Of course." Miles bowed, his manners always impeccable. "Until then."

After Miles had been shown out by the butler, Jillian's mother whirled on her. "Have you lost your mind?"

Jillian's gaze flew to her mother's. "I beg your par — ?"

"I'd originally initiated your journey so that you might grow out of your childish notions about Mr. Bassett. But it seems to me my stratagem has backfired. Is this what sending you abroad to school four years ago achieved? A young woman who dresses scandalously and speaks of things which should be beneath her notice?"

Jillian decided it best to ignore the comment about her and Miles and lifted her chin a notch. At university, she'd been warned of impending encounters with the dissatisfied, older generation about the contemporary way of thinking. "Mama, you must understand. My eyes have been opened. There is a brand-new century looming before us, and we must progress along with our surroundings."

"I should like to protest vulgarity if I live until the century after the next, and so should you!"

"Mama, there is nothing vulgar about being a modern woman." Jillian folded her arms across her chest.

"Don't you dare take that stance with me!"

Jillian lowered her hands to her sides contritely as her mother continued her tirade.

"I raised you! I provided you with the money to attend Moravian Female Seminary! I—"

Jillian held up one hand. "On that note, there is something I need to tell you, Mama, and I'm afraid you may be displeased."

A huff of air escaped from her mother in lieu of laughter. "I doubt anything could disappoint me more than the display you've shown since your arrival this morning."

Clenching her fists then releasing them just as quickly, Jillian readied herself for a championship match between herself and her mother. "Then you'd better sit down, because you are about to endure an atrocious setback."

* * * *

30 June, 1895
Dear Mr. Townsend,
I must apologize for last night's little indiscretion following the alumnus party for Oberlin College. I never meant to be so very drunk in your presence. The fact is, I've never allowed myself to become that foxed before, although I'm sure you must feel that it was common practice for me, especially because of the way in

which I conducted myself in the circle of your arms.

Please know that I hold you in the highest regard and don't at all lay any blame on you for the irreplaceable loss of my virtue. I do also wish to express my regret for running out before you roused from your slumber. I must meet the morning train to New York to catch a steam ship for my home in St. Helens, where I would be happy to receive any letters you may wish to exchange with me. In the greatest humility and harboring no regret whatsoever,

Jillian Kelley of Fairfield Court, St. Helens, England.

In the week or so since he'd received the letter from atop the silver tray which his butler, Bingham, had ceremoniously held out to him on that fated morning, Bradley must have read it three thousand times. Assured that his memory had thoroughly absorbed every word, he refolded it and placed it in the inside pocket of his waistcoat as he disembarked at dockside in Liverpool, England.

The first order of business was to find a decent inn where he could wash the sea salt from his skin, gorge himself on a civilized meal that didn't involve fish and get an absurd amount of sleep on a large, soft bed. Then he planned to set out via rail to find the feisty, midnight-blue-eyed, brunette enigma that had cost him several nights of lost sleep and an innumerable sum of cockstands which demanded his not so tender attention.

Regardless of his newly appointed position on the board of directors at Oberlin and the agreement he had yet to sign pertaining to a teaching position there, he needed this holiday. And if it included Miss Kelley and the delights of her person, then he'd be a very happy tourist.

Just then, a young boy held up a fistful of different colored ribbons for Bradley's perusal. "A pretty for your girl, sir? Each only a ha-penny."

The lad was thin, his skin pale, at least, in places where one could see through the soot smeared across his face. Bradley's heart went out to the boy. It was likely that the ribbons were stolen, but he was certain that the child was only selling them to avoid the workhouse.

"How much for all of them?"

"A-all?" the lad stammered.

He smiled. "Tell you what. I haven't had a chance to change my money yet, but here are two silver pieces." They swapped the goods for the coins. "Now, go on home and give these directly to your mother. Understand?"

Shoving his hand deep into his pocket, he replied, "I shall, sir. Me ma's gonna cry for joy when I give 'er these."

The boy ran off and as Bradley watched him go, he wished he could do more. But he hadn't brought all that much money with him to begin with.

Bradley sighed. He hadn't really thought about what the outcome of this impromptu journey should be. Whatever the case, he wouldn't go home without some sort of closure. He was owed at least that much.

* * * *

Jillian took a deep breath and turned to fully face her mother who had thankfully taken her request to be seated seriously. "I never attended Moravian, Mama. I took the money and enrolled at Oberlin College in Ohio." Jillian could feel the sting of her mother's glare from where she stood.

"But the postmark on your letters—"

"I asked a friend from study hall, who had family in Germantown, Pennsylvania, if she would have one of her sisters forward my letters to you."

If a single glare would've had the power to end a life… "Do you know how long it took me to find a decent school for you over on that…that island of thieves?"

Her mother's voice shook with fury, but Jillian knew there was nothing that could be done about it now. "Mama, firstly, the United States is not an island, and they haven't shipped criminals there for at least—"

"Do not bore me with details!" her mother snapped,

then calmed considerably. "Tell me." She placed a serene, wooden smile upon her face. "Just why did you find yourself compelled to change schools?"

"Honestly?"

"If you please."

Jillian licked her dry lips as she considered her answer. She could lie and say that the academics were of a higher caliber, but she knew her mother had done extensive research on the academics of every school on the east coast of the United States before choosing the seminary, and could likely find out about universities further inland. "Oberlin College is..." She paused. The next words out of her mouth were sure to open a terribly foul can of worms. She rushed through the term, practically spewing it from under her breath. "Co-ed."

Her mother leaned forward just a tad. "Code you say? Code for what? Code for a place which charges one for robbing them of their generally rational behavior?"

Gritting her teeth momentarily at her mother's sharp jab, Jillian shook her head. "No, Mama. I said 'co-ed'."

"And this means — ?"

"Co-educational."

Jillian's mother merely blinked at her, which she knew, from years of conversing with the matriarch of the family, meant that she required, no, *demanded* more information.

Taking one more deep breath to calm her nerves, Jillian expounded. "Oberlin College is a co-educational institution where both sexes can attend classes."

"Together?" Her mother's eyes widened and the volume of the query turned out to be much louder than a prestigious lady in a feminine parlor would normally allow.

"Yes, Mama."

Coming fully out of her seat, Jillian's mother persisted with her outburst. "Such practices should be illegal!"

"Well, Mama, with all due respect, they are not. At least, not at Oberlin."

"And what, may I ask, was your line of study?"

Jillian swallowed. She knew this would not go over well, either. "Literature."

It looked to Jillian as if her mother wasn't breathing, so still did she stand.

Finally, just when Jillian was about to take a few steps forward and feel for a pulse, her mother spoke. "Literature."

"Yes, Mama."

"Why?"

"It interested me."

Her mother blew out a frustrated breath then continued her narrow-minded lecture. As much as she loved her mother, Jillian mentally shut her elder out and fancied herself elsewhere. Jillian understood why her mother might feel this way. She had been born almost sixty years prior to where they were on the calendar now, and back then, men and women didn't do anything together which didn't require meticulous supervision, a string quartet in a room full of their peers or a marriage contract. At least, that was what she'd steadfastly declared since Jillian had been a child.

"…And so it will be up to me to assist you in recalling your societal manners."

This statement brought Jillian straightaway back to the conversation at hand. "Pray, Mama, just how do you hope to accomplish this?"

Her mother paced the length of the room and ended facing the window which overlooked the front lawns. "First and foremost, we'll have Fletcher pull your old gowns down from the attic and see if anything can be salvaged. Once that is accomplished, I shall have to refresh your current wardrobe. I dare say, you won't have any suitable gowns, having come from the unfashionable side of the Atlantic."

Jillian clasped her hands together to keep them from shaking. She had not spent her money frivolously on gowns and such. In fact, she had pinched her pennies and even returned home with a decent sum in her purse. Besides, it wasn't as if she'd had no dresses at all. Aside from the two blouses and three pairs of trousers, one in buff, one in light blue and one in brown for riding, she had two other gowns which would suffice. They weren't trimmed with lace and satin bows, but they were comfortable. "I don't think that will be necessary, Mama—"

"You will let me be the judge of that, I'm sure. In addition, tonight after you have finished with your evening toilette, I want you to send Anne, your new maid, to me. I have a few things I wish her schooled in as far as your future practices."

Her mother had always appeared to be the epitome of good manners—and conducted her staff to comply as well. There existed a cutting undercurrent to her comments and opinions when one paid attention, which seemed quite the opposite of good manners.

"We shall bring a few of your peers together, perhaps a few properly schooled, hand-selected society girls for a house party. I dare say the example of their behavior will turn you back into your old self in no time." Jillian's mother glided over to her writing desk and sat.

Jillian looked down at her bloodless, wrung-out hands. What was so terribly wrong with the woman she'd become?

"Let us begin with a guest list."

Swallowing, Jillian released her hands and took a seat across the room as far from her mother's desk as was possible. "The Mayhew girls?"

"No, that won't serve. All three daughters have made spectacular matches since you have been gone." Jillian's mother's gaze swept from her head to her toes and back again. "They each live elsewhere now."

She hadn't conveyed the information in a negative way, but Jillian could detect overtures of jealousy in her statement. "The Newtons then?"

"I understand that the Newtons no longer accept weekend invitations. Their entire family is very involved in the church and I definitely wouldn't expect them to approve of"—she looked her daughter up and down again—"of how things have progressed with you."

Jillian swallowed and felt the sting of tears behind her eyes. She wasn't so very appalling, was she? One thing was for certain, her mother had no idea, not even an inkling of suspicion that the night before she'd begun her journey home she'd lost all reason and had become fully introduced to womanhood in the arms of a man.

A very handsome, dark-eyed, sandy-brown-haired man.

She pushed the thought from her mind and addressed her mother. "The Youngers then."

"Certainly not."

Expelling a breath, Jillian turned away from her mother and offered half-heartedly, "Then perhaps you could think of someone to invite."

Mrs. Kelley replaced her writing implements without having written a single name. "I shall think on it. In the meantime, I'll send Fletcher to arrange an appointment with the seamstress."

Allowing herself to relax against the back of the chair once her mother had quit the room, Jillian closed her eyes. Her return home wasn't going at all the way she'd planned. Miles was supposed to have taken one look at her and fallen to his knees with a marriage proposal dangling from his lips. But that had been one-hundred and eighty degrees from what had happened. In actuality, Miles hadn't said all that much to her, nothing meaningful, anyway.

And it smarted something awful.

Refusing to cry, Jillian pushed herself out of the chair. She needed to take her mind off of her sad predicament. A smile parted her lips. "Maid Marian."

Chapter Two

It must have been near suppertime when Jillian led her beautiful white mare back into her stall after a rousing tour of the grounds. She was sure Maid Marian hadn't benefited from that quality of exercise since Jillian had left for the States. One of the stablemen, the one she'd argued with for at least twenty minutes about the fact that she'd wanted to use her late father's saddle, offered to give the horse her rub down. She agreed and relinquished the reins to him. With a pat to the mare's side and a promise that she'd come for another visit soon, Jillian then headed for the house.

Fletcher, Fairfield Court's head butler, approached Jillian moments after she'd entered. "Your mother awaits you in the drawing room."

She smiled at the older man. "Thank you, Fletcher." As they strolled through the house to the formal sitting room, Jillian conversed with Fletcher. "What do you think of Maid Marian's foal, have you seen him?"

"Indeed. Rancor was broken and has been accommodating riders for many months now."

Stopping at the entrance to the drawing room, she turned to Fletcher. "*Rancor*? Who on earth named him that?"

"Your mother."

She wrinkled her nose at the pessimistic name. "Why?"

Fletcher cleared his throat. "You see, Miss Jillian, one of the Bassett's prize stallions, uh…*got* to Maid Marian while she was in season. Your mother felt it an appropriate name at the time of his birth."

Jillian laughed aloud, finding more levels of humor in the situation than she was at liberty to discuss. "Well, Fletcher,

I suppose we can no longer call Maid Marian a *maid*, now, can we?"

Jillian could have sworn Fletcher's eyes went wide. Still smiling, Jillian turned to step into the drawing room and froze in her tracks. Inside the room sat her mother and her mother's best friend, Lady Bassett, Miles' mother.

And they had heard every word. She could tell by the sour looks upon their faces.

Jillian's mother's gaze raked her from head to foot. "You look a fright," she forced out with no small amount of venom in her voice.

Glancing at a large gilt-framed mirror on the wall, Jillian assessed that not only was her face and hair speckled with tiny splatters of mud, but her blouse and brown trousers were, as well. Loathing to do so, she glanced down at her equally muddy boots. She groaned inwardly.

"Fletcher!" her mother barked.

He appeared in the doorway instantly. "Yes, mam." He delivered the inquiry as a statement as opposed to a question, in the way of all good butlers.

"See that a bath is drawn for my daughter and the kitchen sends her supper up later."

Fletcher bowed in acceptance of her command and Jillian, assuming she had been dismissed as well, turned to follow him out of the drawing room.

"Jillian. A moment, please." Her mother had employed the same tone she'd taken with Fletcher.

Her spine stiffened and she turned back to her mother. "Yes, Mama?"

"I will take your behavior today as a sign that you are not yourself because of your strenuous journey. But tomorrow, I will expect the Jillian I raised to meet me at breakfast."

Her gaze slid from her mother to Lady Bassett—who hadn't said a single word—and back again. "Yes, Mama. If you will excuse me." Jillian posed a curtsy, turned on her heel and exited the room, her cheeks burning in utter humiliation.

* * * *

Jillian's hot bath hadn't calmed her down one little bit. She stood at her window tapping out an irritated cadence with her fingernails on the pane, looking out over the lawns which were illuminated by the moonlit sky. "Behavior, behavior, behavior," she murmured to herself. Her entrance into the drawing room not two and a half hours ago, accompanied by the conversation about a couple of randy horses had not, she was sure, done anything to win Lady Bassett's affinity.

Regardless of what her mother thought, she liked who she was. True, she wasn't the quiet little girl who used to follow Miles around, peeking around corners at him and making faces at the other girls who'd had crushes on him. But she had found her voice at Oberlin and an independent side she couldn't believe she'd lived without before.

So what if she'd been tempted to lie with another man? *Who just happened to be wonderfully handsome.*

And intelligent.

And gallant.

And had made her head spin with the things he'd said and done to her.

Jillian redirected her thoughts with a shake of her head. Nevertheless, she didn't think she'd changed very much. Even now she loved to ride horses, take long walks and read. And she still held a desperate attraction to Miles. She smiled. No matter what sort of growing and changing she did, she'd always love Miles.

Disappointed in herself, however, not nearly so much as her mother was, Jillian turned to her bed. On the nightstand sat one of her favorite books, in which she was more than happy to lose herself.

* * * *

Jillian gave her riding trousers to Anne to be laundered. This morning, and for the sole benefit of her mother, she'd donned a simple day dress in which to attend the meal.

Not two steps into the breakfast room, Jillian's mother began assessing the dark-blue cotton ensemble.

"You do realize that your *serviceable* gown isn't anywhere near fashionable."

It didn't take a PhD to figure out that what her mother had meant by 'serviceable' was that the only place it would be acceptable was *below* stairs. "Really, Mama, it's—"

"Furthermore, your sleeves do not belong pushed up to the elbows, and why isn't there a bustle or even a sash to be found?"

"Good morning to you, too, Mama." Refusing to be moved, she sat and focused on choking down her breakfast, astonished that her mother didn't comment on the low neckline —of course, Jillian had decided against pointing it out to her for fear of just what might be implied about her person. In spite of the torment, she sat with her mother for the rest of the morning and into the afternoon. She'd even endured the tedium of an hour-long meeting with the seamstress.

By the time the luncheon dishes had been cleared, Jillian was of a mind to quit the house as fast as she could. Her own sanity demanded it. Determined to do so precipitously, before her mother drove her straight to Bedlam with her relentless needling, she excused herself and made for her room.

After changing into her buff trousers and white blouse combination, Jillian set out, with book in hand, and headed for her favorite spot at Fairfield Court, the west gazebo.

She let Fletcher know of her destination, and he in turn informed her that the west gazebo had been recently swept, the bench and chair coverings laundered and the cushions re-stuffed. He also mentioned the flowers that had been planted all around the perimeter were in full bloom. Jillian couldn't wait to spend the rest of the day immersed in her book, napping off and on, and listening to the buzz of bees as they circled the blossoms.

She hurried along the old path to her retreat, the worn trail in the grass barely visible. Now that she was home again, there could be no doubt that she'd reestablish the footpath in no time. The day had turned warm, but not overly so, mostly because of the breeze.

The sight that met her made her tear up. Since her childhood, the west gazebo was the place where she came to be alone and dream. Most likely everyone in the household knew it would always be her favorite place of refuge—it was perhaps the reason they'd spruced it up upon her arrival. She settled herself on one of the wide cushioned benches and opened her book. She sighed. This was as good as life could get.

She'd been reading for almost an hour, and even though she'd come to a particularly exciting chapter in the book, Jillian could barely keep her eyes open. Placing her bookmark between the pages, she then set it upon the floral cushion next to her. After removing one of the pillows which had kept her head elevated, she settled in for a nap. The warm sun occasionally dappled through the heavily leafed branches far above the lattice roof of the gazebo, and the breeze, which rustled the leaves, released the scent of summer blossoms to roll over her body. Very soon she drifted off to sleep.

A dream-like, rumbling, thoroughly male voice whispered softly in her ear, reading the very words aloud she had been relishing, simply devouring.

"Psyche felt something soft and warm sweep down her naked thigh. She shivered. Ensconced in total darkness, it was impossible to see who had approached her. She blinked rapidly to assist her plight. 'I am here to consummate our marriage, Psyche. But first, let me worship you the way a woman as beautiful as yourself should be worshipped.' Her breath caught in her throat and she strained to see the man who'd spoken, whose heated breath she could feel caressing her legs as it traveled higher and higher. Ever so gently, Psyche's legs were parted and something warm and wet touched the juncture of her thighs. Unimaginable bliss engulfed her when he covered her with what was surely his mouth. Within

seconds, his lips surrounded the bud of her most intimate flesh, causing it to surge and fill. She heard her groom's voice groan and the sound reverberated through her sensitized sex straight to her womb."

When the voice paused, Jillian stirred, gooseflesh covering her body at the wicked words her memory had echoed from her reading. Expecting to see no one, as it must have been her mind playing tricks on her the way it sent that deep-toned, American accent over the breeze, Jillian opened her eyes languidly.

With a squeak, she sat bolt upright. Her feet came to rest on the floor directly in front of the man to whom she had lost her virginity...or perhaps *given* her virginity to, would be a better description, J. Bradley Townsend. His recumbent position next to her on the floor of the gazebo whispered of his undeniable confidence, and her book in his masculine hands shouted his utter gall. She swallowed hard.

He grinned. A dazzling, toe-curling smile it was. "Why, Miss Kelley, I had no idea you enjoyed sensational fiction."

"What are you doing here?" she scolded, not intending for her voice to be quite so loud.

He lifted the book and took a breath to continue reading when she snatched it from his hands. The very rare, sensationally written book of Greek mythology had been a gift from a friend at Oberlin who had studied literature along with Jillian. She'd warned Jillian that this particular mythology book was even more explicit than a novel. However, Jillian treasured it all the more because of the fact. The thoughtful gift was rather valuable and not at all something she would be willing to part with. Not that the man before her had asked her to. "What I read is none of your business. Answer my question, Mr. Townsend, this instant!" She shoved the book behind her on the bench.

"Now is that any way to welcome your lover?"

Jillian sucked in a breath, but her mind was yet reeling at the fact that he was here, before her in the flesh, and at the same time, scrambling to find just the right stinging retort.

"Perhaps we should get reacquainted by acting out the lovely scene I just read to you." His smile widened and he bent his head just enough to nudge the top of one of her knees with his chin.

The rat!

"I could peel these trousers off the way I did in my bedroom after Oberlin's alumnus party and we could get right to it." His voice rolled over her skin in the same manner a warm afternoon breeze would.

Jillian opened her mouth. Nothing came out but an unintelligible stammer.

Rogue! Cur!

"Perhaps I should fetch a bottle or two of wine. A few toasts and we can pick up where we left off."

Shooing at his face before he began gnawing on her knee, Jillian then shot to her feet, took a few steps toward the stairs that led out of the gazebo and spun on her heel to reprove him. "What are you doing here, Mr. Townsend?" This time, she'd meant to increase the volume of her voice.

Once he'd risen from his kneeling position, he turned to face her. "I've come for a visit. I'm on holiday, you see."

"Yes, I see," she murmured, not allowing the thoughts that nagged at her to be voiced, such as how handsome he looked, how he made her tremble and that the obvious bulge in his trousers seemed to call to her. She jerked her chin in the opposite direction before she looked at it again.

He stepped forward and reached for her, but she moved away just in time. "You can't be here—we can't be here. *Together. Alone.*"

"Why?"

She whirled on him. "The rules are different here."

"Since when do you adhere to rules?"

Jillian's jaw dropped open at the indignation she felt. Granted, he was right.

His gaze fell to her gaping mouth. He smiled again, this time a languid smile, an indolent smile, a smile of remembrance.

Without warning, he took her by the upper arms and kissed her full on the mouth.

Jillian felt the buzz of excitement, or was it fear of being caught? Her mother would have his head if she found them like this, alone together. She'd demand the entire story, perhaps even an engagement, and Jillian, God help her, would never hear the end of it.

She attempted to pull out of his arms. "You can't be here!" she rasped, her breath sounding as if she'd been running. Or dancing. Or kissing a very desirable man.

Mr. Townsend released her and folded his arms across his chest. The chest she knew for a fact looked much better without clothes hindering her view.

"What of all this lovely hospitality England is so popular for?"

"You can't just waltz in here and—"

He interrupted, pressed his lips together, his wonderfully luscious lips, and tilted his head—of thick luxurious sandy-colored hair. "I'm afraid I already have. Your man, Fletcher, I believe is his name, took my bags to—the east guest suites on the third floor. Yes, that is what he said."

"What!" Jillian's voice rose in pitch.

Mr. Townsend shrugged a shoulder. "I told him you and I were old school chums."

A wave of nausea overtook her. She placed a hand over her forehead. "'Old school'—My mother is going to go into fits."

He chuckled. "I doubt that. Fletcher said that Mrs. and Miss Kelley were planning a house party. He must have figured that I am early, is all."

"Early? The party isn't supposed to begin until Saturday. It's Monday."

He shrugged again. "Call it *very* early." He grinned. "Fletcher didn't seem disturbed about it in the least."

"And for your information, sir, you and I are not old school chums."

"I beg to differ, Miss Kelley."

"No, you may not. You and I never took a single class together. In fact, if my memory serves, you graduated years before I came to Oberlin!"

"Only six."

"Six years is a very long time."

He's smiling again, the blackguard.

"If my memory serves, we did a bit of learning together." Before she could protest, he stepped forward and took her by the arms again. He continued speaking in that deep, rich voice of his, which had never failed to persuade her when he'd used it with such expertise against her dangerously immodest sensibilities. "I learned to lick a pathway to your soul."

Jillian's mouth hung open again, she knew, but this time she didn't care. She was seething. Or was that smoldering?

Whatever the case, his words caused a tremendous excitement within her.

"And you learned what certain parts of your body are for." His face came precariously close to hers. "How they like being touched, tickled, tasted."

Bloody hell, he's kissing me again! His lips are so… No!

She broke out of the kiss. "We can't do this. You must release me this instant and leave Fairfield Court!"

He did release her but looked at her as if questioning her logic.

She took a step backward. "I have plans for my life – plans that don't include being seduced at every turn."

"Is that why you think I'm here? To seduce you?"

"Well, frankly, yes," she said, calming considerably now that more than a foot of empty space could be detected between them.

At least the look he gave her was thoughtful. "Very well."

She let out a breath.

"I shall endeavor to live up to your standards."

"What?" Jillian shrieked.

Chapter Three

Mr. Townsend's lips quirked. "I said, I shall endeavor to live up to your standards."

"I know what you said! I meant—"

He went on as if she hadn't spoken, which pricked her ire something awful. "If you think me the rogue, I shall be that man. It's your fantasy, after all."

"Fantasy? I never said—"

"You may not have used that exact word, Miss Kelley, but what is a fantasy but a made-up scenario?"

"I—"

"You've set the tone. Let's play." He smiled. "Games are my specialty, as you may recall."

It was the wickedest grin she had ever beheld. She reached out to a sturdy, cream-colored post to steady herself. "Mr. Townsend, please. I don't have time for this."

"I do. I'm on holiday," he reminded her smugly, his straight white teeth showing between smooth lips, the happy creases around his mouth assisting in forming perfect dimples.

With determination, Jillian straightened her spine, having realized her salvation. Her next bit of news should send him running from Fairfield Court. "If you act the scoundrel in front of my mother, you will be out on your ear before the sun sets."

He nodded. "I thank you for the warning."

But he didn't run. Instead, he came to stand directly in front of her and set his forearm on the post above her head. Leaning in, he whispered, "I do love a challenge"

She could sense his body moving slowly toward hers for

what she imagined would be another heart-melting kiss, so she escaped, stepping around him.

Needing a moment, she shut him out as much as humanly possible. She had to think and do so with a clear mind. She blew out a breath. He'd never get past her mother's astute nose. Not in a million years. Good God, he was an American, for Heaven's sake! Jillian walked over to the bench and snatched up her book.

"I wouldn't unpack if I were you, Mr. Townsend." And with that, she quit the gazebo.

Her skin tingled with awareness as he followed her back to the house and up the stairs. Fletcher greeted them and escorted Jillian's guest to his suite.

Once they made it to the landing where the stairs split, one set to the west and one to the east, Jillian turned on her heel and continued up the west staircase to her room without a word.

Once she arrived, she slammed the door shut. Stalking to the window, she then gazed unseeingly over the lawns. Thank God, the gazebo couldn't be seen from the house.

Jillian couldn't believe he was here. J. Bradley Townsend, the most handsome man in the entire United States of America, if not the most arrogant. Here. In England. In her house.

Next to the window sat a salmon-colored, velvet fainting couch with lacy, ivory satin pillows nestled invitingly at the head. Using it for what it was named for, she collapsed onto it.

Bradley.

She cursed under her breath.

* * * *

Bradley stripped himself of his traveling clothes then made use of the washbasin. He lay down upon the bed, the cool brocade satin soothing his heated skin.

Miss Jillian Kelley. He sighed. *Sassy, intelligent, beautiful.*

And they were once again under the same roof. He'd acted the rogue with her just now. It hadn't been his intention, but one look at her lovely face, so peaceful as she'd napped, had turned his insides out.

Truth be told, he hadn't really come here to seduce her. Well, not as such, anyway. The second he'd recognized the book she'd been reading—the story of Eros and Psyche—it had pushed his sensibilities over the top. Had he not spent the last six years after he'd graduated traveling through the near and far East, studying cultural conduct, with emphasis on the most interesting part, the history of human sexual behavior? The story she had been reading was one of the first Greek myths he'd ever picked up—the one that had sparked his interest in the subject. The version Jillian had was far more detailed, more arousing than the one he'd read. It was like some sensual, banned novel, completely scandalous.

How wonderful that her passions reached beyond a deliciously drunken romp which had lasted only one night.

* * * *

As Jillian patted the last curl into place, her stomach grumbled. Teatime had arrived and aside from being famished, she was sure that J. Bradley Townsend hadn't a clue about English tearoom manners. She smiled to herself so as not to raise questions from her maid while she replaced the rest of Jillian's hair pins in the drawer of her vanity.

Jillian's mother would strip Bradley of his arrogance. And at the very least, it would defer her mother's scrutinizing attentions from her.

"You look lovely, miss," Anne murmured when Jillian rose and headed for the door. The rosy-cheeked Irish girl's age must have been around the same as Jillian's.

Jillian turned to her maid. "Thank you for your help, Anne, and if I've been remiss, forgive me. Welcome to Fairfield Court," she replied sincerely then made her exit.

Downstairs, she paused just outside the parlor where she heard her mother asking questions. Jillian grinned, feeling giddy. This was it. The humiliation of Mr. J. Bradley Townsend had commenced. She swept into the room and over to the tea tray.

"And what do you plan on teaching, Mr. Townsend?" Her mother's voice sounded tight, as if she were trying to make pleasant conversation out of something that was beneath her notice.

"Cultural behavior, Mrs. Kelley. I've been abroad and have some interesting curriculum I'd like to share with the students pursuing history majors."

Bradley had stood when Jillian had entered the room, but she refused to acknowledge it. Jillian took her tea to a seat by the window. On this unusually clear day, the warmth of the late afternoon sun seeped wonderfully onto her neck, back and shoulders. She tried to focus on matters outside of the room rather than the apparent fact that Bradley was to teach, most likely at Oberlin.

Professor Townsend. She admitted—however begrudgingly—it had a nice ring to it.

So much for trying to employ my thoughts elsewhere.

"Who on earth would want to study history?" her mother asked with a wave of her hand.

Jillian shifted her gaze to Bradley, expecting him to falter under her mother's interrogation.

"There are those who say that in order not to repeat history, one must be familiar with it." Bradley turned to look at Jillian to include her in the conversation, she imagined. He grinned. "Then there are those who wish to repeat successful events of the past."

Jillian jerked her chin away and her teacup clattered atop the saucer.

"What sort of events, Mr. Townsend?"

It was apparent to Jillian that the snake had successfully secured her mother's interest. But just how far would he go? In a snap, Jillian turned back to glare at him with a warning in her eyes.

"Well, Mrs. Kelley, things such as pleasant encounters" — his gaze locked with Jillian's and he continued — "between countries, triumphant peace treaties, annual celebrations, significant discoveries, the great romance of ink and paper."

Her mother cleared her throat. "'A romance of ink and paper'. What, precisely, does that mean, sir?"

His gaze slid back to Jillian's mother. "Literature, madam. Anything from fiction to historical accounts of great countries such as this one."

"Ah," was all Mrs. Kelley offered.

At that moment, Fletcher stepped into the room. "Mr. Bassett," he announced.

Jillian came to her feet as Miles strolled into the room. Out of the corner of her eye, she saw Bradley rise from his seated position. *Well, he may have a few tearoom manners after all*. She set down her teacup and rushed to greet Miles. "Miles." She smiled, reaching for him.

"I hope you don't mind if I'm early for supper, Jillian, Mrs. Kelley." He bowed to her mother. "I thought we could spend some time chatting since we didn't get a chance to yesterday."

"Of course we don't mind." She took him by the hand and led him to the opposite settee from where her mother and Bradley sat.

Before lowering to sit, Jillian made the introductions. "Miles, this is Mr. Townsend. Mr. Townsend, may I present my —" Lord, she'd almost said 'my fiancé'! "My very old and dear friend, Miles Bassett."

While the men shook hands, exchanged pleasantries, Jillian sat. How strange it felt to have both men in the same room.

"Mr. Townsend, I can tell from your accent that you are an American."

Miles is so very clever. Jillian smiled while she poured him his tea.

One point for Miles.

"I am. Have you visited?"

"America?"

"Yes."

"No."

Jillian stirred a few dribbles of milk into his cup, turned toward the window to conceal her shamed expression. Well, that was that—the extent of Miles' conversational skills with total strangers. He'd have never made it at Oberlin. She handed Miles his tea and returned to her seat. Perturbed that Miles may not be able to hold his own with such a highly educated man, she glanced out across the lawns as if to find assistance for him.

When Bradley spoke, it drew Jillian and her mental state of annoyance back into the room.

"What do you do, Mr. Bassett?"

"Oh, well, my father owns a good deal of land." He turned to Mrs. Kelley and smiled. "Outside of Fairfield Court, of course." Sipping his tea, he returned his gaze to Bradley. "I help him manage things."

"Hm." Bradley thought for a moment. "Do you hunt, Mr. Bassett?"

"Not really. Although I have ridden to hounds a few times in my life."

Jillian thought she'd seen a flash of apathy in Bradley's eyes as he drank his tea and it caused her to feel sorry for Miles in a way that made her nearly physically ill. She smiled encouragingly, then returned to her comforting beverage.

"Do you shoot archery? I understand that our Miss Kelley here"—Bradley indicated to Jillian with a tilt of his head—"is very good at exercising the implements of Eros."

"Eros?"

"Cupid." He clarified then turned to Jillian. "As in Cupid and Psyche."

Before Miles could ask Bradley to elaborate upon the relationship of Cupid and Psyche, Jillian shot to her feet. "Perhaps we should have Fletcher set out a few targets before supper. Would you enjoy that, gentlemen?"

"I would very much enjoy that, Miss Kelley, if it's not too much of an inconvenience to Mrs. Kelley's staff." Bradley looked at Jillian's mother and smiled.

"How very thoughtful. Of course not." Mrs. Kelley leaned over and tinkled a little silver bell which sat upon a table to the right of her, calling Fletcher into the room.

Jillian sat her half-finished tea on the tea cart. "I should wish to change first. Do feel free to precede me to the field." She turned toward the doors when Miles' voice stopped her.

"Will you be changing into those trousers again?"

She couldn't tell if Miles had been happy or disgruntled about her wearing trousers. If he decided to be of the same mindset as her mother, his manners must have gotten the better of him to have delivered his inquiry with such ease, she mused.

"I'm curious about that as well, Miss Kelley," Bradley asked with a mischievous twinkle in his eye.

Jillian knew exactly what *he* thought of her trousers.

Her cheeks warmed and her gaze slid to her mother, whose single raised eyebrow threatened retribution if she answered incorrectly.

Absorbing the contradictory expectations of the entire party, Jillian lifted her chin. "I haven't decided yet what I shall wear." And with that, she made her way out of the room.

Chapter Four

Jillian approached the targets Fletcher had set up on the west lawns with her head held high. A few clouds had gathered and it was misting slightly, but nothing to be alarmed about. Both Bradley and Miles turned to her the moment she came to a halt between them.

Miles frowned.

Bradley's eyes traveled from the top of her head, down her wool-encased legs to her boots and back again. He smiled as though he appreciated her choice.

One point for Bradley.

Earlier, when Jillian had arrived at her room, she'd felt the need to push at the boundaries that threatened to keep modern women, not unlike herself, so locked up. Not only did she don her light-blue trousers and white blouse, but she'd removed every pin that held her hair in place. She'd brushed out her tresses, allowing them to flow freely down her back — then fled the house as not to incur her mother's wrath if she were spotted.

Jillian strode over to stand before the middle target. Her quiver and arrows had been set a mere forty yards from the round, hay-covered, color-banded objectives. She strapped on her guards as Miles and Bradley did the same.

She placed an arrow onto the string of her bow. "Are we ready then, gentlemen?" To her right, Miles nodded. Turning to Bradley at her left, she found him perusing her figure. She could practically feel his hands where his eyes wandered.

She cleared her throat and his gaze snapped to hers. Raising her brow, she sent him a look of warning, then she focused on the targets. Grasping the arrow with her fingertips, she pulled back, aimed, then let it fly.

Gold. The center of the target.

Miles' arrow struck between the red and blue — the second and third sections of the target, respectively.

Bradley's arrow hit the center's outer gold band.

Notching a second one, he whispered to her, "How about a little wager?"

Jillian released her second arrow. "No." Gold.

"Scared?" He let his projectile fly. Gold.

"Not in the least." She prepared a third arrow.

"Good, here are the details. If I shoot better than Mr. Bassett, you have to meet me at the gazebo tonight at midnight," he whispered as he positioned his next instrument of assault.

Jillian held her stance, the bowstring taut in her grip, her back muscles straining to hold still. She glanced over at Miles' target. An arrow bounced off and landed on the ground. "Absolutely, no bet," she murmured and hit the outer red band with her arrow. She gritted her teeth and reached for another.

"All right." He notched his next arrow to the string. "If my grouping is tighter than yours, you have to meet me at midnight." He released and hit the center gold.

Before she answered, both she and Bradley shot three more arrows. They were now tied as far as groupings went.

"Well?" he asked quietly and struck red.

Jillian felt good. She felt the wind wasn't too strong, the misting had ceased and the sun was low on the horizon, unable to impede her line of sight. "Fine. Twenty arrows. When I win, you leave and never return."

"Done."

As the eighteenth and nineteenth arrows were placed, both Jillian and Bradley's groupings were rather snug.

Bradley released his twentieth arrow. Gold. He replaced his bow and glanced over at Mr. Bassett, who had been trying very hard to catch up. He was about ten arrows behind.

As Jillian placed her last arrow on the string, Bradley leaned over to whisper in her ear. "I can't wait to hold you in my arms tonight."

Jillian's hands instantly began to sweat. She paused to wipe each palm down the side of her trousers, hoping to deter the perspiration.

"You haven't won yet, sir."

"No? Look at my grouping. One can see less gold on my target than on yours. I've already won."

"I have one more arrow," she whispered harshly. He was trying to make her nervous. Well, it wasn't going to work. Carefully disconnecting her arrow from the string, she turned fully to Miles. "How are you doing, Miles?"

"Well, good enough for someone who hasn't shot in over four years."

His grouping was spread pathetically over the face of the target, two of the arrows lay on the grass in front of it.

Jillian took a breath. "It's not so very bad, dear."

With determination, she turned back to Bradley. She re-notched her arrow and aimed.

On the light breeze, his words drifted to her ears. "It has been too long since I tasted you."

Jillian released her arrow. Gold.

"I win." Bradley's insolent whisper made her want to prepare another arrow, light it on fire and send it hurling his way.

Instead, she set her bow into the quiver and placed it into the holder before her. She then stripped herself of the guards and turned to Miles. "Miles, I need you to tell me which grouping is tighter. Mine or Mr. Townsend's?"

Miles placed his bow into his empty quiver and peered at the targets. "Well, they both look better than mine."

"Yes, but on which target can you see the least amount of gold?" If Miles chose hers, it meant he loved her. If Miles chose Bradley's, he may as well hand her over to the braggart naked, atop a silver platter.

After glancing down the row at the empty quivers, he

went to stand in front of each target. He then turned back to them. "I think it's a tie."

Both Jillian and Bradley deflated.

At once, Jillian saw Fletcher heading toward them. She crooked her finger at Miles and Bradley, directing them away from the quivers.

"Fletcher," she called to him to hurry him along. "In your opinion, which of these targets has the tightest grouping?"

Fletcher assessed the groupings with a discerning eye. "Why, the end one, Miss Jillian."

Bradley smiled triumphantly and Jillian felt the air leave her lungs.

She swallowed. "Thank you, Fletcher. That will be all."

"Miss Jillian, your mother sent me to fetch you and your party. She'd like you to join her for cards in the drawing room before supper."

Jillian nodded. "Straight away, Fletcher." She turned to follow him when in two strides, Bradley caught up with him.

"Tell me, Fletcher, what time is it?"

"Nearly half-past seven, sir," Fletcher offered amicably.

Bradley thanked the butler and slowed his pacing to look at Jillian.

He grinned.

She glared back.

* * * *

Surprisingly, Miles was as bad at cards as he had been at archery. Jillian had teamed up with him against her mother and Bradley for bridge. And they'd lost nearly every hand. She didn't recall Miles being so awful at gaming but, then again, if she thought about it, she couldn't remember playing with him all that much growing up.

Thank God, the quarters were so close that Bradley was unable to make other licentious wagers with her. And thank God, her mother didn't comment on her appearance, although after looking her daughter up and down upon entry to the drawing room, and visually taking particular note of her hair, she barely met her gaze again.

When Fletcher announced dinner, Miles helped Mrs. Kelley from her chair and led her out of the room.

Bradley did the same for Jillian but stopped just six steps before they entered the dining room.

"What are we, down to four hours now?"

"You can wait all you want, I won't meet you tonight or any other night for that matter."

"Yes, you will."

"No, I won't." She declared.

"Then you give me no alternative."

Jillian turned to him and glared, waiting for his ludicrous statement which she was sure he thought would make her change her mind.

"I shall have to tell your mother you made a bet with me and won't honor the wager."

Pulling her hand from his arm, she protested, "You wouldn't dare!"

"Oh, yes I would. It's your honor at stake here, and I'm sure your mother would agree that one should follow through with their promises as polite society would dictate."

She laughed at his absurd reasoning. "I won't go, and that is that."

"Then I'll come to your room and carry you down." At her offended intake of breath, he smiled smugly. "Wouldn't your mother just love to see that?"

"Damn you, Bradley Townsend," she hissed.

"Don't forget. Midnight." He placed his hand on the small of her back and propelled her forward into the dining room.

* * * *

From the time the clock in the hallway had chimed eleven, Jillian had been pacing. She'd sent Anne to bed shortly after retiring, and was glad of the respite from all humans, both male and female. She certainly didn't need someone poking and prodding at her with Bradley's threat looming before her.

Initially, she'd planned on not going. She had washed, put on a clean nightdress and loosely plaited her hair, preparing to crawl into bed. And then reality set in.

Now, at five minutes to midnight, she became exceedingly anxious. Bradley Townsend was just the sort of person who would storm through the halls of Fairfield Court and drag her down to the gazebo — most likely by her braids, the big Neanderthal. And he wouldn't care who knew about it.

With a curse, she quickly donned a trouser ensemble and fled the house, walking with purposeful strides to the west lawns. Upon arrival, she planned on telling him a thing or two about his conduct.

Her heart beat akin to wild druid drums as she stalked up the four steps of the gazebo and looked around.

He wasn't there.

Not sure if she was happy or disappointed, but determined to sort it out later, she turned back to the steps.

Bradley Townsend blocked her escape with his wide shoulders and a smile that radiated confidence even in the dimness of night.

There was no doubt in Bradley's mind of her anger as she stood there, arms akimbo similar to some dark, brooding, feminine warrior, in the trousers and blouse combination which showed every one of her lush curves. Hell, she'd not said a word since that milksop, Miles, had departed after supper. But she'd come to the gazebo, swooping out of the night like some outraged goddess to meet him, the lowly Bradley Townsend. His grin widened.

"All right. I've honored the bet by meeting you in the gazebo. Now if you will excuse me, I'll just go back to my room." She made to go around him, but he stopped her by stepping directly into her path.

"What is your hurry? It's such a beautiful night —"

"Mr. Townsend, I have no desire to be out here unchaperoned with *you*."

He took a step forward. "Regardless, I have a great desire to be out here with *you*."

Bradley's gaze fell to her mouth and he watched as her tongue darted out to moisten her lips.

She shook her head. "I — I can't — I must leave. Now." Jillian sidestepped, but Bradley's hands came to rest on her shoulders.

"What are you afraid of?"

She tilted her face toward the ceiling of the gazebo as if in contemplation of her answer and she sighed a very frustrated puff of air. Her neck was long and smooth-looking. Bradley longed to place his tongue there for a taste, to inhale her warm scent. He could almost smell her now, but the light waft of her perfume wasn't enough. No, he wanted to drown himself, to cover his body with hers.

"I am not afraid. I just do not wish a repeat performance of what happened between us after the alumnus party."

He pulled her chest against his. "Then how about a reminder of the first or perhaps the second act?"

"Mr. Townsend, please." She tried to shrug out of his grip but he held fast. Her gaze came to rest on his shirt front.

"Tell me you don't desire me — that you don't wish to feel my lips on yours."

Jillian did her very best not to allow her breathing to become as swift as her heartbeat. Bradley's chest was hard, all male. And he smelled as wonderful and spicy as she remembered. Her head swam with the close contact of his body, so much so that she might topple over. She couldn't deny that she longed for such attentions from him. What woman wouldn't? He was strong and tall and — and so very handsome.

Suddenly, his hands were on her cheeks, tilting her face up to his.

At that moment, he kissed her.

The shock of Bradley's lips touching hers was devastating. When his hands slid down her back, gooseflesh spread over her shoulders, arms then, like a warm wave of pleasure, over her breasts. She'd not donned a corset in her haste to dress, so her breasts were free and pushing against the solid warmth of him. From deep in the back of her throat came a moan that reverberated against his mouth.

When the bones in her legs seemed to dissolve, Bradley caught her and in moments, they were kneeling on the floor of the gazebo, his body pressed to hers.

It wasn't as surprising as it should have been that Jillian's body chose to ignore every verbal protestation she'd uttered up until now. She now wanted nothing more than to be possessed by this man. It had occurred to her, more times than she could count since she'd left America, that he knew exactly how to get under her skin.

She felt one of his hands slide down her back and take hold of one of her buttock cheeks. He gently kneaded, lifting and spreading it away from its twin. At once his hand slipped into the crevasse, holding her open and pressing his long fingers lower and lower until they acted as a saddle.

God, he was almost touching… He was so close to… She arched her back and the tips of his fingers grazed her vaginal lips through her trousers.

The vibration of his chuckle tingled and skidded across her chest. "Do you want more, my little vixen?"

Jillian couldn't answer. If she were to engage her vocal cords, the only sounds that would've emerged would've been more moaning. And that just wouldn't do.

As if through an intoxicating haze, she felt him begin to undo her blouse. To her surprise, she leaned back just a bit to allow him access to all the hooks and eyes. She wanted to feel him pressed to her skin with a desperation that took her aback.

One shoulder of her blouse fell away and his hand immediately went to cup her exposed breast.

This time, it was *his* moan she heard. He hugged her to him, sensually compressed to his body, between the hand that held her between her legs from behind and the breast he so tenderly kneaded. Her insides shook with need, and the juncture of her thighs went moist from the heat of his skin.

Bradley abruptly let her go and dragged one of the large cushions from a nearby bench to the floor of the gazebo. He maneuvered her backward until she rested upon it.

He lay down next to her, his fingers returning to caress her breasts, and his lips drew a path to her earlobe.

She closed her eyes languidly. God, but he knew what he was doing. His intrepid confidence only proved the fact. He exhaled near her ear, the air from his lungs producing a shuddering sigh.

Bradley's mouth sought hers and he kissed her the way he'd taught her — their tongues intertwining, a soft dance, boldly begging permission to stroke then shyly doing so.

His ragged breath matched rhythmically with her own. She reveled in the fact that she'd been the cause of his excitement. It was then that she noticed her trousers were down around her knees and his hand was petting her privates that up until a moment ago had been hidden from his touch.

Jillian broke out of the kiss and kicked her trousers off the rest of the way. She refused to acknowledge that *his* trousers were being stripped off at the same time.

Bradley returned to his position next to her on the cushion. He groaned deep within his chest and gently urged her thighs apart.

She spread for him, welcoming his attentions.

When his fingers found her pearl, she moaned loudly, the sound soaring toward the ceiling of the gazebo.

There wasn't terribly much she recalled from the inebriated night they'd shared together, but this, she remembered.

Chapter Five

A river of pleasure ran between Jillian's thighs, and Bradley tested the waters with his fingers at every opportunity, dipping low, then back up to tease her rigid flesh. He repeated this until she was out of her mind with sensation.

"You are so wet, Jilli," he whispered in her ear, using the same nickname he'd given her the night they'd slept together. She shuddered in response, his voice sending sensual electricity that lanced all the way down her spine. "Will you come for me?"

His soothing voice floated almost unheard past her ears. Jillian nodded, afraid of what would tumble from of her mouth.

"Then let me stroke you until you do, like this."

His wicked fingers gently tugged and released her, gaining speed. It must have been mere moments until Jillian cried out in pure bliss.

Barely a second after her tremors stopped, Bradley settled between her thighs, sinking slowly into her.

Oh, God. She remembered this intense sensation, too. Remembered it as if he'd done it to her yesterday. She bore down on him, squeezing her insides. He gasped and she reveled in his responsiveness.

"Yes, that's it," came his agonized voice.

He pressed harder into her and Jillian's insides trembled gloriously.

"God, I love to feel you come."

Unable to quell the tide, Jillian took a deep breath and allowed her feelings to control her voice. What came out was primitive, half-gasps and moans that didn't mean anything but what she felt. He carried her over orgasmic waves and rode her hard, deep. He still had the most glorious physical cadence — and she couldn't imagine anything more perfect.

Just when she felt she could catch her breath, he whispered, "My turn, Jilli."

He slammed into her, unleashing his passion again and again, his precision incredible, the aftershocks nothing but pure pleasure.

He took his release, growling through clenched teeth.

They lay together, hearts pounding, skin slick, limbs shaking, until they were able to breathe normally.

Bradley rolled onto his side, his face serene, as if sleeping with a slight grin on his face.

Jillian pushed herself to a seated position, her blouse open and, hanging from one shoulder her hair, that had long since escaped the plaiting in the melee of activity, fell over the other. The air was balmy, and a breeze which smelled faintly of rain and roses stirred her wavy tresses. Behind the gazebo and beyond the trees, the stars twinkled as if nothing of significance had happened. Her gaze wandered across their impromptu nest. She observed the cushion under her bare legs and the pile of their clothes.

She felt her eyes go wide. *What have I done?*

Bradley reached for her and almost took hold of her hand, but she pulled away.

His head came up. "Wha — ?"

Jillian was already reaching for her discarded garment. "This wasn't supposed to happen." she whispered with acute aggression, mostly to herself, then turned to Bradley. "You shouldn't be here in England!" She rose and shoved a leg into her trousers followed by the other one.

"Jillian — "

"No. I don't want excuses. The first time, I was drunk, lonely for male company. This time the blame lies completely on your head, you — you loathsome seducer!" A sob escaped her raw throat. "I have plans for my future, plans that don't include the infamous J. Bradley Townsend! I never ever intended to see you again, to do *this* with you." She fastened the buttons of her trousers and shoved her blouse down the front and back of them. *How could I have been so reckless? How could my flesh completely ignore the logic of my head?*

"Jillian, I'm sorry —"

"As well you should be." she nearly shouted as she fastened her blouse. "I am already in enough trouble without your help."

His eyebrow quirked but then he held up his hands. "All right. All right. Just allow me to stay until the end of the party —"

Jillian didn't allow him to finish. "Do what you will, Mr. Townsend, just don't do it to me." She spun on her heel and took the steps down to the lawn where she ran the rest of the way toward the main house.

Bradley fell back upon the cushion and sighed in frustration. They were supposed to be snuggling together right now. Dozing in and out of sleep. Blissful. Content.

But instead, he lay there, painfully aware of her absence from the now cold spot next to him.

She'd at least stayed a while the last time they'd been together.

He laced his fingers behind his head. He understood that he probably should not seduce her anymore, which would be near impossible, but the rest of what she'd said didn't make sense to him. What had she meant by plans that didn't include him? And just what sort of trouble was she in?

He stood and pondered the possibilities as he replaced the cushion upon the bench. He reached for his trousers and slid his foot inside. But as he attempted to slip the other foot into the adjoining leg, he found that the garment only went to his knees. His head came up as the realization hit him.

"Shit! She has my trousers!"

* * * *

Jillian rounded the corner to her room when her mother opened her door.

"Mama, what are you doing up so late?"

"I was just about to ask that of you, Jillian." Her voice sounded raspy and tired.

Jillian stood there, unable to answer her mother — all the while holding back her own accusations. Had her mother been waiting for her? For how long? Had her mother been awake when Jillian had flown down the stairs just before midnight? She wasn't a child for Heaven sakes, nor was she under some sort of curfew.

Jillian's mother's gaze suddenly traveled down to her bare feet, but not before pausing at her hips. She knew it could be considered odd to go about without shoes, but what was her mother staring at?

She looked down at her legs and felt her eyes go wide.

Jillian was wearing Bradley's trousers.

Setting a serene smile upon her face, Jillian looked up at her mother. Before she could comment, Jillian bid her mother a good night then strode to her room.

* * * *

Bradley's shirt tails barely reached the bottom of his buttocks. The breeze which blew wasn't helping matters, either. Draped over his arm were Jillian's trousers. Disallowing the blame to be placed on either of them for the absurd situation, he marched across the west lawn to the main house, his shirt tails flapping, giving anyone who might look a good show.

He slipped unnoticed over the threshold, beyond the foyer and up the split stairway to his room.

Shutting the door, he considered himself lucky that no one had witnessed his journey from the gazebo. He couldn't imagine how much more Jillian would hate him if he was forced to explain why he appeared naked from the waist down, carrying her trousers.

Bradley tossed Jillian's garment onto his bed, stripped off his shirt, washed at the basin and fell atop the bed. He noticed belatedly that her trousers were trapped under his thigh.

He grinned, imagining it was Jillian herself ensnared there.

* * * *

Breakfast found everyone red-eyed and not very sociable. Everyone, that was, but Miles, who had come from Thornton Manor to join the Kelleys and their guest.

Unable to speak to Mr. Townsend about the fact that he still had her trousers, Jillian simply ignored his presence. She wished everyone would vanish but Miles. He seemed to look at her with compassion and she found herself desperate for his temperate company. With him, she could be herself and not be on her guard, worrying if he was out to seduce her or not. She figured that Miles would engage her in the sport of seduction after they were married.

"Miss Kelley." The silence of the room was shattered by the sound Miles' voice.

Jillian's gaze flew to his—unruffled, though how she accomplished it, after her insides seemed as though they were lurching through her skin, was beyond her reasoning.

His manners, she supposed, caused him to refrain from comment. "Might we take a turn in your garden maze after breakfast? I'd like to have a chat with you if I may."

Thankful that she had an excuse to get away from both her mother and Bradley, she accepted. "That would be lovely, Miles."

Jillian's mother spoke up, "Mr. Bassett, if she insists on wearing trousers again, perhaps you could talk her into, at the very least, a parasol?"

Jillian slid her mother a weary look. "Mother, there is no need to speak as though I were not in the room." She stood and placed her napkin on the table. "Do finish your breakfast, Miles. I will meet you in the garden maze in thirty minutes." She quit the breakfast room without so much as a, 'by your leave' from any of them.

* * * *

Not a word that hadn't to do with the weather was spoken after Jillian had left the room. Bradley brooded during the meaningless conversation. Jillian's mother pushed her food from one side of her plate to the other. Miles ate as if he were going to be executed. What was so private that the milksop couldn't say it in front of everyone? That he wanted to marry her?

Bradley somehow evaded an audible intake of breath at the idea. That must have been it. Sweet Jesus, it had to have been the trouble Jillian had spoken of! She and Miles must have formed some sort of attachment. And, because of that one night they'd shared in the States, she was no longer in possession of her virtue. Yes, Bradley could see how that could be a definite problem.

Regardless of her lack of purity or depth of passion— however one wished to label it— the situation was perfectly unacceptable. No one was going to marry Jillian. No one but—

Miles stood, bringing Bradley out of his thoughts. He placed his napkin on the table and turned to Mrs. Kelley. "Mrs. Kelley, thank you for the lovely breakfast. I'll just run along and wait for Miss Kelley out of doors."

Mrs. Kelley dismissed him with a smile and a friendly wave of her hand.

Positive Miles was out of hearing distance, Bradley addressed Mrs. Kelley. "Madam, do you think it wise of me to be concerned about Miss Kelley?" He didn't allow her to answer. "After all, both she and Mr. Bassett are of age and— well, let's just say that a discreet chaperone might keep things from becoming...you know." He finished by raising his eyebrows high.

"Good thinking, Mr. Townsend. I shall ring for Fletcher —"
She reached for her bell.

Placing his napkin atop the table and standing abruptly,
Bradley stayed her hand. "No need. I will be happy to
wander in the maze." He smiled at her. "That way Jillian
won't know you've sent a companion and you will be free
and clear of her wrath."

Her face brightened. "You are always so thoughtful, Mr.
Townsend, thank you."

Bradley bowed to her and set out in search of the garden
maze.

* * * *

On her way out to the garden, Jillian fumed. Oh, she'd
brought her parasol, all right, but she'd be damned if she
was going to open it. Using it as an old-fashioned walking
stick, she sniffed delicately. She had become a free-thinking
woman, and she was not about to be bullied or manipulated
in any way. Not, that was, unless Miles himself insisted.

When she came to the east entrance of the maze, she
discovered Miles sitting on a bench in the shade. His very
essence calmed her and she thought it quaint that he wished
to speak in the maze where they'd played as children. They
knew every twist and turn in the hedgerows, and could go
through from beginning to end blindfolded and backward.

"Hello, Miles." She smiled, unconcerned that every
emotion she felt showed on her face.

He stood and reached out his hands to hers. "Come, let us
take our stroll." He gave her fingers a quick squeeze before
releasing them. He then offered her his elbow.

After Miles threaded her hand through the crook of his
arm, they started forward.

They walked along in companionable silence, but by the
third junction, Jillian couldn't help but begin to speculate
about why he'd invited her to take a turn. Was he looking

to further their friendship or reprimand her? Was he going to tell her how lovely she'd turned out to be after the last four years or was he going to admonish her for her fashion choices? Yet she waited, nibbling on the inside of her cheek so as not to blurt the fact that she had become anticipatory, more so with each slow, ill-measured minute, about what was on his mind.

From somewhere nearby, a twig snapped as if trod upon, but Jillian wasn't disposed to comment because at the same time, Miles finally cleared his throat to speak. Forgetting about the noisy shrubbery, Jillian steeled herself and tilted her face toward his.

"Jillian, you and I have known each other all of our lives."

"Yes, we have."

"I am quite aware that there was a time when you wished to be more than friends with me."

"Mm," she agreed, hoping to subdue the emotions which were at present rioting in her stomach. Where was this conversation headed? In the right direction, she hoped.

"I am older now and it is, in fact, time for me to settle."

Settle? Settle down or settle for the next girl who crosses his path? Whatever he was about to say, she knew would alter her future from this moment on. She pulled her gaze from his and focused on the greenery as they strolled along.

"As you know, my father is respected among the people of St. Helens."

She could do naught but agree with a nod.

He took a shuddering breath. "As such, I would be hard pressed to offer for a girl of questionable habits."

Jillian's hand flinched on his arm. Was he insinuating that she had questionable habits or was he referring to another girl? He still hadn't made himself clear on either point.

He continued, "My wife will have to maintain that respectability from the instant we become engaged until death do us part."

"Of course," Jillian murmured. Her mind reeled while trying to unravel his curious comments.

Miles stopped their progress and turned to her. "You understand, don't you?"

Looking into his eyes, she searched for the meaning of his words, but to no avail. "Have—? Have you made any declarations to this girl as of yet?"

He took a deep breath as if to say something of significance and after a pause, he shook his head.

All of Jillian's hopes and dreams began to deflate until he spoke again.

"I am anticipating seeing if her recently acquired ideals will be a permanent addition to her personality "

Jillian opened her mouth to answer, but with what she had no idea. From the other side of the hedgerow, she thought she heard someone sniffle. She lifted her hand from Miles' arm and, by the power of suggestion she was sure, Jillian rubbed her nose back and forth across the backs of her knuckles. It had suddenly become incessantly itchy.

Noticing that Miles was at once disposed to do the same, she spun away, thinking that perhaps he was trying to tell her, ever so politely, that she'd left something unsightly around her nose. Jillian turned and pulled a handkerchief from the pocket of her trousers. From behind her, she heard Miles inhaling once, twice, thrice, getting ready to sneeze. When he did, it seemed that the originator of the idea on the other side of the hedgerow sneezed at the exact same time.

Someone must have been spying on her. Jillian's fury flared.

As quick as lightning, she lifted her parasol and thrust it through the bush as if it were a sword, hoping to chase away the perpetrator. The second her parasol made contact with something solid, a faint whoosh of air sounded and at once the handle was yanked from her grasp. *The vile conspirator has snatched my parasol away!* She suffered a humiliating widening of her eyes, and just as she'd made ready to plunge her hand back through the bushes to retrieve the pilfered item, Miles turned to her.

"Rather dry out today, don't you think?"

Abandoning the idea, she stuffed her handkerchief into her pocket and nodded.

Miles offered Jillian his elbow when her hand was once again free. They took a few steps then he stopped. He peered over his shoulder as if to consider the spot they had just occupied.

Miles looked about then glanced down at her free hand. His eyebrows did a bit of a hitch. Then, as if shrugging off his former inquisitiveness, he presented her with a pleasant, closed-mouthed smile.

She and Miles continued down the path. She'd be eternally thankful that he hadn't seen her parasol disappear in to the hedge. Of course, the probability was high that he had forgotten altogether she'd been carrying it. Even still, knowing Miles the way she did she suspected that he was simply demonstrating his good manners in not mentioning it.

Yes, that must be it.

As they approached the end of the maze, Jillian politely dismissed Miles, saying she'd like to sit upon the shaded bench and nurse her slight headache. Miles bowed to her and headed for the house.

After he had gone, she climbed a trellis attached to a tall stone wall which flanked the maze garden. Arms akimbo, she looked down into the maze from the top of the wall.

"All right, where are you?" A silence followed her inquiry, but she wasn't fooled one little bit. "I know you're there, so you may as well declare yourself."

Seemingly with great reluctance, her parasol rose into the air and waved as if it were a white flag and the person at the handle end had declared themselves surrendered.

"If you can direct me to the nearest exit, I would be most grateful." A penitent male voice rose from the shrubbery.

She didn't miss the fact that this mysterious declaration carried with it an American accent. "And why should I? You were eavesdropping on a very private conversation.

In some countries, a person could face certain torturous reprisals for such an offense."

"If you help me out of here, I will gladly offer myself up for punishment."

"Ha! I just bet you would." She then let him stew while she climbed down and entered through the west end of the maze.

Making a few turns, she spoke into the air. "I'm considering letting you dwell within the walls of this maze for a few days."

"Have I acted so very wrong as to deserve that?" He took a few steps in her direction.

"You have, indeed." Jillian turned a corner, taking herself farther away from him.

After a few moments, the accused came up with a defense. "I was only looking after your best interests."

"You were spying, sir, deny it if you dare!" *How on earth could he still believe himself free from blame*? She hurriedly made her way to the spot exactly on the opposite side of the maze from him.

"Where did you go?" he asked, his voice muffled by at least seven walls of shrubbery.

"I am on the innocent side of this haven, a place where you shan't be allowed to tread." When he hesitated to reply, she held her breath to listen. His footsteps tapped out a swift beat down the path and she stifled a giggle with her hands. He was going farther into the center, not toward the outer edges, the simpleton.

As if reading her thoughts, he addressed her. "I'm afraid you have the advantage over me, Miss Kelley. I'm sure you've known your way around this maze since you were a babe."

Jillian took the passageway that sent her a bit deeper into the center, but then cut south toward the wall. "There is where you're correct. Pity you couldn't use your intuitiveness to get yourself out of this maze."

At that point, his heavy footfalls became hurried and

desperate-sounding. She smiled. He was running around in the maze.

"Do you have any idea what I'm going to do to you when I catch you?"

Carefully stepping toward the exit, she laughed. "When? Don't you mean if?"

"No. I mean when."

Good lord, he was in the next row over! Down a few steps and around the corner and they'd be face to face. Jillian recalled a hiding place that she'd used as a child, deep inside the maze. She hurried around two more corners then ducked into a particularly thin place in the hedgerow, whispering a prayer of thanks that it still existed after all these years.

When she stood and opened her eyes, Bradley Townsend was there, taking hold of her upper arms.

"I win." His serious countenance melted into a wicked smile.

Jillian gritted her teeth. "You and your games and wagers. Bradley Townsend, you let me go this instant!"

"Not on your life. I would, however, like to discuss that punishment which has intentionally transferred from me to you."

"I was not spying on *you*!" Jillian protested and tried to shrug out of his grasp.

"No, but you threatened to leave me in this maze to die."

"Not to die!" She pleaded as if for her own life. "Just to give you a bit of your own medicine, that's all."

Bradley pulled her close and wrapped his arms around her. "The only medicine for my ills is you."

Then he kissed her.

Again.

Chapter Six

She had to admit it to herself, standing there being kissed by Bradley Townsend, cut off from the possibility of prying eyes by at least ten if not more hedgerows on three sides of them was rather thrilling. Her mind spun in lazy circles. Miles would probably never have thought to kiss her in the maze. No. Inside Bradley Townsend smoldered a scorching fire which Bassett just didn't possess — in fact, it may have been possible he didn't have the capacity for it.

Another point for Bradley.

However, this new revelation did nothing to dissuade her from her duty of marrying Miles. Bradley was going to have to stop taking liberties with her. Right now.

This instant.

Just as soon as he's finished kissing me.

Jillian's breath was ragged and desperate-sounding, and Bradley deepened the kiss. *He is entirely accurate in sensing what I need.* Without the permission of her own wits, Jillian found herself giving in to the diversion.

God, his tongue. She knew exactly what it was capable of, and the memory almost made her swoon. Several times, she'd thought about beginning a diary and jotting down the sensational exploits they'd shared the night of the alumnus party, but she figured it would be unreadable and dreadfully fragmented as Jillian only recalled the more volatile points of the evening.

Yes, her mind echoed. *Just like this.* Jillian was vaguely aware that Bradley had unbuttoned her blouse, released her breasts from her corset and had a nipple in his mouth. There played that tongue again — and those fingers kneading the pliant, excitable flesh.

All at once, Jillian wanted to lie down, to spread herself naked upon the ground and let him have at her body like on that wonderful night all those weeks ago. She opened her eyes to find a spot where they could stretch out when she realized her iniquity.

Miles.

It aggravated her to no end that the very presence of J. Bradley Townsend could make her forget her duty.

Pushing at his head she gave a squeak of pleasure-pain when she tore away from the suction he had on her nipple. With great determination, Jillian held him at arm's length.

"You rake! You've done it again!"

His line of sight languidly dipped to her exposed breasts and she followed. The tip was rosy and puckered, as if happy, even satisfied. Her whole being indulged in a strange sensation of elation which made no sense at all. It should be Miles here with her, not Bradley! She made to cover her chest and her gaze snapped back to his.

Bradley shrugged. "We enjoy each other's company. It's a simple matter of coming to terms with the fact."

She narrowed her eyes as she tried to tuck herself back into her corset. "We enjoy each other's bodies, I think you mean."

"There is little difference. In public, we call it 'company', in private… Well, let's just say, 'clothes are optional'. Here, allow me." He swept her hands away and took hold of a breast. Pushing it against her body with one hand and tugging at her corset with his other, he managed to tuck both the breast and his hand deep inside. Ever so slowly, he pulled his hand out, scraping her nipple down the entire length of his fingers.

Jillian closed her eyes and her head fell back slightly, but she managed to stifle the moan that would have been very loud, she imagined.

"I apologize if that was a bit rough."

She opened her eyes. "No. Fine—it was fine." She felt

insane heat creep up her cheeks while protesting. Somehow, she managed to right the other without a show. The moment his hand was away from her person she buttoned the blouse.

"Was it? Of course, I remember." He snapped his fingers as if it were a new revelation. His voice dropped to a dangerously sensual reverberation. "You like it a bit rough up top."

With an indignant inhalation, Jillian hastily made her way to the exit, knowing full well that the arrogant J. Bradley Townsend was, much to her embarrassment, entirely correct and additionally, hard on her heels.

She managed to refasten her blouse and, spotting her parasol that he had so unceremoniously discarded at some point, she scooped it on the way to the exit.

Outside the maze, as Jillian passed the bench, Bradley stopped her. "Jillian, wait."

Strictly out of courtesy, she paused and waited for him to say his piece.

She suffered through several moments of his hesitation, until finally he spoke, "Look at me."

Jillian took a breath and spun toward him. "Yes? I'm looking."

He closed the distance between them and glared down at her without touching her. "Bassett is trying to change you."

A laugh erupted from Jillian. "He is not. You have no idea what you're talking about."

"No, it is you who has no idea."

She narrowed her eyes, wishing she could block him from her sight. "I don't have to stand here and be insulted." She turned to go.

Bradley quickly sped up and stepped into her path. "I'm not trying to insult you, Jillian. I'm trying to show you what's happening here."

She waved away the notion with a sweep of her closed parasol. "How could you possibly know what Miles is thinking when you've just met him?"

"You are correct. I don't. However, one cannot ignore the facts. He spoke of respectability and questionable habits. He made it perfectly clear that settling down topped his agenda, and yet he did not declare his intentions to you."

"That says nothing of significance to me."

"Perhaps not to you, but I happen to be a man, and I know where his golden speech was headed."

"Nonsense." She made to pass him but once again he impeded her departure.

"Jillian, listen to me. Bassett is waiting for you to transform into something you are not."

She laughed. "You have it wrong, Mr. Townsend."

"Bradley."

Stepping around him, she ignored the invitation to call him by his given name. She turned to watch at him as she set out back toward the house. "Miles loves me and will be offering for me by the end of the weekend. You'll see."

"If that is what you want, you will have to burn your trousers and not speak your mind, which will be quite a loss for those of us who possess a higher intellect."

His compliment went mostly unnoticed as she strode up the sloping lawn. Stopping in her tracks, she then glanced back at him. "Perhaps I will change, Mr. Townsend. Shouldn't one adapt to one's surroundings?"

"In some instances, yes. But love is different, Miss Kelley. Love, and loyalty, should remain constant no matter its environs."

"I have nothing further to contribute to this discussion, sir, so I'll be off." She headed home, pretending not to hear his closing comments, which he freely and rather loudly submitted.

"You'd be wise to remember this. One's love is only as deep as one's personality will allow."

* * * *

For the entirety of the next three days, Bradley somehow

quelled his lust for the brazen Miss Kelley. Instead of concentrating his efforts and thinking of ways to corner her, he observed as Jillian, Mr. Bassett and Mrs. Kelley interacted. He hadn't supplied much conversationally, either, but did his best to apply his expertise in the usual parlor distractions — cards, backgammon and reading aloud. There wasn't a single doubt in his mind that both Miles and Jillian's mother longed to have their little girl back — the girl Jillian must have been before her experience at college had opened her eyes to the world.

Friday afternoon, Jillian's mother had Mr. Bassett's mother, Lady Bassett, over for tea. Miles was noticeably absent. However, this being a delightful happenstance, Bradley hadn't mentioned it.

After tea, Bradley listened patiently to the conversation as the elder women announced the invitees for the weekend house party, glancing up at Jillian every so often while he played at solitaire on a small tea table.

Mrs. Kelley sipped her tea while Lady Bassett addressed Jillian. "Miss Prudence Dearborne and Miss Audrey Van Amberg will be arriving tomorrow after breakfast."

Jillian sent the woman a closed-lipped smile as though she had no idea who these girls were.

Lady Bassett continued. "Both of them will be coming all the way from Brighton and have been properly introduced into society in London this season past."

Mrs. Kelley bobbed her head in approval.

Abandoning her card game, Jillian made her way over to a small book case and perused the titles with a pointed index finger.

"Additionally, we will be privileged to have the Honorable Miss Mary Eberhardt in attendance. Just yesterday I received her mother's response." She looked over at Jillian's mother. "The Honorable Miss Mary Eberhardt's father is a Baronet, don't you know." Lady Bassett nodded once in affirmation.

Both older women directed their gazes to Jillian, who held tightly to a book she'd chosen, but seemed to have no reaction whatsoever for her mother and her mother's friend.

"Jillian dear, aren't you excited about your house party?" She didn't allow her daughter to speak before continuing. "As hostess, you will provide entertainments, diversions, and see that nothing untoward or scandalous happens." As if she knew Jillian didn't have an opinion, she went on. "Do thank Lady Bassett for arranging the guest list for you. I dare say she's done some wonderful research on the girls in a very short amount of time."

Bradley watched Jillian press her lips together for a fraction of a second before she answered. "Of course. Thank you, Lady Bassett." When the two women turned back to continue chatting, Jillian cleared her throat, gaining their attention. "Are there no other gentlemen on your list?"

Clearly in on the so-called research of guests and apparent conspiracy, her mother answered. "Well, we already have Mr. Bassett and your friend, Mr. Townsend, from the States. I think that will be sufficient enough."

"But that leaves three females and two males. Surely one can see the scales are tipped slightly toward feminine influence."

Both Mrs. Kelley and Lady Bassett looked to Bradley for his opinion.

Following a brief silence during which Bradley glanced from the older women to Jillian and back again, he grinned. "I shan't be upset by the imbalance, I assure you." Then he nodded a slight bow to the ladies. Returning his attention to the game before him, he could feel the heat of scorn radiating from Jillian. He barely contained a grin let alone the chuckle that threatened to bubble up from the depths of his soul.

"If you will excuse me." Jillian crossed the room. The skirt of her gown she wore, most likely at her mother's request, nearly overturned the table on which Bradley had placed his cards.

When she was gone, Bradley looked sheepishly up at the

two older women. "I suppose I've upset your daughter, Mrs. Kelley."

Mrs. Kelley addressed Bradley. "Sir, it seems whatever we say these days has an adverse effect on the girl."

He smiled sympathetically. "She's of that age."

"Indeed," her mother agreed.

"However, I feel that I should at least apolcgize. I wouldn't want to dampen the spirit of the impending party with ill feelings."

Smiling, Mrs. Kelley gestured toward the door through which her daughter had fled. "That is very thoughtful of you, Mr. Townsend."

Bradley stood, bowed then departed to find Jillian.

* * * *

Beside herself, she'd fled to her favorite refuge, but somehow, the west gazebo didn't feel like the sanctuary it used to. The very thought of her safe haven shifting to the status of a public place, where any sort of person could venture, further stirred her anger. Having overturned every cushion and pillow within reach, she felt a pang of guilt, then set about righting the abused items.

With a sigh, she hugged the last of the pillows she'd thrown on the floor to her bosom in an apology. Tossing it onto a nearby bench, she stared off beyond the west lawns. "They have no idea as to the kind of people I would wish to entertain. Where are the scholars, the learned and the forward-thinkers? Had I kept my hand in the matter, I wouldn't have ended up with two bits of fluff and an aristocrat."

At Oberlin, she'd inadvertently drawn to herself wonderfully witty people. They'd compliment her by saying, "Birds of a feather, you know," which had pleasantly surprised her. Then, on that fateful night Bradley had appeared. How had it happened all those weeks ago?

She remembered the joy and tear-filled farewells of her

classmates, the well wishes from the alumni she'd met that evening, and hearty handshakes from the staff she'd be leaving behind when she left for home the next day. One of the alumni, a Mr. Townsend, had struck her as quite pleasant to be around, not to mention handsome. All this had occurred even before dinner had been served, well before they'd begun sampling the wines donated by various east coast vineyards, anyway. He'd asked if he could sit next to her for the meal, and she'd acquiesced.

If anyone would have told her that mere hours after the conclusion of the party she'd be lying in his arms naked, sated and forever changed, she would have laughed in their face.

In the back of her whirling mind, Jillian knew she must come to terms with the fact that Bradley knew what he was doing, physically speaking, of course. Perhaps that was the reason she couldn't withstand his charms. *Yes, that had to be it.* He embodied heat and cold, elation and anguish, whimsy and reality. And Jillian, apparently, was addicted.

What else could one call it but an addiction? She didn't crave him, per se, but each time she'd been presented with the temptation, she'd never been able to resist.

It was a crying shame that Miles hadn't wielded his allure to her in this manner. Perhaps she should encourage him to do so.

Jillian stiffened when she heard a masculine chuckle behind her. Already knowing exactly who loitered there, she slowly turned toward him. Her mood was sour and she didn't care if it showed or not. "I do not remember issuing an invitation requesting your presence at my gazebo."

He sobered, but not enough for her taste. He yet smiled. "Miss Kelley. I must confess to feeling a stitch of self-reproach here. Is it because of me that you are upset at this moment?"

She turned away and sighed. "I-I will admit that it would have been better if you had gone home when I told you to. However, now that I have been made aware of my guest list for the weekend, I will acknowledge that you will probably be the most entertaining of the lot."

"What, even more so than your darling *Miles*?"

She whirled on him. Jillian had just bared her soul to this rake. Could she even hope for a crumb of civility from him? "Don't you *dare* mock Miles. He's a perfect gentleman, which is more than I can say for *you*. Why, you haven't even offered to return my trousers?"

"Your latter statement is terribly unfair, for neither have you offered to return my trousers."

Jillian's mouth opened, but having no retort, she shut it just as quickly and jerked her chin away.

He sighed and rested his hands on her shoulders. Just how the stealthy cur had gotten across the gazebo without her hearing his footsteps, she'd never know.

"Perhaps we can come to an agreement."

"An agreement, with you? Well, you certainly have proven yourself worthy of my trust up until this point, haven't you?" Jillian's venomous sarcasm, she hoped, hadn't gone unnoticed. Ignoring the lack of warmth she felt when he lifted his hands from her person, she took a step away from him.

"In any case, if you don't wish to hear my offer, then perhaps you don't want the trousers after all."

She turned to him. "Of course I do," she snapped.

He indicated to one of the benches with an upturned hand. "Then perhaps you should have a seat and we can discuss the matter."

Jillian eyed Bradley with a shrewd gaze, hoping with all her heart that he got the message that she didn't trust him as far as she could carry him upon her back. Still watching him, she proceeded across the gazebo and lowered herself to a cushioned bench.

"Much better."

Bradley sat beside her. She couldn't shake the feeling that he was, in fact, the spider from the *Little Miss Muffet* nursery rhyme. Not that she portrayed herself as some prim Miss to go scurrying away because he had eight arms that seemed to wrap about her every single time her guard was down.

"Now." As if adjusting to a more comfortable position, Bradley inched closer to Jillian. "We must agree upon a discreet time and place to do the switch."

"Why can't we just meet on the landing, mid stairs?" Trying to look nonchalant, Jillian leaned in the opposite direction, distancing herself as much as possible from Bradley.

"No." He shook his head. "What would happen if someone were to see us exchanging trousers? That wouldn't do at all." He placed his hand behind her on the railing.

"The stables, then." She tilted away again. One more subtle move and she'd be flush to the post behind her.

Bradley pressed his lips together for a brief moment. "Still too many people lurking about." He reclined upon the cushions.

"Our staff doesn't lurk." She inched forward this time and felt the edge of the cushion against her bottom. If he made one false move, she would still be able to escape.

He partially stood, then sat directly next to her, their thighs touching from hip to knee, her skirt trapped under his muscular leg. *Blast!* She wouldn't have been able to move now even if the gazebo caught fire.

Currently at the obvious advantage, Bradley leaned into her — she closed her eyes. What wouldn't she do to once again to shut him out of her sight? Would he take the hint this time?

"I'm afraid you'll just have to meet me here tonight. At midnight," he whispered then nipped at her earlobe, which sent sparks beneath her eyelids and tingles up and down her body.

"No," she choked out, unable to move for reasons in addition to the confinement of her skirts. He did smell utterly clean and male and quite wonderful, after all.

"Yes," he murmured then nuzzled her neck. "It won't take long." His lips grazed the side of her neck. "I promise."

At once, Jillian felt as if he were sitting on her corset too, for her lungs refused to cooperate with the amount of air her brain needed. He was virility and fire and just plain dangerous. Sadly, the danger was not enough to make her demand that he release her from her trapped position. As if issuing a response out of habit, she spoke. "I cannot meet you." Then, as her conviction made for the exit for no apparent reason other than the mere proximity of him, she whispered, "I *will* not."

The thought, as well-founded as it was, fled her mind as she turned to Bradley. She offered him her lips and as expected, he made use of her moment of weakness rather thoroughly.

Chapter Seven

Seduced.

Again. And this time, in broad daylight. What a shameless woman she'd become.

Ever since Bradley had shown up on her doorstep and gotten within two inches of her, the second he gazed deeply into her eyes or smiled that roguish grin of his, Jillian couldn't help but shove all duty, sense and reason out of the window. Was it completely her fault, though? If he were more of a gentleman, perhaps she wouldn't succumb so easily.

Jillian needed to come to terms with the fact that Bradley, if given the opportunity, would probably try to seduce her many more times before the weekend was over. As hard as she tried, she couldn't think of a way to avoid his advances without looking like a green-skirted maid.

Jillian's thoughts drifted back to the gazebo and to the man delighting her with his lips and a tongue so competent in its engagement with her own, it practically made Jillian lose her mind. Well, perhaps not practically, *most assuredly*.

She'd have to put her foot down. Miles was her one and only love — they had a history, numerous events and holiday celebrations which they'd experienced together which stretched back as far as she could remember. The Bassett family had never missed a family gathering. Lady Bassett and Jillian's mother were best friends, after all.

What she had with Mr. J. Bradley Townsend was purely physical. A silly chemical reaction. Some sort of primal instinct.

Miraculously, she raised her hands and placed them

against his chest. Pushing away, she broke off their kiss. "I'm sorry. I will not meet you tonight or any other night. Now release me this instant, Mr. Townsend." Her voice had been steady, the speech short and to the point—and she was amazed that she wasn't shouting or in tears. This seemed to have an effect on Bradley, as he rose to his feet, allowing her liberation.

Ha! Finally, she'd earned a point in her struggle to break away from this seductive, virile male. She'd have to remember this emotionless tactic in future.

His back was to her as he stared out at the west field, running a hand through the top of his thick hair. He sighed, a frustrated sound. "How can you be so cold to me?" he murmured.

Jillian would have laughed had her breathing returned to normal. "Cold, Mr. Townsend?" She strode over to stand next to him. "Look at my cheeks." When he glanced at her, she continued, her voice remaining as steady as it had been. "I can feel the fire in them. A fire you yourself started like some stark, raving arsonist."

"I won't deny my feelings for—"

"Feelings are not something we should act upon on a whim. The discernment of such is one of the things which separates us from the beasts of the field."

Bradley exhaled again and with a seemingly great effort, he tore his gaze from her and looked out at the lawns. "I concede," he said with a dismissive shrug of his shoulder.

Jillian relaxed. "Good. Now, in case I have not made myself perfectly clear, I am going to marry Miles Bassett."

At that moment, Bradley whirled on her. "Am I correct in the fact that Miles has not made any declarations as to an understanding between the two of you?"

"Yes you are," she said calmly, not allowing the pain to show on her face at Bradley's candor. "But I'll not indulge in a dalliance with you whilst I wait for him."

Jillian turned and walked toward the stairs that led out of the gazebo, pausing only to answer his next question.

"And how long, Miss Kelley, do you intend on waiting?"

"However long it takes." And with that, she continued up the lawn toward the house.

Near exasperation, Bradley dropped onto a cushioned bench in the gazebo. Something needed to be done about Miss Jillian Kelley. He'd not allow her to waste away waiting for the milksop to make his move, nor would he sit back and watch as she retreated into the clamshell this tedious English society forced upon its women.

Jillian Kelley deserved more than either two of those fates would afford.

Bradley closed his eyes and, in searching for a solution, tried to imagine himself at Jillian and Miles' wedding. Aside from every thought and feeling revolting against even a single vision, he knew in his heart he'd never allow such an absurd event to take place.

When he opened his eyes, his gaze trained on the floor of the gazebo, the same floor where he'd made love to Jillian what felt like moments ago and eons ago all at the same time.

"Two days," he murmured. He'd give himself two days to win her, and if he couldn't do it in that amount of time, he'd head home straight away and dive headlong into teaching at Oberlin.

Bradley looked up as Fletcher approached the steps to the gazebo. "Sir, Mrs. Kelley wished me to remind you that an early supper would be served tonight, seven o'clock instead of eight."

He smiled at the butler. "Thank you, Fletcher. I would imagine this household would be run with much less efficiency were you employed elsewhere."

Fletcher bowed. "Thank you, sir."

Bradley rose and walked alongside Fletcher back to the house. "May I be so bold as to put a few questions to you, Fletcher?"

"You may, Mr. Townsend."

"You've known Miss Kelley for a long time, yes?"

"I have, sir, for most of her life."

"Can you perhaps tell me — that is, enlighten me — as to what the story is behind she and Mr. Miles Bassett?"

Fletcher's pace slowed and he placed his hands, one inside the other, behind his back as they strolled. "Mr. Bassett has long been a favorite of Miss Kelley's, even before I came to Fairfield Court. As I understand it, they've known each other since they were babes, due to Mrs. Kelley and Lady Bassett being best friends and the like."

One thing for sure, the butler was telling the truth. Everything had fallen into place from Mrs. Kelley allowing Lady Bassett the liberty of creating a guest list for the Kelley's house party, to Jillian's insane desire for the milksop. She may have even felt obligated in some deep-seeded way to wed her mother's best friend's son. "I see." Bradley nodded. "Do go on."

"Ever since she could walk, Miss Kelley followed the young Mr. Bassett around. When nature ran its course as it usually does and Mr. Bassett discovered the fairer sex, he saw our Miss Kelley as a little sister, and not so much a prospect for marriage. At least, that was how myself and others in the household saw it. We were all rooting for our dear Miss Kelley to win Mr. Bassett, who would inherit upon his father's death, but it seemed fruitless. When it became near certain that Mr. Bassett was looking to reach higher than Miss Kelley, Mrs. Kelley sent her daughter off to school — even so far as across the Atlantic. Mrs. Kelley, if truth be told, hoped to get the love-struck girl out of Mr. Bassett's way, as well as to cleanse the girl's heart of him."

"One would think Mrs. Kelley would have been upset with Lady Bassett," Bradley commented.

"Not in the way of things here. In fact, she didn't blame her best friend at all because she would have expected no less if she had had a son."

"Tell me, Fletcher. In your opinion, why is Mr. Bassett not married after all this time has passed?"

"Well, sir, it has been rumored that he did make his intentions known to a girl from Kent whom he had met during the recent season, but she refused him."

"Why? I thought the Bassetts provided a superb match for anyone."

"Not the daughter of an earl, apparently."

"My, that was high," Bradley murmured mostly to himself.

"Indeed, sir. Now if I may put a question to you?"

Being obliged to the man for the information he'd divulged, Bradley could hardly refuse. "Of course, Fletcher."

"Do understand that I only have Miss Kelley's happiness in mind." At Bradley's nod he continued. "If Mr. Bassett decides against offering for Miss Kelley after all, will you be considering forming an attachment with her?"

"Tell me, Fletcher, if I give you my answer, how many others in the household will I have to depend upon to keep the secret?"

Fletcher nodded in understanding. "Only myself, sir. Your answer shan't go any further than that."

"Can I have your word on that?"

"Indeed you may."

"Then my answer is— Good Heavens, I don't think I've ever said it aloud." To be honest, Bradley had no idea as to what the future held, especially if Jillian was averse to the idea of marrying him. The way things were going with Jillian of late and if her infatuation with the milksop did indeed run so profoundly, it didn't look good for one J. Bradley Townsend.

Chuckling, Fletcher answered for him. "I'll take that as a yes, sir."

"You may, Fletcher, you may." Now to convince Jillian of the splendid match.

By now, the two conspirators were at the front steps of the main house. "I thank you for the insight, Fletcher."

"You are welcome." Fletcher stopped Bradley just before he opened the door. "Would you take a word of advice, sir?"

"Anything if it will assist my cause."

"Even as a child, when it came to something Miss Kelley wanted, it could be said that she enjoys the hunt as much as the catch."

Bradley nodded slowly. "So, if she's allowed to hunt, she may respond."

"Indeed, sir. In addition, if it looks as if you are perusing other game, you may get her attention much more precipitously."

Bradley smiled and reached out to pat Fletcher on the back. "You are invaluable, Fletcher."

Fletcher smiled back. "Thank you, sir."

* * * *

It had to have been past midnight, and Bradley lay in bed, staring at the canopy above in his lavish guest room. Jillian hadn't even glanced his way at supper, but had trained the entirety of her attention on Miles Bassett. When he'd announced where he'd been during the day, Bradley thought she would jump into the Bassett's lap.

"I have a surprise for you, Miss Kelley," Miles had said.

"A surprise?" Jillian sat up a little straighter, if that were possible. She'd been trussed up in a fine dusty-rose silk gown, one of the new ones her mother had ordered and paid dearly for the rushed job. Yes, Jillian looked beautiful, stunning even. All the same, though, Bradley thought she would be appealing in whatever sort of outfit she chose.

"I have secured a string quartet to play during dinner tomorrow night and, if you and your guests are so inclined, an hour or two of dancing."

"Oh, Miles! You are so wonderful to have done this for me!"

She'd simply lit up. Bradley had watched with a rapidly souring stomach as she'd reached her elegant hand across the table and Miles had taken it, giving it a gentle squeeze.

The obsequious twit.

Had his brother Daniel witnessed it, he'd have had the whelp's head on his polo mallet. A grin tugged at the corners of Bradley's mouth. Then again, Danny was a bit more hot-headed than he. Well, to be fair, merely younger, and less experienced in the obtuse British social skills he'd been required to endure since his arrival. No wonder his grandfather had left the *grandeur* of the family's title behind all those years ago.

Bradley sighed, his exhale filtering silently through his nose. His endeavor to divert Jillian's adoration away from the milksop was going to be a difficult one at best.

His next assignment would be to turn her head. And if her heart wasn't going to be the first to turn, perhaps her interest could be piqued another way. The party would commence tomorrow at luncheon. That gave him exactly twelve hours to come up with a 'play for keeps' stratagem.

Chapter Eight

"I am delighted to make your acquaintances, ladies," Jillian offered graciously, even though she felt like being terribly uncivil to all three of the girls who now stood in her mother's formal sitting room. Each one had freshened up after their journey and looked as perky as their youthful appearances would afford.

"St. Helens is just beautiful. Fairfield Court is nothing like I imagined," Miss Prudence Dearborne exclaimed. With her dark-brown, doe-like eyes, she scanned the high ceiling. "I think it's much grander." She smiled at Jillian, conveying her compliment.

"And the grounds seem so lovingly attended to," Miss Audrey Van Amberg remarked, standing as close as possible to her best friend, Prudence. "I particularly enjoyed the rose garden we passed on the way up the drive."

"Thank you so much, we love it here at Fairfield Court." To Jillian, Audrey and Prudence seemed to be as close as sisters, the way they practically clung to each other. Audrey had lovely violet eyes and a cherubic face. Her light-brown hair fell in long curls from her coiffure beneath her stiff, cream lace hat. Prudence's face appeared narrower than her friend's. Her dark, shining tresses, which matched her eyes, fell in front of her right shoulder from under her fashionable bonnet. In fact, her body in general was more willowy than Audrey's soft curves. They were the same height, and had the same porcelain complexion and hint of a blush upon their cheeks. It must have been the air around Brighton.

Allowing the Honorable Miss Mary Eberhardt her chance

to compliment her hostess, all three girls turned to her. Mary's close-lipped smile was received — however, Jillian thought the daughter of a baron could have at least been more generous than merely presenting a demure facial expression. Even if she did appear blonder than any Norse goddess could have possibly been.

Well, who cared anyway? In just three days these chits would be on their way home.

Before she could offer a seat to the girls while they awaited Miles and Bradley, both men strode into the room at the same time.

Introductions and pleasantries were exchanged and at once, a bell rang calling them to luncheon.

While Miles, along with the three female guests, preceded their hostess through the door, Jillian realized she hadn't even acknowledged the rat, Bradley Townsend. He now stood next to her, offering his arm to escort her into the dining room. As manners would dictate, she placed her hand upon his wrist. Her gaze rose from his shoulder up his neck, almost to his face, and back down to his neck. Her stomach lurched, then luckily, she quelled a horrified intake of breath.

"Are those my trousers about your neck?" she whispered incredulously.

"Oh." Bradley reached up and gave them a bit of an adjustment as if it were a perfectly natural occurrence to wear buff-colored wool in place of stiff white cotton around one's neck for a formal luncheon. "Why yes, yes they are."

Whatever points Bradley had earned in Jillian's eyes had just drained like bath water from an overturned basin. He'd spoken matter-of-factly, then made to move forward, only stopping when Jillian stood her ground. "Just what do you think you are doing? What will be your explanation when someone inquires as to the absence of your neck tie?" She tried to keep her voice down, but being so upset it was nigh impossible.

"No one will notice, I assure you." He tried to advance

again, but she wouldn't budge.

"You can't be certain of that!" she said in near panic. "What if they question the fashion?"

"I'll simply tell them I like the way your legs wrap around my neck." He grinned wickedly.

"You will do no such thing!" she rasped, completely mortified.

He chuckled then. "You've made such a fuss about it, perhaps I will, if only to stir things up a bit." Bradley's free hand clamped down atop her fingers and he pulled her forward into the dining room.

Jillian felt as though steam rose from the top of her head. She could likely warm the entirety of Fairfield Court's gate house in the dead of winter with the heat she was generating.

She could no longer think on it. Were she to, everyone within sight would be able to read the mortified, and at the same time murderous, thoughts which swirled in her mind.

Bradley helped her to her seat then went round the table to take his place — directly across from her.

She refused to meet his eyes, and, by God, she was determined to ask him to leave the second she got him alone. She'd make his excuses to her other guests. She'd say he became ill or that his aunt lay upon her death bed. Something. *Anything.*

"I say, Mr. Townsend," Miles asked as finger sandwiches were offered to the party, "is your neck tie there a new American trend?"

Jillian wanted to be struck down on the spot.

Bradley smiled at Miles then leveled his gaze on Jillian. "I'm hoping it will become a trend."

Before Jillian could even think of a reaction, Audrey Van Amberg addressed Bradley. "So, are you really an American, Mr. Townsend?

After what seemed like an overly long amount of time to Jillian, Bradley finally broke eye contact with her to answer Audrey's question. "Yes, Miss Van Amberg, I am."

Audrey looked at Prudence. "How exciting, a real American right here in this very room with us!"

As the two girls seemed to speak one after the other on every occasion, Prudence's turn came next. "Go on, Mr. Townsend, say something American."

Jillian watched while Bradley visibly colored. How appalling that he did so. The two babes in swaddling weren't worth the effort.

"I-I don't know what to say," he admitted with a grin and lifted a glass of water to his lips as if to hide behind the sip.

The near-sisters giggled at Bradley's words and he chuckled, replacing his drink onto the table.

Jillian clenched her hands into fists in her lap. *He actually likes the attention from the two childish chits*!

Miles turned to the Honorable Miss Mary Eberhardt. "And how about you? Have you ever seen a real American before?"

Unbelievable. Miles was engaging the empty-headed aristocrat in conversation! Jillian couldn't have been more livid. Splitting rails with her teeth would have come easily to her.

"No," she replied as if still thinking about it. "I have not."

Mary's demeanor remained perfectly flat, and perfectly English, Jillian observed. She would have been quite lonely were she to attend Oberlin.

"You know, ladies," Bradley addressed all three girls. "Miss Kelley went to school in the States, at the same university I attended. You should ask her how she liked it."

Everyone's gaze shifted to Jillian.

"Oh!" Prudence took a shuddering breath. "And how did you find America, Miss Kelley?"

Put on the spot, Jillian swallowed, searching for an answer and at the same time, thanked God her mother wasn't in the room. This subject would forever be a thorny stem between them.

"Uh —" As she thought, she felt her shoulders relax a bit. "It was…different."

"But how? The people? The scenery?" Miss Van Amberg asked, seeming more excited than anyone.

"Yes, actually. All of it." Jillian grinned slightly in remembrance.

"I heard that there are more men than women in the United States. Is that true, Miss Kelley?" the Honorable Miss Mary Eberhardt asked as she dipped her spoon into her custard.

Jillian glanced over at Miles, who seemed to be very intrigued by Mary's actions. She cleared her throat to gain his attention. "Yes, there were more men than women. It was rather wonderful being amongst all those big strong males," she replied, strictly for the benefit of Miles.

Prudence and Audrey looked at each other, grinning with wide eyes. Mary didn't react, and Miles still watched the pale, stuff-bodiced toad, much to Jillian's annoyance.

"That's right, Miss Kelley," Bradley interjected. "In point of fact, I remember the alumni party we attended together. It seemed as if you were the only female in the room."

Jillian fumed beneath her cool façade. Bradley could take his uncalled-for flattery and deposit it right up his—

"Yes"—she smiled woodenly—"there were times when I was the only female in the room."

Bradley took up his teacup and saluted her. "Those moments, I must confess, were my very favorite."

Before she unleashed her wrath upon Mr. Townsend and his overly big mouth, Jillian raised her water glass and ingested a small number of deep gulps. She would not let the entire weekend proceed in this fashion. She needed to take charge and, as hostess, it was her duty to direct the conversation. Or in this case, *re*-direct it. She set her glass down and cleared her throat.

"Mr. Bassett, I've been away for so long. Why don't you tell us all about Thornton Manor and its tenants?"

For the next hour, Miles Bassett droned on and on about his father's house and the surrounding area. It wasn't five minutes into his oration that Jillian observed Bradley's eyes glaze over. But one detached person in a party of five could still be considered a successful luncheon. The ladies in the room sat and listened with rapt attention to each and every dull detail Miles presented them with.

Ha! Jillian's first social test had been a triumph.

Take that, high society!

* * * *

Jillian's challenge didn't come in the form of conversation. There, she could hold her own. The chief problem was the fact that the two men in the party held exceedingly different interests. Bradley appeared the extrovert, always looking for new and diverse things to experience, while Miles neither hunted nor had a thirst for adventure.

She had to admit, the possibilities of tedium were much higher with Miles than with Bradley. That was not to say that one was better than the other, just that Miles had more of a temperate personality than Bradley did. Therefore, as hostess, Jillian had the responsibility of devising events which hopefully both gentlemen would enjoy doing.

At the moment, the entire party had wandered out to the stables to feed treats to the horses and watch the head grooms exercise the new matching carriage geldings on the track behind where they housed the horses. If anything, it gave her guests a tour of some of the grounds at Fairfield.

"I do love your mare, Miss Kelley," Audrey commented while Maid Marian bit into an apple balanced on the palm of Audrey's hand. "She is entirely sweet!"

"Thank you, Miss Van Amberg. I think you should have a chance to ride her, she really loves to run."

"Oh, I would be very excited to take her round." Then she sobered. "But alas, I hadn't thought to bring a riding habit."

"I'll bet I could find something for you to wear, Miss Van Amberg," Jillian offered.

"And me, too, Miss Kelley? I haven't gone riding in what seems like months."

"Tell you what, Miss Dearborne. Tomorrow after breakfast, we girls will go riding. How does that sound?"

It was clear that Prudence and Audrey were indeed eager for the diversion—however, Mary wasn't so engaged. "I should like to stay behind, if you don't mind, Miss Kelley. I don't like to spend too much time out of doors."

Jillian couldn't have been happier to leave Miss Precious Bloomers to her knitting or whatever it was she did. She smiled at Mary. "If that is what you wish, then I am happy to comply. I'm sure we'll be back before luncheon in any case."

Bradley chimed in then. "I'd be glad to take Mary's place, that is, if Miss Van Amberg and Miss Dearborne don't mind."

Jillian took a breath to unleash her displeasure on Bradley when the girls practically squealed with delight.

Bradley smiled at Jillian as if he knew her precise thoughts. "It's settled then. Tomorrow we shall go exploring."

Jillian felt a headache coming on.

Suddenly, Miles appeared beside Jillian, placing a hand upon her arm. She looked up and smiled at him, knowing he was about to ask her if he could join the exploration party as well. And of course, he could. He could have everything his heart desired, at least, any of which were in her power to give.

"Yes, Miles?"

"Er, may I have your leave to escort the Honorable Miss Mary Eberhardt back inside? I'd not wish for her to be overtired from being out of doors."

Jillian's smile froze on her face. "Of course."

Had Jillian said more than that, she would have choked on the words. She watched as Miles offered his elbow to the Honorable Miss What's-Her-Name, the forgettable, who would simply expire were she to be left to the effects of fresh air and sunshine.

In one fell swoop, Miles had lost his entire store of Jillian's victory points.

Bringing Jillian out of her lethal musings, Bradley came up next to her. "How about if we go and watch the geldings now?"

She knew he was trying to cushion her irritation and her heart softened toward him — if only a fraction.

A half-point for Bradley.

He did, after all, still have her trousers around his neck.

Perhaps a quarter of a point.

Bradley offered her his elbow and over his shoulder asked Prudence and Audrey to join them.

As they walked out of the stable and approached the fence which outlined the track, Audrey and Prudence quickened their pace and climbed onto the first rung of the railing. Taking advantage of the moment, Jillian slowed up a bit and addressed Bradley.

"I want my trousers back, Mr. Townsend."

"What, right now?" he murmured with a grin and a gleam in his eye. "I'm sure you are well aware of the scandal we would cause were I to produce your trousers from inside my shirt."

"Do not play games with me, sir. I demand to have them back the instant we are free and clear of speculation."

"I told you the circumstances of my terms, of which I'm sure you have not forgotten."

"And I've informed you that under no circumstances whatsoever would I join you in the gazebo at midnight."

"Then I suppose we are at an impasse."

Prudence gained Jillian's and Bradley's attention. "You must let me and Audrey in on your discussion, Mr. Townsend. You and Miss Kelley are certainly enjoying a heated debate from which we would be loath to abstain."

They approached the railing and Jillian's thoughts raced in search of an answer that would appease the young busybodies, but when none came, Bradley spoke.

"We were discussing a particularly sticky game of charades."

"Sticky?" Audrey wrinkled her nose. "How can a game of

charades be considered *sticky*?"

"Well, Miss Van Amberg, this is no simple game. The game of charades of which I speak should not be attempted by the young nor the faint of heart."

Having no idea as to what Bradley was going on about, Jillian turned an inquisitive countenance to him.

Prudence leaned toward Bradley. "You have me intrigued, Mr. Townsend. Do continue."

Audrey nodded and leaned in as well.

"It's quite scandalous, I'm sure you will agree."

The girls' eyes widened.

"A selection of mature adults meet in a secret place at midnight in their night clothes."

Jillian's jaw dropped open and the girls tittered.

"Then teams are formed, and the riddles are pulled out of a hat." When no one made an effort to remark, he continued. "Not just any linguistic riddles, mind you." He leaned closer toward the girls and whispered, "Wicked words — words which aren't said aloud in certain circles."

"Oh! I want to play!" Prudence nearly toppled off the railing in her excitement.

"Me too, Mr. Townsend, me too!" Audrey demanded playfully.

"Very well, then. There is a lovely gazebo out on the west lawns that is not viewable from the main house. Meet me there at midnight. And remember, dress code will be strictly enforced."

The girls squealed and giggled.

Jillian couldn't believe Bradley had even suggested such a thing. This wasn't his house party, it was hers! Finally finding her voice, Jillian turned to Bradley. "Mr. Townsend, I don't think — "

Audrey interrupted her. "I know that tone very well, Miss Kelley, for my mother uses it often. Please, oh please don't spoil our good time!" she begged. "Prudence and I are very willing to risk the night air to play the game and it would add some…mature stimulation to our otherwise dull existences. Come now, please, give us your permission to do this?"

Now what, exactly, was Jillian to say to that? Nothing. She could say nothing. If she disappointed her guests, her small triumph she'd had at luncheon would fall to the wayside.

Jillian tossed her head as if she didn't give a fig what they did. "Go ahead then. I don't care."

The girls squealed again, a sound Jillian was becoming more and more annoyed with by the moment.

"Tell us more about the game, Mr. Townsend!" Audrey suggested, her voice low as if she were trying to be seductive.

Prudence matched her friend's tone. "Yes, do tell!"

Jillian turned her face away and rolled her gaze to the sky, unable to form the plea to save her from this situation into words.

"You ladies will hear all the rules and details tonight when you arrive."

Jillian groaned to herself. She knew Bradley enjoyed every minute spent with the girls, and it raised her hackles like nothing else ever had. All she had to do was make it through dinner, the parlor games afterward, then go to bed. She'd avoid the stupid game Bradley so obviously had made up to lure her out to the gazebo, and afterwards suffer his wrath the next morning for failing to engage in the debauched recreation.

Sure, all of it seemed like a mere piece of cake.

Irony or sarcasm, or a combination of both, there was certain inevitability that this house party would be the death of her.

Chapter Nine

Jillian felt much better after a short nap and bath before dinner. So much so that she pleasantly endured the prodding of her head by Anne in order to create the perfect coiffure, and the seemingly endless matching of hooks and eyes her new emerald dinner gown required. Once she'd slid on the matching satin gloves, she had to admit, her mother's insistence upon a few new pieces for Jillian's wardrobe had paid off this time. She swept down to the formal parlor to await her guests and found the string quartet setting up in the corner, with the help of Fletcher.

Slowly, her guests trickled in and, just as the dinner bell rang, the music began. It was like magic. Perfect. A sure triumph.

Once the dessert plates had been taken away, Fletcher announced that the formal parlor had been cleared for dancing.

Terribly grateful to Miles, she offered him the first dance.

"You are my hero, you know, Miles," Jillian whispered as he waltzed her across the small floor.

"How could that be, my dear?"

Jillian's heart fluttered. She loved the fact that he'd used endearments instead of her name. "Because, if it weren't for you, we wouldn't have had this entertainment."

"It was nothing, really. I can't boast of digging them up from the grave, after all. I knew where they were rehearsing and I merely hired them for you."

"Well, you're still my hero. I'd even dance three dances in a row with you tonight and risk a scandal." She smiled and gazed into his eyes.

"Then shame on us, for what of your other guests?"

Truly, Jillian didn't care one little bit. She shrugged the notion away with a toss of her head.

"Besides, I've already promised a dance or two to the Honorable Miss Mary Eberhardt."

It was on the tip of Jillian's tongue to tell Miles that the Honorable Miss Horse Face could take a flying leap from the third floor of Fairfield Court for all she cared, when the waltz ended.

Miles raised Jillian's fingers to his lips and it seemed to her that they lingered in the position a few moments longer than society allowed. Her heart swelled.

Miles's points are on the rise once again.

He saw her to one of the chairs next to the window, and Jillian watched as Miles hurried over to Miss Mary What's-her-Title. She turned away before the couple saw her watching them.

She glanced across the room and noticed Bradley for the first time that night. He was dressed in evening black and speaking to Prudence and Audrey. The girls giggled and simpered at him, but who could blame them? *Very well,* she admitted to herself, *Bradley Townsend strikes a fine figure.* But that was all the admiration she would allow. They were still in possession of each other's trousers and until they exchanged garments back, she refused to show him an inkling of courtesy.

Jillian made sure that each of her female guests danced at least one dance with her male guests. The last waltz of the evening, she'd wanted to dance with Miles, however, he'd already offered his hand to help Mary Mary Quite Contrary to her feet.

Honestly, besides her titled father, what did Mary have over Jillian?

The tears threatened, causing her vision to blur, and she had no idea how to stop them until Bradley stood before her with an upturned hand.

"Dance with me," he murmured.

Jillian saw that Bradley had noticed her watery eyes, but thankfully, he didn't mention it. She nodded, giving him permission by placing her hand in his.

She tried not to observe Miles and Mary, but each time they came into view, her breath caught in her throat. Miles had always paid more attention to Jillian at social gatherings when they had been younger...hadn't he? She couldn't recall any particular instances, but she was sure they had happened. It was impossible that their entire relationship existed entirely in her head...wasn't it? The thought threatened to shred her nerves to bits so she decided to ignore the niggling voice and focus on the dancing. The only hint she'd received that Bradley knew of her distress was that his arm tightened around her waist as if he were giving her a reassuring embrace. However, Jillian figured it must have been her imagination. Bradley couldn't possibly have known what thoughts were going through her mind.

Bradley, Jillian noticed, hadn't uttered a single word the entire time they'd danced, but as the song ended, he whispered in her ear, "See you at midnight."

As if he had burned her, Jillian released him and stepped out of the circle of his arms. "No, you won't," she said with quiet authority then turned to the room and offered a cool 'goodnight' to Miles. After he bowed to her, she herded all three girls up to their rooms.

The girls chit-chatted on the way up the stairs, but the only thing Jillian was paying attention to were her own morbid thoughts.

Bradley Townsend could be so accommodating, so affable, and yet, infuriating, stubborn and arrogant. Who on earth did he think he was? He was so sure that she'd be there at midnight. Why, he'd probably made up that silly game of charades right on the spot when she'd told him that in no uncertain terms would she show up — only to be man-handled, most likely, in her very own gazebo.

Besides, with any luck, Jillian would be asleep by midnight, and this nonsense about being seduced by Mr.

Townsend yet again, would cease to plague her thoughts.

* * * *

"Miss Kelley? Miss Kelley?" Jillian opened her eyes to find Audrey and Prudence standing before her holding a lit match. "It is almost midnight. We must leave now to meet Mr. Townsend." Prudence whispered.

Jillian groaned. "I will not be joining you, ladies." She took hold of her covers in a determined fist and rolled away from her guests and their offending light.

"Oh, but you must, Miss Kelley!" Audrey whined quietly. "What shall we do without you?"

"I'm sure you'll think of something," Jillian said into her pillow but loud enough for the girls to hear.

The door to her room closed softly and Jillian turned back over, smelling the smoke that lingered in the air from the snuffed-out match.

Not showing up to his indecent little midnight tea party would teach the arrogant J. Bradley Townsend a lesson he wouldn't soon forget. He'd be stuck in the dark with two curious girls in their nightgowns. What would he do with them?

Jillian sat bolt upright. She knew exactly what he'd probably do with them — the same thing he'd done to her every opportunity he got!

The second her bed linens were in the air, Jillian sprang from the bed and quit the house as fast as she could, heading with all haste to the west gazebo.

* * * *

Even above the balmy breeze which rushed by her ears, Jillian could hear murmurings coming from the gazebo. When she ascended the steps, Bradley, in a short nightshirt and beige britches without boots or socks, and her two young female guests who stood in their shifts, huddling together and shivering in anticipation, turned to face her.

Bradley's pleasant grin he'd worn for the girls blossomed into a full-blown smile.

Jillian clenched her hands into fists at her sides.

"Miss Kelley," Audrey breathed. "Oh, you've changed your mind!"

Lifting her chin a notch and tearing her gaze away from Bradley, she answered. "Yes, well, had I not shown up, the teams would have been uneven, and what kind of hostess would I be then?"

Jillian felt Bradley's gaze sweep over her body before he spoke. "Then come, ladies, allow me to explain how the game works."

Bradley explained the rules then asked, "Are there any questions?"

"So only one guess per person," Prudence confirmed.

Bradley nodded. "That is correct."

"And points are given for missing your guess." Audrey repeated his earlier statement.

"Correct again."

"The highest amount of points will receive a penalty at the end of the game."

"I believe you have it, ladies." He grinned.

Clearing her throat of nervousness, Jillian remarked, "You haven't named the teams yet."

"You are right, I have not. That is because you will be competing against each other."

Audrey interjected. "So you won't be playing, Mr. Townsend?"

He raised his hands, palms up. "How could I? I already know the answers to the riddles because I've written them. I will, however, be giving you the visual clues."

"Shakespeare himself couldn't have plotted it better," Jillian grumbled.

Bradley glanced briefly at Jillian. She couldn't be sure he'd heard her and she didn't give a fig if he had. What a scoundrel to carry on such proceedings.

"Now, if you ladies would like to have a seat, we can

begin."

Once the girls were settled, Jillian couldn't resist needling Bradley. "Mr. Townsend, didn't you say that the dress code for this evening would be strictly enforced?"

"Indeed, I did, however, I was thinking of my audience's sensibilities. You see, more oft than not, I sleep in the same state in which I entered this world."

"Bloody and squalling?" Jillian shot back.

This dragged a giggle from Audrey on Jillian's left and Prudence on her right.

Bradley grinned at Jillian. "I'm sure, Miss Kelley, you know better than that."

Jillian took a breath to tell him a thing or two, but clamped her mouth shut just in time. What a horrid place for her secret to get out.

"Will there be any more questions or shall we begin?"

Prudence spoke up. "Do proceed, Mr. Townsend. I can hardly stand the suspense!"

"As you wish, Miss Dearborne."

He bowed slightly at the waist and Jillian couldn't help but think of how silly it was to be displaying such manners when all four of them sat outside in their night clothes. Bracing herself for Bradley's unpredictable antics, Jillian inhaled and held her breath.

"Here is your first riddle."

Bradley opened his mouth. His soft tongue lapped once slowly and most seductively at the air.

Jillian shivered.

Prudence bounced in her seat and shouted, "Tongue!"

Almost at the exact same time, Audrey offered, "Taste!"

The game master shook his head at both their answers. Everyone turned their gaze to Jillian who blew out her held breath. "Lick," she murmured.

The girls giggled, but stopped when Bradley spoke. "Very good, Miss Kelley. Have you played at this before?"

"Just give us the next word, Mr. Townsend. Suffering your comments on our experience was not listed amongst the rules," Jillian said with unabashed derision.

He nodded a bow as if in deference to her comment. "You are correct again. I shall have to amend the rules the first chance I get."

Lifting her gaze Heavenward, Jillian motioned to him with her hand. "Do proceed."

"Very well. And don't forget, that is one point each for Miss Van Amberg and Miss Dearborne. Here is the next one."

Bradley closed his eyes and opened his mouth slightly, pursing his lips.

Audrey nearly jumped from her seat. "Pucker!"

"No, lips!" Prudence countered.

Again, everyone turned to Jillian when she didn't offer her answer. She jerked her chin away from the gaping group and sighed loudly. "Kiss."

The girls squealed.

Jillian rubbed at her temples with her index fingers.

"In keeping true to the system, ladies," he said to Prudence and Audrey, "that's one more point for each of you." Then he turned to Jillian. "Now, Miss Kelley, you will have to watch closely to be able to ascertain this next one. The words will get a bit more daring from here."

"Oh, God," Jillian murmured and lifted her head to glare at Bradley.

He grinned at her. "Ready then?" With that, he doffed his nightshirt and stood there, proud as a preening peacock in his breeches and nothing else.

When he reached for the fly on his trousers, Jillian jumped from the bench. "Really, Mr. Townsend, is this necessary?"

He eyed her, his look heated and dark. "Which one of those words is your answer, Miss Kelley?"

"None of them. The word is 'naked', but I really must protest—"

The girls inhaled audibly and far too late, covered their wide-open mouths.

Bradley chuckled. "Now, Miss Kelley, do I have to state

a rule about only speaking to your guests while playing?"

Jillian jerked her chin again and turned to retake her seat only to find that the two girls were now huddled together. She took Audrey's original place.

"Shall we continue?"

"If we must," Jillian said under her breath.

"Good. Now this one is going to be tricky." Bradley kneeled and stroked a hand across the back of an invisible animal.

Prudence was the first to shout, "Dog"

Bradley shook his head and Jillian wanted to fade from existence.

"Cat?" Audrey guessed.

When the entire party once again turned to Jillian, she refused to look at any of them.

"Miss Kelley, I'll have your guess now."

She felt his gaze upon her. Did he not realize that these were sheltered, virginal society girls who would have no idea what he was taking about? Her fingers sought her temples once again. The tension there could have toppled Maid Marian.

"Miss Kelley?"

Jillian crossed her arms over her chest. How could she possibly say the word out loud then answer the question that was sure to follow? Perhaps she would let him give the definition. Or would he mime that too?

She sighed, horrified at the task ahead.

"Do you not remember the word?" His voice rang low and husky.

At his challenge, her gaze snapped to his. "I remember," she barked. "The word is pussy."

"Pussy?" Audrey blurted the word aloud. "What is so scandalous about a pussy?"

That was it. Jillian felt as if she were going to faint dead on the spot. Out of the corner of her eye, Jillian saw Prudence pull on Audrey's nightdress and haul her to her side. Her hand went to cover Audrey's ear and Prudence proceeded, thank God, to give her friend the definition. Jillian could tell because Audrey's eyes went wider than Jillian thought humanly possible.

Jillian's gaze returned to Bradley's. "I think this game is over, sir," she said in a menacing voice.

"I beg to differ. The penalties must be doled out."

She stood, her tone none too soft. "And what horrid, debauched thing will you have these poor girls do?"

Bradley feigned innocence with wide eyes and a slack jaw. "I wouldn't do such to the ladies who were so kind as to come and join the game."

"Oh, please." Then she turned to Prudence and Audrey. "If he suggests anything untoward, you have my permission as hostess to decline." Her voice then lowered menacingly. "You also have my permission to invite the degenerate for pistols at dawn."

"Miss Kelley, really. All Miss Dearborne and Miss Van Amberg have to do is walk the perimeter of the main house and stables, pick up the markers to show they'd been there and come back to the gazebo to present the proof of their journey."

Audrey spoke up then. "Oh, we can do that! What exactly are we looking for?"

"Ribbons. Twenty in all. They won't be all that easy to spot, but they are within your reach.

"You mean like hair ribbons?" Audrey asked, her inquiry directed to the party in general. It was likely that after the explanation of the slang word, she was unable to meet his gaze, Jillian surmised.

"Yes, Miss Van Amberg. And you may keep the ones you find as a reward."

The girls stood and took the steps to begin their quest.

Jillian watched them cross the lawn and didn't notice until it was too late that Bradley had come up behind her.

"And now for your penalty." He slipped his hands around her waist and pulled her up against his chest from behind.

Ignoring the warmth his bare skin provided, she protested

and tried to squirm away. "I won, Mr. Townsend. One would assume that the winner of the game be allowed to escape penalty-free."

He buried his nose in her hair and inhaled before he spoke. "Very well then. If you can't complete this last task, you will have to gracefully receive your punishment."

"Don't be absurd."

"I am not. Don't you want to hear your task before you object? I promise a woman of your education will find it a rather ordinary, simple task."

Jillian blew out a breath. "Very well, what is it?"

"Merely use tonight's words in a sentence."

Chapter Ten

Her jaw dropped open. "I will not! How vulgar of you to suggest such a thing!"

He chuckled against the back of her neck, which caused the fine hairs on her body to rise. "You remember then."

She struggled to escape from his arms, but to no avail. "I'm sure I have no idea to what you are referring."

"Yes you do. In fact, I pulled the very words from my verbal invitation to you all those weeks ago, hoping you would remember. You so readily fell into my arms after I'd whispered the temptation into your ear of what I wanted to do to your body."

"Stop, I'll not hear any more of this!" She tried in vain to squirm from his grasp.

His grip tightened. "Come on, Jilli. The girls won't be back for at least a half-hour, and you know I can bring you to a pleasurable orgasm in way less time than that."

At his low, seductive words, Jillian lost her breath. Of course, she remembered the invitation he'd issued to her in his rooms after the alumnus party. Aside from being sufficiently foxed, she'd been further dizzied with his kisses for at least an hour when he'd murmured in her ear the most seductive suggestion she'd ever heard, or probably ever would hear.

And nothing could be truer than what he suggested now. She was well aware of his skills. She knew exactly what his silken tongue could do to her. A familiar pressure built between her legs, the kind of pressure that begged to be released via sensation. At once she stopped her struggling and stood still as statuary. Her mind whirled at the thought of his mouth on her body and with that, her rebellious knees turned to water.

The next thing she knew he'd sat her down on the edge of one of the benches. He leaned her backward, her feet still on the floor of the gazebo.

She shut her eyes when he slid the hem of her nightgown up to her waist. At once she experienced his hot breath between her legs. He hadn't touched her yet, and all she wanted was for him to hurry and fulfill his promise to make her come. He'd taught her so very much on that one night. It was entirely his fault she craved such illicit acts with him.

"Bradley," she breathed.

"God, Jilli. You have such a sweet, ripe strawberry." Faster than she could react, his mouth descended upon her, sucking on her, his tongue lapping at her. *Such a glorious feeling.*

When he began to ply his fingers she went off like a Chinese firecracker, but longer, louder, like the *1812 Overture.*

Her body still buzzing with sensation, he picked her up. She couldn't react. Couldn't think. And didn't want to, either.

"Put your legs around my waist, Jilli."

When she did, Jillian reaped her reward.

"Yes, that's it." He slid into her and backed her against one of the thick, rounded posts of the gazebo. He took her with blinding blows, his angle perfectly hitting something inside her that made her sing her ecstasy. Still he drove into her, still her insides shuddered and squeezed around his intrusion, causing him to call her name and alternately breathe endearments to her, encouraging her, cherishing her, loving her.

Without warning, he pressed into her, his orgasm reverberating through both of them. The only thing Jillian could hear was the rush of her blood above the gasps for air that came from each of them.

Dammit if she hadn't fallen again.

Bradley nuzzled her neck. "God, we fit so perfectly

together."

She'd barely heard what he had said, but felt his meaning when he began to kiss her jaw, her cheek, then her lips.

Yes, she admitted in defeat. They did fit perfectly together. But who wouldn't fit with a man who knew his way around a woman's body so well?

Jillian closed off the kiss. "You'd best release me now."

"Yes." Bradley complied. "I suppose I should."

Once her feet had touched the floor, she hurriedly righted her nightgown while Bradley buttoned his fly.

"Now that my punishment is complete, where are my trousers?"

"Was it so bad then that you consider what we just did a punishment, Jilli?"

Jillian turned from him and walked over on shaking legs to sit on a bench. "My trousers, if you please, Mr. Townsend," she repeated calmly.

He sighed. "When you told me you weren't coming tonight, I didn't think it necessary to bring your trousers."

Taking a punch at a pillow, she cursed under her breath.

He stood next to her, both of them silent for some minutes.

Apparently, and with full force, Jillian's reason returned. "And what, pray, would you have done with those two innocent girls had I not shown up? Seduce them too?"

"Please," he scoffed. "Don't you think more of me than to assume that I would stoop so low as to bed either one of those little girls?"

"Having just suffered your reckless, passionate side, no."

"Well, then allow me a moment to feel the insult."

Jillian jumped to her feet. "Insult? How is the pot feeling insult when it is called black by the kettle? In fact, I'm not so sure you haven't already bedded the Honorable Miss Mary Hot Cheeks! I dare say she didn't look so ravished the morning we met, at least, not until you—"

Bradley closed the small distance between them and interrupted her. "I am not a seducer of women!"

Too short to be nose to nose with him, she tried her hardest on the tips of her toes. "I hate to be the one to break it to you, Mr. Townsend, but yes, that is exactly what you are!"

"Really? Then can you name any woman at Oberlin whom I have supposedly seduced?"

After a brief pause, she answered, "I cannot."

"There, you see?"

"No. The only thing I see is that you don't need any particular woman to use those skills of yours on. Any one of them would do, and since you've traveled so extensively, I'm sure you've left a trail of heartbroken women all the way around the world."

"And how about you, Miss Kelley. Have you broken any hearts besides mine?"

"Oh, please. I have not broken your heart, if in fact, said heart actually exists. Besides, one has to be in love for their heart to officially be broken."

Bradley retreated a half-step and lowered his gaze to the floor. "Is it not obvious then?"

"Is what not obvious, Mr. Townsend? Or is this another of your tricks?"

Slowly, his eyes rose to meet hers in the semi-darkness. "Isn't it obvious that I—"

"Whoo-hoo, Mr. Townsend!" Audrey hailed from not twenty yards away. "These hair ribbons are lovely."

Jillian and Bradley fell silent.

The girls ascended the steps and fell onto the nearest bench. "Where did you get them?"

Bradley turned to the girls and smiled, woodenly, Jillian observed. "At port side in Liverpool."

Jillian stepped toward the girls then. "Yes, Mr. Townsend is just a living, breathing haberdashery." She hoped her sarcasm didn't go unnoticed by the lot of them. "It is time we went to bed. We have a busy morning ahead of us what with the ride after breakfast and all."

The girls thanked Mr. Townsend for an adventurous, insightful evening and waved goodbye as Jillian practically dragged them from the gazebo.

"I must say, Miss Kelley, Mr. Townsend is surely a handsome gentleman," Audrey said wistfully.

"Yes, well, the status of 'gentleman' is yet up for debate."

"How do you mean, Miss Kelley?" Prudence asked as they walked along. "Has he shown you some sort of disrespect?"

Jillian was loath to discuss the issue any further. "No. What I mean is, is that he works for a living."

"Goodness," Audrey murmured. "At least he has an occupation. My mother has been at her wit's end every day of my life because my father has been under her feet for eighteen years."

Prudence giggled. "It's true. I am witness to their circus daily."

Having nothing to say to that, Jillian kept her strides sure as she and her guests headed for the main house.

"Miss Kelley, one more question, if you please."

"Yes, Miss Van Amberg?" She sent a quick plea to the universe that the inquiry had nothing to do with Bradley.

"Are you and Mr. Townsend — ?"

"No!" Jillian didn't mean to bark the answer, but she knew that if the chit would have been allowed to finish her question, the fact that she and Bradley had been lovers would have shone on Jillian's face like a beacon.

After exchanging a brief glance between the two of them, neither of the girls said another word until they were spoken to.

Once inside, Jillian stopped her two young guests. "Miss Van Amberg, Miss Dearborne, before I bid you a goodnight, I'd like to make sure tonight's little game doesn't go any further than the three of us."

"You have my word there, Miss Kelley." Prudence nodded.

"And mine," Audrey echoed.

"Fine then. I will see you tomorrow at breakfast." Jillian smiled politely and headed for her room.

* * * *

The girls were bleary-eyed the next morning at breakfast, Jillian noted. But even in front of Miles and the Honorable Mary Boring-Head, they were full of questions for Bradley.

After they visited the sideboard, each in turn, the conversation continued. "Now, tell us about your parentage, Mr. Townsend," Audrey, obviously over her shock from last night's education, asked then took a bite of her buttered scone.

"What else can I say but I'm an American? First generation, I'll admit, but there it is." He grinned at the enthusiastic young lady.

"Come now, everyone is from somewhere, Mr. Townsend. For instance, where are your maternal relations from?"

At that moment, Jillian's mother, for the very first time during the party, joined her and her guests. Everyone stood when she entered, and Bradley, being much faster than Miles, jumped up and helped her to her seat.

"I thank you, Mr. Townsend," she said graciously, then after he'd returned to his chair, joined the conversation as if she had been there the entire time. "Are you aware, Mr. Townsend, that your father's family is from England?"

"You've found me out, Mrs. Kelley. How did you know?"

Having never mentioned it to Jillian, it occurred to her that he'd not been interested in his past in the way that her mother's set held the topic in particular adulation.

"Lady Bassett, Miles' mother, told me. She and I are great friends from way back."

"Indeed?" he remarked and took a bite of sausage.

"Yes. She's doing more research on the subject. Lady Bassett has many influential acquaintances, you see."

"Mm," Bradley acknowledged but commented no further.

Unwilling to listen to the praises of her future mother-in-law, Jillian abruptly rose from her seat. Both Miles and Bradley made to stand, but she stopped them with raised hands. "It is time we changed for our ride this morning,

Miss Van Amberg, Miss Dearborne." She nodded to each of them.

The girls agreed and all three of them headed upstairs to Jillian's room.

Jillian shut the door and turned to them. "I'm sorry to announce that I only have one suitable riding habit."

Her guests frowned. "Then what will Miss Van Amberg and I wear?"

Jillian looked at the girls with a conspiratorial grin. "Would you be inclined to wearing a blouse and trouser combination?"

Her guests paled, their eyes went as wide as saucers and they stood there, mouths agape, however, no verbal reaction had presented itself. Now convinced her suggestion would take some time to sink in, Jillian bid them sit upon her fainting couch before it was required.

"Ladies," she said in her calmest, most soothing voice. "I've donned trousers in the past and I must give the fashion credit. There is more freedom of movement in said garment than any riding habit you've ever sat atop a side-saddle in."

"You—you mean you've gone about in man's trousers and—?" Miss Dearborne practically choked.

"Well, not as such." Jillian purposefully omitted the other night when she'd marched across the lawns from the west gazebo in Bradley's trousers. "I had a friend who studied couture at Oberlin. And one of her more outrageous fashion designs involved a pair of trousers for women."

The girls still weren't of the disposition to re-hinge their jaws.

Jillian smiled. "They are really quite comfortable, I assure you."

Recovering from her apparent shock, Miss Van Amberg spoke up. "W-would you mind if I gave them a try?"

"Well certainly, Miss—"

"I'm not saying that I'll wear them outside the confines of this room," she interrupted but sounded far more contrite with her very next breath. "But I must admit, the prospect stirs within me a gnawing curiosity."

Jillian smiled then turned to her armoire to fetch said garments.

* * * *

Miss Audrey Van Amberg stood before Jillian's mirror gazing down at her powder-blue, fabric-encased legs, her eyes wide, the barest hint of a grin on her face.

"Audrey," Miss Dearborne whispered in awe. "You seem so — so modern, so free! How does it feel — you know, to be exposed for all the world to see?"

Miss Van Amberg thought for a moment. "I don't feel exposed at all," she said as she admired her legs. "Why would you say such a thing?"

Her best friend grabbed her by the shoulders and spun her around. "Now take a peek over your shoulder. I dare say you will find at least one item exposed."

Audrey did as her friend bid. "Oh, mercy!" Her hands flew to her bottom, attempting to cover it, her face colored as she glanced to her hostess for guidance.

Jillian, who had stood back to admire her handiwork once Miss Van Amberg had on her outfit, allowed a light laugh to escape. "My dear, you're endearingly fetching."

"Fetching?" she croaked. "I look like a hoyden!"

"Indeed not, Miss Van Amberg." Jillian chuckled. "The wearing of trousers is an acquired taste, apparently."

Miss Dearborne studied her friend for a few moments. "Audrey, I must have been mistaken." She tilted her head to the other side as if considering a different perspective. "Miss Kelley is indeed correct. When I think of how much she knows in comparison to the country manners you and I have been attuned to for the whole of our lives — why, I think — I think you're simply smashing!"

Jillian grinned. She remembered feeling rather exposed herself the first time she'd donned trousers.

"Miss Kelley." Miss Dearborne turned to Jillian. "May I

try them on now?"

Jillian made to answer but Miss Van Amberg stepped in with vigor. "Now, Prudence! You've just gotten me used to these, and now you want me to relinquish them to you?"

"Well—"

"One moment, if you please, ladies," Jillian interrupted. "I happen to have another pair, that is, if you are both prepared to stand by our very modern fashion statement."

At that moment, Miss Dearborne and Miss Van Amberg went giddy, clapping and squealing. The dark-brown trousers were presented to Miss Dearborne and, with much haste, she began disrobing. The two girls chatted away, their voices echoing their excitement, until they noticed Jillian in the process of laying out for herself a feminine riding habit.

"I must admit, I feel quite altered. Quite altered indeed. My entire personality has been improved upon, I dare say," Miss Dearborne said as if astonished.

Miss Van Amberg nodded in agreement. "It does feel that way, doesn't it?"

Miss Dearborne turned to Jillian. "Oh, but Miss Kelley, does this mean you won't be in trousers along with us?"

Jillian didn't allow her irritation to show. If she did, she would have to explain the circumstances, and she was not disposed to doing so. "My third pair is—is in desperate need of being laundered. I hope you don't mind."

Seeming a bit disappointed, the girls shook their heads and returned to the task of dressing while Jillian called for her maid with the bell pull.

Once all three girls were ready to venture forth, they headed out—despite Jillian's maid's protests about propriety. There was still a possibility that Mrs. Kelley might find her daughter and her guests as they made their way to the stables. Oh, the protestations she would raise at Jillian's attempt to corrupt her guests. Jillian made doubly sure that dreaded scenario wouldn't play itself out. She hastened the girls down the servants' stairs.

Chapter Eleven

Surprised Bradley hadn't come early to the stables, Jillian smiled to herself. But honestly, what did she care? Perhaps he would be delayed indefinitely. That would indeed be a boon. Too bad she hadn't thought of a device that could have facilitated such.

She stood between Miss Van Amberg and Miss Dearborne, awaiting the mounts she'd ordered for the girls. Their apprehension was palpable, but she knew once they got used to riding astride, they'd be terribly disappointed returning to the dreadful side-saddle. She'd already explained on the way down to the stables that one had no immediate control over one's mount in a lady's saddle. With a decent amount of reluctance, they agreed.

Miss Dearborne gravitated toward Maid Marian when the groom brought the mare around. Jillian suggested Miss Dearborne ride the horse on the way out, and Miss Van Amberg on the ride home.

When all three girls were mounted, Jillian took the lead. Clicking her tongue, she steered her horse toward the west lawns.

"Hold!" a deep male voice called out.

Jillian engaged the reins and ordered her horse to stand. She didn't even have to turn around to know who'd stopped them.

"So sorry I'm late," Bradley said from next to her. "I'll obtain a mount and we can be off."

Without looking at him, she answered flatly, "Do hurry, I wish to take advantage of the fine weather." Oh, how he irritated her. But she refused to let it show.

* * * *

Jillian led the party, followed by Miss Dearborne and Miss Van Amberg. And by the way the sound of Bradley's voice advanced and retreated, one could only assume that he purposefully guided his horse to the front then to the back of the line again as he spoke with the girls. Jillian was positive he did it to annoy her.

No matter how polite Mr. J. Bradley Townsend acted toward her guests, Jillian could not be put at ease. For the last half hour or so, they'd meandered through the countryside, chatting about superficial subjects such as the weather. Bradley had even offered up his take on terrain throughout the world. However, Jillian had remained silent. She'd felt his warm gaze upon her person ever since he'd mounted.

It was flattering, she had to admit to herself. If he'd been paying attention to any of the other girls in that forward manner of his, she'd probably be jealous.

Lord, but I've turned out to be a fickle bird, she chided herself.

In all honesty, her only goal this morning, now that Mr. Townsend had decided to show up, was to make it through to luncheon — and Miles. She wondered idly what occupied him at this very moment. A bit of reading? Could he be enjoying refreshments? Or perhaps conversing with Miss Mary-Tepid-Tea? That last thought made Jillian frown and she felt it to the soles of her riding boots.

"Miss Kelley?" Miss Van Amberg called to Jillian, interrupting her thoughts of Miles.

"Yes?" Even to her own ears her reply sounded as if it had come from far away.

"Do you suppose we could dismount for a moment? The view from the top of the hill ahead must be wonderful."

Bringing herself mentally back to the small riding party, Jillian turned to answer Miss Van Amberg. "It's called Billinge Lump." She smiled fondly at the name she'd grown up with. "And I think that's a fine idea."

At once, Bradley dismounted and helped the girls down. He then gathered the reins and led the horses to a suitable place to tether them.

"Ah." Miss Van Amberg sighed when they reached the top. "I knew it would be this lovely."

All three girls took seats in the grass underneath a small tree. Looking out across the valley, Jillian could see the border of Miles' estate. On this very spot, they'd visited together just before she left for the States. She'd tried to get him to kiss her that day. He had refused, but strictly on the grounds of honor, he'd said.

What a wonderful man, Jillian mused. Miles was nothing like Mr. Townsend. In fact, they were quite the opposite of each other.

"Miss Kelley?" Miss Dearborne addressed her hostess. "Now that we are well away from the main house and any prying ears, tell us of the latest gossip around St. Helens."

"Yes, do, Miss Kelley. Why Prudence and I have simply been on pins and needles since our arrival."

Jillian looked at the girls. She honestly had no idea of what they were speaking. "I've just recently arrived home and am not privy to the happenings."

"You mean you've received no correspondence from home? Not even from a reliable source?" Miss Dearborne asked, so astonished, a slight breeze could have toppled her over.

Shaking her head, Jillian confirmed their suspicion. But being the curious creature she was, she couldn't help but inquire. "No. Perhaps you could enlighten me?"

Miss Dearborne slid Miss Van Amberg a glance. "Go on, then. Take the wheel of the S.S. Gossip Ship."

Jillian couldn't help but be taken aback at their banter, but the girls seemed to understand each other perfectly.

"Well," Miss Van Amberg began. "We heard that a very prominent citizen, who is now of our acquaintance thanks to you, stands to inherit a nice-size fortune, had occupied his recent season by trying to form attachments."

Unable to do aught but blink, Jillian encouraged her guest to continue with a nod.

"Don't forget about the earl's daughter," Miss Dearborne reminded her friend.

Jillian's gaze flicked from one girl to the other, still feeling out of the loop.

"The first girl he'd offered for was far and above his station."

Miss Dearborne nodded in confirmation.

"When she asked for a few days to think about it, he silently took it as a refusal. And then next thing we heard was that he'd asked to court yet another girl!"

"Can you imagine?" Miss Dearborne chimed in.

Still trying to put the puzzle together, Jillian shook her head.

"So, in the interim, the first girl, the earl's daughter, received a far better offer. Can you guess what happened then?"

Jillian shook her head.

"Why, she took it, of course!"

"Of course," Jillian repeated, as a feeling of dread crept over her like a dark cloud. Only one man in all of St. Helens stood to inherit a fortune, and in addition, if one were to be cruel, could be labeled as a scatterbrain.

Miss Dearborne took the wheel next. "So, due to the apathy of the beau, he'd lost the earl's daughter!"

Miss Van Amberg hastened to add, "It was also said that once he made his intentions known to the second girl, he'd buzz about the others like a bee, seemingly too busy to get back to the previous flower."

"Which, of course, was his downfall. Had he stayed where he originally landed, he would be married and producing an heir at this very moment." Miss Dearborne groaned. "Simply pathetic."

"My, my," Jillian said, trying to detach herself from the subject. She prayed it wasn't Miles — *her* Miles.

Miss Dearborne continued, drawing Jillian from her

thoughts. "Meanwhile, when girl number two overheard the earl's daughter talking to one of her friends about having to send a refusal letter to the lower man, she went from where she sat, found the man and refused him, right then and there, in front of everyone! She would in no way be second choice, you see."

Jillian swallowed. If it was Miles they were talking about and there were two choices in line before her — this would make her his third choice.

"Miss Kelley, are you unwell? You've paled drastically in the last few moments."

"I-I am fine, Miss Van Amberg. Truly." Jillian presented her guests with a closed-mouth smile.

"You do know of whom we are speaking, don't you?" Miss Dearborne asked.

Dear God, the moment of truth. "Uh, no. Why don't you tell me?" There existed a tiny glimmer of a possibility that it wasn't Miles, and she clung to it as if it was a life line.

"Why, Mr. Bassett, of course!" Miss Van Amberg seemed surprised that Jillian couldn't have even guessed.

"Miss Kelley, it is the very reason Miss Van Amberg and I have been so distant to him here at Fairfield Court. Why, he'd probably make one of us his next victim!"

Miss Van Amberg chuckled. "Victim, Prudie? I think not. However, I will say this. If a man is too busy to court and lay all his affections at a girl's feet — one girl, any girl — then he'll hardly be able to give his wife time in the bedroom."

The two girls giggled and Jillian sat there, her head turned away, mortification filling her being.

At that moment, Bradley joined the party sitting at the foot of the tree. He leaned against the trunk and drew one knee up, resting his forearm upon it. "What has you ladies so engaged? Has Miss Kelley been telling you about her escapades at Oberlin?" He grinned.

"Oh, you know," Miss Dearborne said with an air of flippancy. "Just tea talk."

Jillian could hardly pipe up and tell Mr. Townsend

that her guests had just informed her that Miles had the attention span of an insect, nor that Jillian wasn't the first flower in line.

"Ladies," Bradley addressed the girls. "After I tied the horses, I thought I saw a family of wild rabbits just over the south side of this hill."

"Truly?" Miss Dearborne jumped up.

"Oh, let's go have a look, Prudie!"

The girls scampered off and at once Jillian felt Bradley's gaze upon her. If he said but one forward thing to her right now, she'd push him down the bloody Lump. After the information she'd just received, she was in no mood for flirtations.

He cleared his throat before he spoke. "I'm surprised that you would have instructed the girls to don your trousers, Jillian. Your mother will likely have a thing or two to say about it upon our return."

Jillian gritted her teeth. How dare he admonish her! She fisted her hands into tight balls. Apparently, it wasn't a dalliance he was after, but a fight. Who did he think he was, her father? She turned to him and didn't care if he noticed the lightning bolts shooting at him from her eyes. "Well, aren't you the town hypocrite?"

Bradley's eyebrows drew together. "How so?"

"Well, Mr. Townsend, I'm rather surprised Miss Van Amberg hasn't adapted her newly acquired vocabulary from last night and used the word 'pussy' in a sentence!"

He waved a hand. "A mere trifle for fun, and no one but her friends were present. You'd best take note here and now that it wasn't I who asked her to expose herself to the ridicule of your mother for fashion's sake, and in the light of day."

Jillian stood and glared down at him. "You, Mr. Townsend, are the most vile, crass, untrustworthy person ever to walk the hallowed halls of Fairfield Court!"

He stood as well. "Oh, and I suppose Mr. Bassett is the most caring, honorable and loyal man in the county?"

"Indeed he is, sir! I am going to marry him and there isn't anything you can do to stop me!"

"I wouldn't put any money on that wager if I were you."

"What, exactly, does that mean?"

Chapter Twelve

Bradley turned away and took a few steps in the opposite direction. When his heavy-footed strides returned him to Jillian's side, he stared her directly in the eyes but said nothing.

This was more than she could bear.

"Thank you for your silent admission, Mr. Townsend."

He looked mad enough to shake every leaf from the tree under which they'd taken their repose. "I admit to nothing, Miss Kelley." His voice sounded clipped and as menacing as his face portrayed.

"Miss Van Amberg, Miss Dearborne?" Jillian forced a calm façade and called to the girls who weren't but forty yards away. "I think it's time we headed back."

The girls returned without another word of encouragement from Jillian, and they all descended toward the horses, Miss Van Amberg claiming Maid Marian for the journey back to Fairfield.

Jillian was fit to be tied. She could hardly raise her gaze to the know-it-all Bradley Townsend. She allowed him to help her onto the ladies' saddle, turned her horse then headed in the direction from which they'd come, forgetting about him as best she could.

"Good Lord," Jillian murmured to herself. "Miles." He'd proposed to other women while she'd been away at university.

The pain of this situation would surely cause her demise unless — she sat up a little straighter — unless she could get to him and tell him that she didn't care about his other declarations. This entire escapade must have been the reason for his reluctance to ask for her hand in the first place! She would forgive him. She must. Everything would be right again after she told him so.

Jillian felt placated and justified at the same time. Forgiveness would reconcile his fears, she'd make sure of it.

As if the clouds separated and the sun shone through, Jillian felt the urge to return to the house as soon as possible. She glanced back at the girls behind her, ignoring Bradley's scowl. "Come, girls, let us give proper employment to these beasts."

She refused to let on that one of the beasts, to which she referred, took up the rear of their riding party. With that thought, she gave a hearty kick to the side of her horse and they all bolted toward home.

As they rode back at a hearty gallop, Bradley fumed. He'd almost told Jillian of the debauchery of Saint Miles Bassett but had decided not to at the last possible moment. He wouldn't have been able to bear the disappointment which was sure to blossom upon her beautiful face, nor was he disposed to doing so in front of the girls. As a result of his analysis, he'd kept the information to himself. The odds of Jillian falling into his arms no matter what he'd told her were slim to nil at best and therefore, there would be no point.

At the stables, he offered to rub down his horse. The small exercise would temper his inner tantrum. He informed the party of ladies that he would join them indoors shortly.

Much to his disappointment, Jillian didn't seem to care, one way or another, what his plans were.

* * * *

Jillian had forgotten completely about avoiding her mother until they entered the house and by then, it was nearly too late. As they crossed the foyer, Jillian frantically attempted to herd her two guests up the main stairs when Miss Van Amberg spotted the tea cart being wheeled into the parlor.

"Oh, capital. I could use a spot of refreshment."

"As would I," replied Miss Dearborne. "You don't suppose we've missed luncheon, do you?"

"My stomach says we might have!" Miss Van Amberg quipped.

The girls changed directions and followed the tea cart before Jillian could stop them. If her mother took her ease within that room... *Heaven forbid.*

"I will have to admit," Miss Dearborne said upon entering, "the sheer freedom one has in Miss Kelley's trousers does give me a mind to dismiss my crinolines and bustles for more snug-fitting garments."

"I couldn't agree more with you, Prudence. In fact, I may order a few pairs myself, once we arrive home."

Jillian entered on the heels of her chattering guests only to see Miles' overly widened eyes as he observed Miss Van Amberg and Miss Dearborne. Miss Mary-the-Sensitive inhaled an audible breath, stood and turned her back on the room.

Wholly unconcerned with what the Mary chit thought of her other guests, Jillian poured herself some tea, secretly thankful her mother was nowhere to be seen. Prudence and Audrey helped themselves each to a crumpet.

Miles visibly noted Mary's embarrassment and strode over to comfort her. As Jillian watched, she could have bitten through the china cup in her hand. *Oh, boo-hoo-hoo, Miss Mary-Can't-Wait-to-Read-her-Obituary has been exposed to unfashionable company! What ever will we do?* The thought actually caused Jillian to turn her head and smile.

But her smile soon faded as Miles barked — actually *barked* at her, "Miss Kelley."

She spun on him in surprise. A wave of hot tea splashed over her fingers, but that wasn't what made her flinch. He had never spoken to her in that tone before today. *Ever.*

"It would behoove you to escort Miss Dearborne and Miss Van Amberg upstairs and direct them to their armoires. I believe that proper afternoon dresses are in order here."

Jillian made to answer but he cut her off. "I shan't hear any excuses, either."

Embarrassed to her core that Miles would speak to her thus, and in front of company, Jillian re-deposited her teacup onto the cart. Once the girls set their refreshments down, she led them out of the room.

At the foot of the stairs, she addressed the girls, her cheeks burning and her hands folded repentantly in front of her. "Please forgive my thoughtlessness. I seem to have subjected you to ridicule."

"My dear Miss Kelley," Miss Van Amberg said and placed a hand on Jillian's shoulder. "Prudie and I knew what we were doing this morning when we donned these wonderful garments. Mr. Bassett is merely an overbearing male, not unlike our own fathers."

Miss Dearborne nodded and added to the discussion. "And as strange as it may seem, we hold our fathers in a much higher regard than Mr. Bassett."

The girls laughed heartily and Jillian could do naught but smile at them. They just didn't know Miles the way she did. Why, he was only looking after Jillian's reputation. "Thank you, ladies. Go on up to your rooms and rest a while. I'll have the kitchen send up what we missed from luncheon, then have Anne come help you dress later."

Miss Van Amberg and Miss Dearborne chatted while they ascended the stairs as if the scene with Mr. Bassett was of no more consequence than a dish of spilled tea.

Jillian turned for the parlor to apologize to Miles and Miss Mary Throw-a-Fit, when Miles himself entered the foyer. He strode directly to her as if purposefully seeking her out.

"Oh, Miles," Jillian began, her voice a sweet supplication, but he interrupted her.

"I know. I suppose I shouldn't have been so harsh with you in your own home, but the Honorable Miss—"

She held up her hands. "There is no need to mention it, Miles. In fact, I would like to speak to you about this and several other subjects." She glanced around to make sure they were alone. "Do you think you could meet with me, away from everyone else, say, around eleven o'clock tonight, at the west gazebo?"

"Miss Kelley, I hardly think —"

She resisted the urge to stomp her foot at his protest, as it would surely have gotten his attention in earnest. "Really, Miles." She sobered. "Address me as Jillian. We've been calling each other by our given names since we could sit up and take notice of our surroundings. Why, wasn't it only a few days ago that we were alone in the maze where we used to play as children? There is no need for decorum between us. Not now, not ever."

Something akin to fear had flashed in his eyes while she'd spoken, but she must have imagined it.

"I'm not sure —"

Jillian took a step closer to him. "Oh, Miles. Please say you will meet me tonight? I shall be so disappointed if you don't."

"I —" He paused as if weighing a terribly political answer. "I suppose so," he ended feebly.

Sighing in relief, she threw her arms around him and felt his shoulders stiffen. Jillian merely hugged him tighter. "Thank you so much, my darling."

Miles cleared his throat and shrugged out of her arms. "Once you've changed out of your riding habit, come have some tea with Miss Mary and me. And do me the favor of easing her anxiety."

Miss Mary? The realization of her Miles using Mary's given name flitted out of her head in a flash, replaced by an agreement which chose instead to be spoken aloud. "Indeed, I shall."

It was most fortuitous that Bradley came in when he did. Not to mention that, had his steps been any louder, both Jillian and Mr. Bassett would have detected his presence not five feet away and around a corner.

What did Jillian think to do at the gazebo, seduce Mr. Bassett the way Bradley had seduced her? He cringed. He hated to think that way, but if he looked at it from Jillian's point of view, his behavior toward her in that locale in the cover of night was exactly that. A seduction.

Well, one thing was for sure. He wasn't about to allow this liaison to happen. Not if he had anything to say about it.

"Eleven o'clock," he murmured. "I'll be there."

* * * *

Having taken the time to not only don a proper dress but have her hair curled and piled meticulously atop her head, Jillian returned to the parlor, and confronted her offended guest. The apology she had given to Miss Mary-Sour-Face was sure to go down in history as the best theatrical performance in history. She had oozed remorse as if she were a sap-filled tree on a particularly hot summer's day. And she'd done it all for her beloved Miles.

The Honorable Miss-Pudding-Brain had taken Jillian's apology like a well-bred lady, which burned within Jillian's stomach like so much smoldering coal.

Having refilled her teacup, Jillian now sat near the window, looking out over the lawn in a daze. The things she'd done—and would continue to do for Miles Bassett. She shook her head slightly.

Miles and Miss Mary-Good-Manners chatted away, and all too soon, Mr. Townsend joined the party. But Jillian hardly noticed. She focused on tonight, when she'd have Miles all to herself. She'd have to perfect a speech so that every second they were together would be employed advantageously and not squandered away.

"I understand it is supposed to rain tonight," Mr. Townsend commented in a casual tone.

Miles slid Jillian a glance and she spoke up to quell his uneasiness. "Yes, well, it is impossible to believe everything one hears about the weather." She shot Bradley a sardonic smile and returned her attention to the view of the lawns.

"Although" — Mr. Townsend walked over to the window out which Jillian gazed — "the sky does seem to be graying up a bit."

Jillian gritted her teeth. He would spoil everything if he kept up the Edgar Allen Poe act. She'd have to lighten the mood, even if she had to fabricate a scenario. "It only looks gray because of the thin layer of clouds which will, I'm sure float away. Besides, you have nothing to worry about. We will all be inside and cozy in our beds."

From the corner of her eye, she thought she saw little Miss Mary-Mind-Her-Manners flinch, but couldn't ascertain for sure as Mr. Bradley Townsend was now so close to her that the toes of his boots were hidden under her skirt.

"Will we now?" he all but whispered.

Whether he'd asked rhetorically or not, Jillian didn't give him the benefit of an answer. She did kick at his shins though, as she lifted her foot to cross her legs.

Bradley chuckled quietly and strode over to the tea cart.

After a couple of agonizing hours passed from the time Jillian had begged forgiveness from the Right, Honorable, Pain-In-The-Arse, Miss Dearborne and Miss Van Amberg entered the room, properly attired to Miss Modist's standards and broke up the monotony.

"That was delightful, Miss Kelley, we are quite refreshed" Miss Van Amberg spoke to Jillian without even acknowledging or apologizing to the titled blonde whom Miles had seated himself next to on the plush pink and cream striped divan. Not that Jillian cared, even if she was the hostess. The girls had no reason to kiss the hem of her other guests' dress — or trousers, for that matter. "So, are you up for any amusements before dinner?"

"I'm so sorry, Miss Van Amberg. I am quite exhausted from today's ride and I have completely forgotten to schedule something."

"Perhaps we could read out to each other." Miss Dearborne suggested.

"Now there's a promising idea." Of course Mr. Townsend had to toss in his two pence. "Miss Kelley has a very interesting book of Greek myths where—"

"No," Jillian said flatly and with vigor, squashing the subject like an overly annoying beetle.

"There is always charad—" Miss Dearborne began, but her ribs were introduced to Miss Van Amberg's elbow, and not for the first time, Jillian guessed.

Jillian glanced up at Bradley to gauge his mood. He grinned at her and she felt as though she had been caught with her hand in the sweet jar. She jerked her chin away as fast as she could and viewed the lawns once again. However, as fate—or was that luck, *bad* luck—would have it, he'd come to stand next to her once again.

She moved to the edge of her seat, just in case she was forced to bolt. She had no rational reason to, but just in case.

"Well, I can't think of a thing," Miles said with a sigh.

"Was there ever any doubt?" Bradley said under his breath, certainly for Jillian's benefit.

Jillian made to quit the chair in which she sat when Bradley stood directly in front of her.

He looked down at Jillian. "How about if I read everyone's cards? Would that suffice?"

"You know how to read cards, Mr. Townsend?" Miss Dearborne asked with no small amount of awe.

"Of course, doesn't everyone?"

"No, indeed, I do not. In fact, the only person I know of who has any idea about such things is Grandmother Dearborne."

Bradley smiled. "Funny you should say so, for it was my grandmother who taught me."

Mary turned to Miles. "Hm. I think this would be an acceptable diversion, don't you, Mr. Bassett?"

So, the title speaks. Jillian had to direct her attention to a vacant corner of the room so that no one would catch her look of disgust. When she turned back, Bradley smiled at her. *Damnation*. He'd seen her in yet another weak moment. Well, she bloody well didn't care.

"Fine, Mr. Townsend." She nodded. "Choose a table and we'll rearrange the room."

The second Bradley stepped away, Jillian shot to her feet, but alas, she was not to be free of his presence just yet. He pivoted on his heel and placed his hands on his hips.

"Are you sure you want to do this?" he warned aloud so everyone could hear. "I may reveal secret things about you and your guests."

Ignoring the excited energy and endless fidgeting coming from Miss Dearborne and Miss Van Amberg, Jillian chuckled and picked up the gauntlet that he'd thrown down. "There are no such secrets here, Mr. Townsend."

A pair of dark-blond eyebrows rose above a cool chocolate-brown gaze and an insolent dimple appeared in Bradley's cheek. "Aren't there, now?"

Chapter Thirteen

Jillian ignored Bradley's rhetorical challenge, if in fact, there was such a thing. It really bothered her when he spoke aloud, but not to anyone in particular. The distasteful situation worsened when she appeared to be the only person alive within hearing distance, but had no inclination whatsoever to answer him.

Jillian rang for Fletcher to help with the room and in no time, they were sitting in chairs which encircled a round table. Bradley placed himself in the largest wingback chair, shuffling the deck of cards he'd retrieved from his room.

"What curious cards, Mr. Townsend," Miss Van Amberg commented. "Where ever did you get them?"

The cards weren't everyday playing cards, nor were they elongated like normal tarot cards. These cards were perfectly square, about the size of a saucer, and twice as thick as a regular playing deck. His big hands, Jillian noticed, cradled the cards with a delicate efficiency. The same he'd used when handling her body.

Jillian dismissed the tingling sensation that traveled across her skin and made the hairs of her arms stand on end.

He smiled. "These are the very ones my grandmother taught me with. I carry them when I travel as sort of a—a good luck charm, one could say."

"And have you had any good luck by them, do you think?"

"Well, Miss Dearborne, I'm still here, aren't I?"

Jillian harrumphed and Bradley chuckled. "Well, perhaps not everyone would call that good luck."

"Indeed not," Jillian murmured. She jumped when he called her name.

"Miss Kelley. You are the hostess. Therefore you should go first."

"What a silly notion. Everyone knows the hostess is supposed to indulge last."

"But, in this case, you must set the example for your guests. Am I right, everyone?"

Like a bunch of anarchist rebels, each and every one of Jillian's guests agreed.

"Very well. I'm not afraid." She shrugged.

"Good," he said with no hidden amount of candor. "Please take the seat next to me."

Not wishing to drag on the slight hesitation that reared its head at the way he smiled at her, she settled into the chair and he continued his directions. "Now, take this deck of cards and begin shuffling."

Again, Jillian complied, although begrudgingly. The cards were awkward in her hands, but she managed.

"When you feel that they are sufficiently mixed, set them down before you."

After a few more rounds, Jillian set the cards face down.

"So, Miss Kelley. Do you have any questions you'd like answered or do you wish for just a general reading?"

Jillian glanced around the table, but when no one encouraged her one way or the other, she spoke. "A general reading, I suppose."

"Very well, give me your hand."

If Jillian's suspicion had been a lion, it would have roared loud enough to irritate every eardrum in the room. "Why?" The question purred in a sinister way from her throat and her eyes bored into his. Honestly. It wasn't her fault he'd not gained her trust in the last week.

Obviously paying no heed to her wariness, Bradley held his hand out to her as if expecting her to comply without protest.

Jillian refused to move. "You haven't answered my

question."

His hand remained steady as he continued to look at her.

"Come now, Miss Kelley," Miss Van Amberg encouraged. "I pledge here and now that your company will make sure nothing untoward happens."

Miss Dearborne nodded in agreement.

Unable to quell a weary sigh, which she was sure irritated the dickens out of Miss Mary-the-Delicate, she reluctantly placed her hand in Bradley's. It was warm. Soft yet strong. She hoped no one noticed her heated cheeks.

He enclosed her hand in both of his and after his gaze met hers for a brief moment, he began speaking. "By shuffling the cards, you have transferred your energy to them." He looked around the room at each person. "And every one of you will have your chance, but you must be patient. This process is…"

He droned on and on, but Jillian could no longer concentrate on his speech. He toyed with her hand while occupying everyone else with his eyes. His actions were a study in the art of duality. He drew lazy circles in her palm, pinched at the pads of her fingers and pressed his palm to hers in what seemed a very intimate dance. By the time his oration came to an end, he held her hand as if it were nothing more important than a finger sandwich.

He fixed his stare on her, and for a brief moment, she would have vowed a flame had shone in his eyes.

Jillian shifted in her seat, and Bradley guided her hand palm-down atop the deck on the table, his hand covering hers. Together they fanned out the cards in a wide arch. The action seemed strangely intimate, but perhaps it was his touch alone which made it so.

"All right. Now allow your hand to hover over the cards until you feel a pull toward a particular card. Draw the card and then place it face up in front of you. This will be your card, which will allow me to see into your soul."

With all eyes on her, Jillian felt as if she were a bug under microscopic scrutiny. Her curiosity, however, won the day.

She shut her eyes and concentrated on the cards until her fingers delved down into the pile as if by their own accord. Pulling out one, she set it face up on the table before her.

The card displayed a lovely blue and gray watercolor of a pond as rain splashed into it, causing endless rings which canceled each other out.

"Ah, the changeling."

"I don't think I follow you. The card seems to be depicting rain. Shame on you, Mr. Townsend, mustn't be so enigmatic." The irritation in her voice reflected her true feelings. If only she could have disguised it, he wouldn't have that smug look on his face.

"Yes, rain. Or more accurately, water. Water is essential to the earth, and yet at the same time can drastically alter its environs. It can divide mountains by carving out canyons, tumble rocks together until they are smooth, define coastlines — however, it is also replenishing and refreshing. It freezes, boils and dissipates into steam. Water is quite a versatile, volatile force of nature." He smiled. "How very accurate that you chose this card."

"So you are saying water is going to define me or change my future?" Pleased that her perturbed voice had evolved and even leaned toward the slightly sarcastic, she gave him a close-lipped grin.

"I think a more precise description is that you are the water."

She considered his words and could only concede that they were the truth, which further annoyed her. "In any case, you haven't told me anything I didn't already know, Mr. Townsend. Perhaps you will have more luck with your next victim." She stood and pushed her chair back.

"Victim, Miss Kelley? I'm not sure that's terribly fair. In what way were you victimized by me?"

She gave him a don't-you-dare-attempt-to-broach-that-subject-with-me look then addressed her guests. "Who would like to be next?"

"I will be next." Miles stood and took the seat Jillian had

vacated. She watched with a jaded attitude as Miles copied her actions from before. Mr. Townsend couldn't have any idea how to read cards – it was an impossibility.

Miles frowned when he flipped his card over. "Leaves?"

"Hm. Yes, Mr. Bassett, but I think that your card is revealing the wind, the carrier of the leaves more than leaves themselves."

"Ah, yes. Of course, I see it now. Wind is strong, I mean, it can't rearrange mountains and such, like Miss Kelley's water, but the wind will bend trees well enough. I say, I'm rather pleased with that."

Jillian watched Bradley carefully, looking for any sort of emotional break in his cool façade. She might have witnessed the flash of humor in his eyes, but it past so quickly that she could never be pressed to accuse him of it.

As Miles stood, Miss Dearborne asked to be next. "This is all so fascinating, isn't it?" she asked the room in general.

Bradley handed her the cards and she found hers right away. "Oh, this is a lovely picture. What does it mean?"

"Before you sits a serene highland valley."

"Does it mean I'm pretty?"

"Yes, and more."

"More?"

Bradley grinned. "You see the loch at the far end?"

Miss Dearborne nodded.

"That is the edge of Loch Ness, one of the largest, deepest lochs in Scotland, and as mysterious as the creatures that dwell beneath the surface."

"Oh, I don't think I'd like to be mysterious."

"Ah, but Miss Dearborne, it is a woman's prerogative to be mysterious." He reached out and clucked her on the chin. "It may entice your soul mate to find you and investigate."

Miss Dearborne blushed prettily. "Tell us, Mr. Townsend. Which card is yours?"

Chuckling, he gathered the cards. "My card is of no consequence."

"Oh, but it is! Come now, tell us," Miss Dearborne urged.

"I must admit to being curious myself, Mr. Townsend." The Honorable Miss Eberhardt, who had spoken — indeed a rarity, since the beginning of the festivities--was at present leaning forward in her chair, gazing intently at Bradley.

Jillian clenched her jaw shut. A girl like that would never catch the fancy of Bradley — er, Miles, she corrected herself. She took a breath in the hopes of sounding far calmer than she felt and, in the midst of everyone else's promptings, added her own. "Indeed, Mr. Townsend. Tell us. One mustn't keep one's audience on tenterhooks, you know."

"All right, all right." He grinned sheepishly. "If you must know, my card is the rampant stallion."

While everyone else offered their speculations on what the rampant stallion meant, Jillian quelled a sarcastic, verbal lashing by pressing her lips together. *How utterly ridiculous. He must have been making that up.*

The party fell silent and Bradley confessed, "I'll tell you exactly what my grandmother told me. The stallion is nigh untamable — at first, that is. Free, beautiful and eventually" — he looked Jillian directly in the eye — "entirely loyal in the hands of a kind mistress."

To that, and not caring what anyone else thought, Jillian harrumphed aloud.

"Come now, Prudence, my turn to have a go." Miss Van Amberg shooed at her friend, took the newly empty seat and made quick work of the cards.

Bradley observed her choice. "We have here an open carriage — at night time. This shows an open, agreeable temperament. The card says you are a good companion to anyone, especially a man."

"How could a carriage tell you that I would be a good companion for a man?" she asked as if she didn't believe him.

"See the full moon peeking out from behind the clouds, just there?" He pointed to the upper right hand corner of the card. "This indicates passion. Apparently, Miss Van Amberg, you are a very passionate woman."

"Mr. Townsend." She looked at him through her lashes. "If that is in fact the case, then I wish to employ a stallion to pull my carriage."

Bradley smiled at her and gathered the cards. "I'm sure you will find one soon enough who isn't otherwise occupied."

Jillian had to admit, it was quite admirable of Bradley to have offered Miss Van Amberg such a diplomatic answer to her flirtatious question. She also acknowledged that his words the other night must have been true — he did think of Miss Van Amberg and Miss Dearborne as little girls.

Miss Van Amberg raised halfway out of the seat when she paused. "Mr. Townsend. You did say it would be soon, did you not?"

He chuckled. "How could it be otherwise?"

She thanked him demurely and vacated the chair.

"It seems that the Honorable Miss Mary Eberhardt is my last customer for the afternoon," Bradley teased as he addressed her directly. "Are you still game for this diversion now that you've witnessed its affects?" He held out the deck to her.

She smiled, tossed a pale-blonde curl from her shoulder and took up his offering. "I am ready, Mr. Townsend."

Jillian quelled the urge to heave her gaze to the ceiling. It seemed that everyone in the room had flirted with Bradley, save for herself and Miles. But she had no fear of Bradley running off with Miss Mary-Empty-Head. She knew for certain, and had gotten it straight from the man himself, that he had an aversion to uneducated, dull-witted women in frothy pink frocks. She'd give her guest credit, though, that in most situations, Mary'd had the good sense to keep her thoughts to herself. Were there any to begin with. But on the other hand, Miles seemed to be her carrier pigeon. It was as if both of them consulted with the other more often than not.

This thought alone pricked at Jillian's pride. The fates didn't play fair — she was his best friend, not Mary. Wasn't she? They'd played together as children, after all. He'd been at every one of her mother's parties since she could remember. She shifted in her chair in frustration, unable to think of a time where Miles verbalized the status of their friendship. But things like that weren't spoken aloud... Were they?

Jillian watched detachedly as Mary shuffled the cards, and stifled an impatient sigh. This game of Bradley's seemed to go on and on, when all she wanted was to get to the gazebo after everyone retired. It occurred to her that she had just over five hours before her liaison with Miles. A trial for her patience, for certain.

Mary pulled her card and set it upon the table.

"You chose the bolts of fabric card. Silk fabric, to be exact — fine, expensive, however, unstructured."

She looked at him with a blank expression that Jillian had half-anticipated.

He continued. "There is an art to weaving such rich fabrics, Miss Eberhardt. Any sort of rush, and there are sure to be flaws. The same can be said for the dressmaker. Rush a pattern and your patron will have an ill-fitting gown."

Mary's pale brow wrinkled. "What on earth does all that have to do with me?"

Bradley tilted his head as if carefully weighing his answer. Then he smiled at her. "Pray the right tailor takes you up."

"I'm sorry?" Mary shook her head as if she hadn't heard right.

"I know," offered Miss Dearborne. "Weigh your choices carefully before you cut into your fabric, or, to be more precise, before you choose to follow one path or another." She smiled. "How was that, Mr. Townsend?"

"Miss Dearborne, you are a natural. You should consider reading cards for a living."

Even Jillian smiled at his silly statement.

Miss Dearborne laughed. "Surely, sir, you cannot be serious."

"Indeed I am," he said with a definite twinkle in his eye.

She considered him for a moment then stood. "Very well. Let us trade places and I'll read for you."

He shook his head. "No, no. That would never do."

"Why ever not?" Miss Dearborne frowned.

"Well for one thing—"

Jillian interrupted. "As hostess, I must insist that you allow my guest to read your cards, Mr. Townsend." And like citizens with no country, everyone in the room agreed in harmonious accord, taking up her side. *Ha!*

Bradley shot her a look she was unable to interpret. "Very well, Miss Kelley. If it will please you."

"Now that's what I call taming the stallion." Miss Van Amberg made everyone in the room laugh—except for Jillian.

Miss Dearbonre took the head seat as Bradley gathered the cards.

"How very intriguing," Miss Van Amberg exclaimed.

Jillian noticed that Miles had on his public face—the one he used when he was agitated or bored. It was absurd to imagine Miles being jealous of Bradley. His mood must have been caused by something else. She was drawn from her musings the moment Bradley's card was revealed.

Chapter Fourteen

"Mr. Townsend! You peeked!"

"Peeked, I? Never." His tone could be interrupted as teasing, but Jillian knew something wasn't quite right.

"Oh, come now, Mr. Townsend. It is impossible that you have just pulled the rampant stallion after shuffling the cards so thoroughly."

"As I said before, Miss Dearborne, it is my card."

Miss Dearborne held out her hand. "Give me the card, Mr. Townsend. You will have to choose another."

Bradley made to protest.

"I will have to agree with Miss Dearborne, Mr. Townsend." Jillian couldn't help but chime in if only to assist in raising his hackles.

"I think he knows his cards so well that he can tell which card is which by merely looking at the back," Miss Van Amberg added in a joking yet accusatory tone. "Perhaps we should blindfold him."

Jillian agreed, but Miss Mary-the-Dull stopped her by placing a hand upon Jillian's. "Don't you feel that it would be rather scandalous of your guests to do such a thing, especially to a member of the opposite sex?"

Upon opening her mouth to speak, Jillian experienced a flash of memory. She was in Bradley's room back in America, sprawled naked across a mussed bed with her wrists bound loosely above her head by his silk tie.

She came out of her seat, partly gasping for air, partly coughing.

The next thing he'd done to her had been to cover her eyes. And after that...*Good God*! Why, she couldn't even allow herself to relive the drunken abandon she'd experienced. And certainly not in front of her guests.

Miss Dearborne took Jillian by the arms to steady her. "Are you unwell, Miss Kelley?"

"Miles, perhaps you should bring Miss Kelley something to refresh herself with," Mary suggested.

However, Mary's idea had come too late. In an instant, Bradley was there with a glass of water, holding it up to her lips, his other hand supporting her back. "And a bit of air may also do the trick." As she drank, he ushered her over to the window and tossed it open. He returned his hand to the small of her back.

In seconds she got hold of herself, downing the entire glass of water. "You are a wicked man, Mr. Townsend," she whispered harshly. As angry at herself as she was for acting as she had that one fateful night, she didn't wish for all of St. Helens to overhear what she had to say.

"I, madam?"

"Of course you, who else? You've come here to my home, staged scandalous games and intrigues, introduced finer society to your debauchery, and now this. Next, I suppose, you will teach them how to tie someone to the bed!"

Bradley faced Jillian's anticipatory guests. "She'll be recovered in no time." He smiled and turned back to her, his eyes now intense. "I see. You feel that you have fallen from grace and now I am to be punished for it."

"It wasn't my idea to bring a blindfold along for the fortune telling!"

"Neither was it mine."

Recalling the conversation, she froze.

"It was Miss Van Amberg's suggestion, and an innocent one at that," he stated quietly.

Damnation! He was right. She cleared her throat, feeling contrite, but not ready to let him off the hangman's scaffold just yet. "Fine. I will allow you that. However, you will not go any further than a blindfold at my party. Additionally, I must insist that you return my trousers as soon as possible."

"The very second the opportunity arises." He took the glass from her hand and showed her back to the table.

Jillian politely dismissed her guest's sympathies, which were appreciated yet unnecessary, and returned to her seat.

"Miss Kelley," Miles addressed her so formally she nearly cringed. "Miss Mary is right, you know. Perhaps Mr. Townsend could cover his own eyes and choose a card."

Honestly. Nearly sighing out loud in exasperation, she didn't really care what transpired next. She wished to remove herself completely from the room anyway. Nodding, she gave her acquiescence.

Miss Dearborne bade him close his eyes, spread the cards and choose one.

He hovered his hand over the arch for a few moments, then he drew.

Everyone looked at the card with an anticipation which fell flat when no one could distinguish the animal.

"Is it a cat with a mask on?" Miss Mary asked.

"It seems to be stuck up in a tree," Miles pointed out.

"Or it is sleeping there?" Miss Dearborne added.

"No," Bradley corrected gently. "That is a procyonidae."

Miss Dearborne pulled a sour face. "I've never seen one before. What can you tell us about them, Mr. Townsend?"

"Procyonids are nocturnal. They are, for lack of a better term, scavengers."

"Well, one thing is for certain," Miss Van Amberg observed. "We already know what the moon means." She smirked.

Fletcher stepped into the room and announced that dinner would be in an hour and a half, and Mrs. Kelley would be joining them.

Relief flooded Jillian. She stood, but Miss Dearborne stopped her.

"Don't you want to hear what I think the card means, Miss Kelley?"

She smiled woodenly. "Indeed. Do go on," she murmured as she lowered herself back to the chair.

"Well, I think that Mr. Townsend is resourceful. He's clever, and he sometimes puts up a mask in front of people to hide his true feelings."

Bradley nodded. "Yes, Miss Dearborne. But then again, don't we all hide our feelings at one time or another?"

Miss Dearborne grinned at him. "Indeed, Mr. Townsend. However, you plucked the card from the deck, and no one else."

"*Touché*, my lady." He smiled back.

"Well." Jillian rose and indicated that the other girls follow her lead.

"Miss Kelley." Bradley garnered her attention. "May I have a word before you change for dinner?"

By this time, Miles was already at the door guiding Mary into the foyer.

Chafed that Miles didn't chose to escort her, Jillian agreed. "Miss Dearborne, Miss Van Amberg, would you please wait for me in the foyer? I shan't be but a moment."

When the girls exited the room, Jillian turned to Bradley. "Yes?" she asked, her voice purposefully cold and unfeeling.

"Jilli, I know you feel the card reading was indeed a silly diversion. But some of what I said is true."

She reached up to pat the back of her hair into place. "It matters little to me if the girls find husbands or not, Mr. Townsend."

"That's not what I meant. About Mr. Bassett—"

"I think that will be quite enough, sir." She made to walk away but he stopped her.

"He doesn't love you, Jilli. He can't."

"And what sort of enigmatic statement is that supposed to be? You are jealous and that is the end of the subject." She stepped around him, but again, he stopped her.

"Please, just listen to what I am saying—"

She whirled on him. "Our conversation is through. Now if you would allow me to change for dinner, we will have emerged from this unnecessary interview with a shred of our dignities intact."

This time he took hold of her arm. "Jillian. I know what's happening here, *tonight*—it's much more than meets the eye."

She jerked from his grasp. "I don't care if you really are psychic. No matter what you say, my plans will not change." She headed for the door. "I shall see you at dinner, and I will expect your good manners, *if* you can find them."

* * * *

Bradley was beside himself. He needed to reveal Miles to Jillian without splintering her hopes and dreams in one harsh blow. But how could he? He was never one to sit back while a woman cried—not even his own sister, let alone be the cause of it. Odd, but he never thought Jillian would have needed to be saved from anything. Which was one of the reasons he respected her. Admired her.

Lo—

Cared for her.

He sat on the bed and pinched the bridge of his nose. No matter what he did, Jillian would hate him. If he interrupted her little ploy at the gazebo tonight, she'd toss him out of her house. If he revealed Bassett's dishonorable character, she'd probably demand that he leave England behind entirely. Something had to be done, and *fast*. She should be in his arms enjoying his attentions, not pining away for that weasel of a milksop.

Bradley kept silent all the way through dinner. As the party chatted, he pondered his predicament. Only once did he join in on the conversation which swirled around him. It was when Mrs. Kelley addressed him directly.

"Mr. Townsend. I want you to know that Mrs. Bassett and myself have been doing some research."

"Oh?" he asked detachedly.

"Yes, on you."

Bradley looked up then. "And your findings?"

"You, sir, have not been forthcoming with us."

The moment seemed frozen in time, along with everyone at the table, each in various eating positions. All eyes were on him now, some expectant, some inquiring.

Without squirming, which in his estimation, he could have been granted a trophy for such a feat, he asked, "How do you mean, Mrs. Kelley?"

"Your grandfather, when he lived here in England, was a Viscount."

"Ah." He'd wondered if this would ever come up. "You see, madam, when my grandmother married my grandfather, he didn't have any sons of his own. My father was from my grandmother's first marriage."

"But he should have been able to inherit, surely."

All this talk about his ancestors made him uncomfortable. A flash of memory had him at his parents' table as a boy, his little brother on one side of him and his baby sister on the other. There existed no ranks, titles or social ladders to be climbed, merely love and loyalty. He sighed, looking forward to providing that sort of atmosphere for his own children someday.

He shrugged, hoping to convey to Mrs. Kelley without offending that it no longer mattered. "With all due respect, Mrs. Kelley, the soil had become depleted around my grandfather's northern estates. Having no way to support the entire household, he cashed in, as it were. Beyond that, my father explained to me that the family considered it an extinct title. He moved to America and started a business. And the rest, as they say, is history."

"I dare say that if you wished to revisit the title, Lady Bassett and I—"

"Thank you, Mrs. Kelley," he interrupted as graciously as possible. "However, to revive the title would be of no interest to me."

"But—"

"Mama, *please*."

Bradley's gaze snapped to Jilli, surprised that she'd come to his rescue.

"Pursue the subject no further. If Mr. Townsend is satisfied with the outcome, then so should you be. Americans look at societal positions differently than we do."

Mrs. Kelley pressed her lips together. When she recovered, she smiled woodenly. "Very well, Mr. Townsend. You know to whom you may turn if you ever change your mind."

"Thank you, Mrs. Kelley." And that was the last of the evening meal interactions with him. Not that he minded. Jillian had, in essence, saved him from at least a two-hour debate with the venerable matron. But had she done it for him or was it that she didn't wish to have the final dinner of her party ruined by two headstrong bulldogs?

No. It was unfair of him to steal from her the glory of a hero's triumph.

The more he thought about it, the more Bradley felt as if he had won an important battle in the conquering of Miss Jillian Kelley's heart. She had indeed stood up for him, and against her own mother, no less. Even if she was forced to choose sides, never in a million years would she have crossed the line to his side unless she harbored some sort of feeling for him, no matter how trivial.

His gaze rose and locked with hers, but he could not read her mood. He wished he could make everyone disappear so that he could scoop her up and carry her away to his rooms. And oh, how he would reward her for this trifle, then.

"Miss Kelley, Mrs. Kelley. As it is Sunday evening, mine and Miss Van Amberg's carriage should be here in the morning. And before the sad event of our departure takes place, I wanted to be sure to thank you for the most wonderful party Audrey and I have ever attended."

"You are too kind, Miss Dearborne," Jillian offered with genuine humility.

"It's true," Miss Van Amberg chimed in. "It's been a most educational event. We must keep each other abreast of our situations via the post." She nodded to Jillian then added wistfully, "Oh, how I shall miss the adventurous ways of our lovely hostess."

Out of the corner of his eye, Bradley saw Jillian shift in her seat. She had every right to be nervous, he speculated. The two girls had been exposed to a good many new experiences here at Fairfield Court over the past seventy-two hours.

"We only wish we could be as fortunate as the Honorable Miss Eberhardt, for she will be staying on a full day beyond our exodus." Miss Dearborne pouted.

He watched Jillian fake a smile, that didn't quite reach her eyes, if for Miss Mary's benefit.

"Then we shall have to find amusements for Miss Eberhardt, for the duration."

"Please, Miss Kelley. No need to do so on my account. I'm sure I can keep myself occupied."

The second Jillian's gaze broke with Miss Mary's, Bradley observed Miles catch Mary's eye.

The fury boiled in his belly, but he said nothing. Apparently, the milksop could do no wrong in Jillian's eyes. Either that or her love for him was entirely blind. Yes, that had to be it. Unadulterated blindness.

Chapter Fifteen

A light summer rain did moisten the yard beyond the cozy parlor, but it didn't hinder Jillian from her purpose. After bidding everyone goodnight and promising Audrey and Prudence she'd see them off in the morning, she went straight away to her writing desk to decide exactly what to say to Miles tonight.

A small voice in the back of her mind echoed that it seemed as though she was trying to manipulate Miles, but she quieted that voice with all haste. Miles just didn't know his heart. He didn't realize that he and Jillian were cut from the same fabric. Someone had to make him see that, for Heaven sakes. Regardless of how logical the match obviously was, Miles seemed to be dragging his feet — and time was running out. He just needed a nudge in the right direction, that was all.

Having rehearsed her oration for at least an hour then, leaving specific instructions with Fletcher, she tiptoed downstairs and out to the west gazebo.

Acute elation blazed through Jillian when she found Miles waiting for her. Her confidence soared to dizzying heights as she ascended the stairs. "Hello, Miles."

"I must say, I'm glad for your promptness. Now what is this all about?"

"Please sit. I'm sure we have time for a nice long chat."

Miles sat, but not without protest. "I don't think it wise to linger too long out here. The night air after all is —"

"Yes, I am well aware of the possible effects of the weather." She waved off the subject, sat beside him and continued. "Dear, I've been thinking about our conversation the other day in the maze and I believe I have a solution to your dilemma."

"Really, Miss Kelley, it is unnecessary to — "

"But it is." She ignored the fact that he was being so formal to her when here they were, all alone in the dappled moonlight. "I must tell you what is in my heart, and it has to do with our future."

She paused, giving him a moment to take the lead in the conversation had he a mind to, but he merely shook his head as if he was about to object. She refused to allow his fears to interfere tonight. "Miles." She leaned into him. "Kiss me."

He made to rise but she wouldn't let him. "Please, darling. You and I understand each other. We've grown up together. An alliance between us would be entirely logical! Let me show you how much you mean to me. Make love to me, Miles. Here. Now — " She reached up and removed a yellow scarf from around the collar at her throat. Her blouse parted in a wide V, exposing her chest. She'd purposely omitted her corset to entice him.

Miles jumped up as if he'd been burned. "Miss Kelley!" he growled. "This is indecent — cover yourself immediately!" He reached for the yellow tie as if he wanted to replace it from whence she'd taken it, but she pulled it away, sliding it through his grasp.

"No," she protested and tossed the yellow scarf as far from her as she could. "I am a woman whose passion will no longer be denied. You must make love to me. You love me, don't you, Miles?" As she spoke, she fumbled with the fly of his trousers.

"You must curb your ardor," he practically barked and pushed her hands away.

She went to him and snaked her hands up his chest to entwine them behind his neck. "After all we've been to each other, you must understand my position."

"Miss Kelley, the other day in the maze, I-I hadn't meant...that is, I — " He attempted to remove her hands but she wouldn't allow it. She curled her fingers into the lapels of his coat. "I never meant to mislead you. You must understand that."

"You haven't, you can't. I know your mind as I know my own." Regardless of their hands in the way, she snuggled closer to him.

"Please, Miss—"

At that very moment, Fletcher ascended the steps to the gazebo holding a tray with two steaming cups on top of it.

"Oh, Fletcher!" Jillian feigned being flustered and clung to her blouse to keep it closed. She'd set the entire thing up and it was working like a charm, but Miles wasn't responding as she supposed he would. However, Fletcher's perfect timing would secure an offer from Miles once her mother found out. And she certainly would find out. Fletcher had been hired by her mother, after all. There was no doubt he'd passed her examinations.

A pang of embarrassment shot through her. What a perfectly horrifying way to gain a husband. But if this was her only option in such desperate times, what choice did she have? She managed to shake off the lingering effects of her shame just as Fletcher spoke.

"Miss Kelley. I'm so sorry. Did you not say—?"

"Yes, Fletcher. You did just fine, thank you."

Fletcher put down the tray and turned to leave.

"Fletcher," Miles called to him. "I shall walk with you back to the house. I have no desire to remain out here."

"As you say, sir." And with that, Miles followed the butler toward the house.

Jillian's mortification manifested again. This time, in the form of a headache. Her seduction tactics hadn't worked on Miles. She sat down to cry, but the tears wouldn't come.

She'd been too forward with him. Yes, that must have been it. Miles had an even temperament. Perhaps he'd fall more easily if she were to come to him simpering and ensconced in white lace from her chin to her toes.

Surely, he'd fall into my arms then.

Jillian got up and headed for the house to choose her next steps carefully.

Bradley took up Jillian's discarded scarf and dropped onto a cushioned bench. Jillian's seduction hadn't worked to her advantage. And how could it with a cold fish like Miles?

Good God, had she come to Bradley like that, he'd have given her the moon were she to ask it of him.

Bassett must have been insane to have rejected such a lovely, passionate creature. Bradley hadn't witnessed such blind stupidity in all his travels.

Honestly, Bassett would never be able to make Jillian happy. Bradley had only known him for a few days, and aside from the bad taste in company he'd witnessed from the twit, there was no way in Heaven that Bassett's soggy personality would be able to stand up against Jillian's fire. In addition, there could be no doubt that his Jilli would have worn out the milksop the first time they fell into bed.

Thank God that will never happen. Had things gone as Jillian planned tonight, Miles would have ended up with bruises around his neck the exact size of Bradley's hands.

This whole dream of hers stank of folly. When would she realize that Bassett didn't love her, and he did? And when that day arrived, would he be around to reap the rewards?

The earth shifted beneath Bradley, his heart and soul echoed in agreement. Lord help him, he really did love Miss Jillian Kelley.

* * * *

"Goodbye, Miss Van Amberg, Miss Dearborne. I do hope your journey is pleasant." Jillian hugged each of the girls before they were handed into the carriage. Upon reflection, the two young ladies hadn't turned out to be mere sticks in the mud as she'd imagined in the beginning. They were curious and rather accommodating when it came to new things, and for that, Jillian would always consider them friends.

"Farewell, Miss Kelley. Thank you again for a most entertaining weekend. I feel my life has been enriched just by knowing you. I must say, Prudy and I are sorely tempted to hop on a ship to America so that we may know all that you do!" Miss Van Amberg grinned.

Jillian smiled. "I highly recommend it. And I promise you wouldn't regret it were you to choose to do such."

As the carriage drew away from the house, Fletcher addressed Jillian. "Miss Kelley. Your mother requests your presence in the study."

Regardless of his dire tone and the location of her mother, which spelled certain doom for anyone who was unlucky enough to be summoned there, Jillian smiled. Fletcher had done exactly as she thought he would. He'd gone to her mother with the news that he'd found she and Miles alone together in a potentially scandalous situation. She turned to the butler. "Perfect, Fletcher. And no matter what happens, I don't hold it against you for going to Mama. In fact, if truth be told, I'm quite grateful." She didn't wait for Fletcher to reply, but pivoted on her heel and strode boldly toward the study where Miles would be — as predicted when she'd hatched the scheme, under the watchful, hawk-like eye of her mother, waiting to offer his undying affection. And, directly following the fated meeting, not until death would they part.

Chapter Sixteen

"Yes, Mama. Everything Fletcher said is true." She stood before her mother who sat behind her father's desk. Miles was to her right not two feet away, but he hadn't looked Jillian in the eye nor said a word since she'd entered the study. It seemed he wanted to be somewhere else, *anywhere* else but in this room with Jillian and her mother. Well, the blame lay entirely with Miles. Had he offered for her last night after she'd poured her heart out to him, this tribunal would not be taking place.

"I've heard from Fletcher and now you and Mr. Bassett have both given your testimonies. But there is one more party to be heard from." Mrs. Kelley turned her head toward the door. "Enter, Mr. Townsend."

Jillian blew out an exasperated breath. *Why on earth did he need to get involved with this?*

He came to a halt before the desk and bowed to Mrs. Kelley. He then nodded coolly to Miles. To Jillian he merely glanced.

What is his game this time? Jillian wondered, but had no time to ponder the question.

"Mr. Townsend. Would you please tell Mr. Bassett and my daughter what you confessed to me not an hour ago?"

Bradley cleared his throat. "Well, the fact is that you two were not entirely alone last night. I happened to be in the vicinity of the west gazebo during the incident, and I can attest to the fact that nothing untoward happened between you."

It was then that Jillian's world began to unravel. "Wha—?" she began, but her mother held up her hand. Jillian glanced at Miles, whose shoulders drooped in what could have been considered relief. "No, I'm sorry, but I don't believe him. What proof does he have?"

"He could indeed provide proof if I asked him to, am I not correct, Mr. Townsend?"

Bradley glanced at the floor and nodded.

"There, you see?" Mrs. Kelley announced.

Just once Jillian would've liked for her mother to be on her side.

"So, Mr. Bassett, I would caution you to be more careful when you agree to meet and with whom you do so, in the future, however clandestinely."

"No." Jillian took a step forward and turned to Bradley. "I want this proof my mother is so certain you have."

His countenance portrayed an apology, but she didn't believe it for a second. "Miss Kelley, please be assured, I never meant to—"

"I am not interested in what you did or did not mean. Just prove to me that you were spying on us."

"I wouldn't call it spy—"

"Do not mince words with me, Mr. Townsend. I've not the stomach for it today. Where is your evidence?"

Bradley didn't seem disposed to do as she asked. Probably because he had no such proof. Well, that was just fine with her. She would be the next Lady Bassett, and nothing would stop—

Bradley turned to Miles. "Mr. Bassett. Please tell us the color of the scarf Miss Kelley wore last night."

Jillian's gaze flew to Miles.

"Scarf. Er, yellow, I believe."

From out of Bradley's pocket he pulled the scarf she'd discarded last night. "Is this the same yellow scarf, then?"

Miles stepped toward Bradley and received the strip of silk. "Yes. Yes, I believe it is."

"And from where did she—that is, she wore it how?"

"'Round her neck, I'm sure of it."

"This is Mr. Townsend's proof?" Jillian protested with an

accusing upturned hand.

"That will be enough, Jillian. Mr. Townsend has already informed me that the scarf came from around your neck."

Miles dropped the scarf like a dirty handkerchief onto the desk and Jillian tore her gaze from the scene in shame.

Her mother dismissed Miles. As he passed by, he murmured in her direction. "I'm sorry, Miss Kelley. I have great expectations that this little event won't distress our friendship."

Staring at the floor, Jillian swallowed the lump in her throat hoping to answer, however, she didn't trust her voice. A barely imperceptible nod would have to do as her acquiescence.

"Thank you, Mr. Townsend, you may go as well."

Although she felt him pause next to her, Bradley didn't say a word as he took his leave.

When the men had vacated the room, Jillian turned to her mother and steeled herself for the lecture that was sure to leave her already shredded ego battered and bruised.

Bradley's agitated steps as he paced outside the parlor echoed off the walls. He fumed, completely beside himself. Not because he'd stopped a shotgun wedding, and not because the milksop fit the role of idiot to perfection, but because he himself had been the instrument which pierced the heart of Jillian, foiling her plans, no matter how ill-fated, for the future.

He walked across the foyer toward the front doors to exit the house and fill his aching lungs with fresh air when Bassett stopped him.

"I say, I wish to thank you for getting me out of that sticky situation with Miss Kelley. I'm not sure about her, but my life would have been in a shambles had her mother pressed us to marry."

Without even blinking, Bradley drew back a fist and slammed it into Miles' jaw.

Bassett staggered back, however, the wall behind him

kept him upright. "What was that for?" he asked rather stiffly and holding fast to his injury.

"That was for being the undeserving twit that you are." Bradley stormed out of the foyer via the front doors.

He walked along the pathway, shuffling his feet, chastising himself for pouting like a spoiled school boy. At the edge of the path, he paused and shoved the annoying voice to the back of his mind. So what if he brooded? He deserved to. His Jilli loved another man. He sighed and shoved his fists into his pockets. Perhaps he'd go lose himself in the maze or hang himself from the gazebo. Pity it was too difficult to shoot one's self with a bow and arrow. And just where was that damned wine cellar, anyway?

* * * *

Jillian had endured her mother's lecture for over an hour. Finally allowed to take her leave, she went to her room and changed into her riding habit, as all three pairs of her trousers were unavailable at the moment. Intent on taking Maid Marian out for the remainder of the day, she didn't give a fig if Miss Mary-Perfect was still around or not— and as for Miles... Well, she still hadn't quite absorbed everything that had transpired.

She was positive that shock had overridden her senses, for she'd not shed a single tear since Miles had left her in the gazebo the night before. Her stomach was acting uppity, but beyond that, nothing. During her analysis of the situation, she realized her suffering resulted in a stung ego, as opposed to a case of utter devastation. But still... *Why do people have to act so uncivilized?*

Her entrance to the stables brought to her the familiar smell of horse and leather that comforted her abused sensibilities. She rounded the corner into Maid Marian's stall but stopped just short of her beloved companion.

Bradley Townsend, who should have been working for the Pinkertons instead of considering a teaching position at

Oberlin, stood next to Maid Marian, petting her and feeding her treats. He'd won her mother's affections. Did he have to stoop so low as to gain the favor of her horse as well?

As fast as she could, Jillian pivoted on a pointed toe and quit the stall.

"Jillian, wait."

She would have laughed at his absurd suggestion had she not been so vexed at him. "Go home, Mr. Townsend. You are not wanted here," she tossed over her shoulder.

Of a sudden, he stepped into her path. "Please, just listen to me."

She pushed past him. "I don't believe I owe you that courtesy."

Bradley spun her around by her shoulders. "He doesn't love you, Jilli. He could never be loyal to you."

"You know nothing of his heart," she said forcefully, hoping to get her point across then knocked his hands away from her shoulders with her fists.

"Perhaps what you say is true, but I know mine."

"What is that supposed to mean?" When he didn't answer, she continued. "Miles and I belong together, whatever his imperfections. And I don't need you to stick your indelicate nose in and spoil my future with him."

"It is only your girlish dreams which have caused you to think you have a future with Miles Bassett."

"Nonsense. I'll not participate in this conversation with you. We've come to an impasse and this is where I leave you, Mr. Townsend." She made to turn and walk away, however, Bradley closed the distance between them and her steps were forestalled.

He lifted his hands either in supplication or to hold her, but they dropped to his sides without any sort of contact, which surprised Jillian. He gave every impression of being the kind of man who took what he wanted, when he wanted it. Without warning, he frowned darkly. *Good. He needs to be put into his place for once.*

He took a deep breath which seemed laborious then

spoke. "You will never be free of the memory of me, of us. No matter where you go, you will hear my voice, see something which reminds you that you and I were lovers, and how perfect we were together. Your lust will burn for me, and you will think of only me when you lie with another. You will never be free, Jilli. Never."

Jillian felt tears sting her eyes. Refusing to squeeze them away, she suffered them shimmering on her lashes. "How on earth could you have an inkling of what I will and won't remember?" Her voice was raw, but with each word she uttered her confidence came rushing back. "Are you putting a curse on my head? Do you truly have *the sight* and are wielding your powers?"

As she expected him to do earlier, Bradley pulled her close. "I know because it will be the same for me about you." Bradley released her as if he could no longer look at her — as if it churned his stomach to do so. He exited the stables, his strides taking him away from her and surely, out of her life for good.

Jillian fell to her knees and wept.

Chapter Seventeen

What seemed like an hour later, Jillian dragged herself from the ground and headed for the house. She was decidedly too embarrassed to be in the same room with Miles any time soon and if one were to be blatantly honest, were she forced to converse with Miss Mary-One-More-Day, it would surely push her over the edge.

On the way up the main staircase, Fletcher let her know that Mr. Townsend had left, having given his compliments to her mother.

The announcement suited her just fine. The odd scalding she felt in her breast was merely an after-effect of their stormy exchange in the stables.

She closed the door to her room and leaned against it, trying to figure out who vexed her more, her mother or Mr. J. Bradley Townsend-the-Terrible. Her head pounded and she covered her eyes with her hands. There she saw a brilliant, thoroughly masculine smile, framed by laugh lines which merged into dimples beneath each of his prominent cheekbones. His eyes, his hair, the whole bloody package was simply perfection.

Mr. J. Bradley Townsend, the terribly handsome.

And he was gone.

"Damnation!" she exploded and pushed away from her door to pace the room. "I refuse to think on him anymore." With each step she took, her anger flared anew. What had he said to her, that she never be free of the memory of him? "How dare he presume to tell me my own thoughts, the cur." She turned from the window to retrace her steps. "And I don't give a fig if he hates me. He's gone, thank

Heavens, and therefore, has seduced me for the last time. And frankly, I'm quite relieved." She blew out a frustrated breath. "I will put him out of my mind for good and will never, ever entertain the thought of his kisses or caresses—"

A vision of the night they'd played that wicked game of charades flashed through her mind, causing her cheeks to burn something awful and her body to react even worse. He'd taken her against one of the gazebo's posts as if he was a wild man. She cleared her throat and continued her tirade. "I don't have to…to—" Her voice faded away to nothing, her anger fizzled out not unlike a spent firework.

"Anyway. I have Miles. We are still friends, and love can always bloom from a deep-seated acquaintance such as ours. Miles is cleverer by far than Bradley—"

If you don't count out of doors events.

Or cards.

Or simple conversation.

Or kissing.

Grinding her teeth until her jaw ached, Jillian stripped out of her riding habit, popping a few hooks in the process, then threw herself onto the bed to escape her wayward thoughts. Not long afterward, a soft knock came at the door.

"Who is it?"

"It's Anne. Is there anythin' I can do for you, Miss Kelley?"

Had the comfort come from a tall, thick-haired male with an American accent…? *No!* Jillian grabbed a pillow and hurled it to the floor. After heaving in a shuddering breath, she replied, "Perhaps some tea."

"Shall I make your excuses to your guests, then?"

"Oh, of course, Anne. Thank you. Have Fletcher tell Mr. Bassett and the Honorable Miss Eberhardt that I'm…I'm overwrought from the party."

* * * *

The tea Anne had brought had gone cold hours ago. In addition, both luncheon and afternoon tea had gone untouched. Jillian lay on the bed, her drapes wide so she could watch the scattered clouds slowly change color until the sun was well beyond the horizon. However, even a full moon which had crossed her view, passed by without import.

The damnable Bradley Townsend's face, person — even his scent invaded her thoughts every time she began plotting how she would win Miles back.

Something should be done about it, and fast, for it was grading on her nerves like several overly-loud frogs in a pond set too close to one's window.

Well-aware that this would be the last night Miles would sleep under her roof, she concentrated on hatching a plan. Once the party totally disbanded and Miss Merry Mary took her leave of Fairfield Court, Miles would go back to Thornton Manor. It would be much harder to win him back from there, that was for certain.

It must have been close to five o'clock in the morning by now, but she rose and bathed at her basin. She slipped on a fresh nightgown, and, steeling herself against yet another rejection, she made her way to Miles' room.

"Miles dear, I want you to know that I am terribly sorry for acting the way in which I have lately," she whispered to an empty hallway as she rehearsed the entreaty she'd deliver to Miles. "I heartily apologize for my little stunt last night, and now that the despicable Bradley Townsend — "

Quite uninvited, Bradley's face flashed for the hundredth time through her mind. She blinked hard several times to clear her vision.

"Now that he has left Fairfield Court, I promise to be on my very best behavior. I shall never don, for any reason mind you, another pair of trousers as long as I live."

Bradley never did give them back, the rat. A squeak of anger eeped out from between her lips at the thought.

She now stood before the door behind which slept her darling, Miles. In her mind's eye, she envisioned him, sleeping peacefully, his regal head atop soft white pillows, a pleasant smile about his lips as he dreamed. She took a breath to calm her thudding heart, turned the knob and stepped into the room.

A single candle still burned upon his bedside table.

"Miles?" she'd spoken softly, but he jumped as if she'd screamed.

"My God—w-what are you doing here?" He sat up. It must have been his modest sensibilities which prompted him to tug the fluffy linens to his chin.

She stepped closer to the bed. "Miles, I must apologize for last night. I—"

"You must leave, is what you must do." He pointed to the door with his free hand.

Jillian sat on the bed next to his hip and felt it a very intimate thing to do. "Darling, if you would give me just a moment to explain—"

"Leave this instant, Miss Kelley! Really, this is entirely indecent."

He was so sweet when he was being proper. She leaned toward him with much more confidence than she'd ever thought possible, and kissed him square on the lips.

One, two, three… She counted to herself. If she reached to ten and their lips were still engaged, she would slide under the covers with him and spend the rest of the morning there in his arms.

Two things happened at once. Miles came up sputtering as if he was a water fountain clearing a clog, and from beneath the covers sprung the Honorable Miss Mary Eberhardt.

"I'm sorry, Miss Kelley. But Miles is otherwise occupied."

Beyond horrified, Jillian stared wide-eyed at the sight before her. Miles was in bed with Mary. And neither of them were the least bit repentant about it.

Unaware how long her jaw had been unhinged, Jillian stood and shut her mouth.

"Miss Kelley, please—" Miles began, but Jillian would have none of it.

She'd interrupted him, but felt a serenity she'd on no

occasion known before. "I have never felt more the fool than I do at this moment," she said evenly. "You don't love me. You never have, and you never will." Once again, it struck her how opposite Miles and Bradley were.

"Jillian—"

"No. Don't." Somewhere in the back of her mind she realized that this was the first time since the beginning of the house party that he'd used her Christian name. Jillian backed toward the door of his room. All of her life, it had been her own imagination telling her that she and Miles belonged together—that they were destined to be married—that they were best friends. With staggering clarity, she realized that she had set the stage for her own deliverance. "I'd like to remember you just the way you are. So, that in years to come, when I look back on my life, I will be able to distinctly remember why you and I would never suit."

"And why is that, may I ask?" His voice reminded her of the way it had sounded just before she'd left for the States, as they'd said their goodbyes.

A tiny hint of bittersweetness clouded her revelation, but only for a second. "Loyalty, sir. You are simply incapable of it." She then flicked a pitiful glance at Mary. "Good luck, Miss Eberhardt." And with that, she closed the door behind her.

She drew in a soul-cleansing breath and exhaled an inner peace which up until a few moments ago had been foreign to her. What folly had she almost fallen into because she felt it her obligation to marry Miles?

Duty and honor are terribly overrated.

Aside from unearthing how wrong—no, *blind*—she'd been for more than half her life, Jillian knew she should have been experiencing chaos, a devastating storm of emotions intense enough to put the largest, most stubborn stallion in the stable, down. However, in the dim light of pre-dawn, serenity encompassed her. It was more than she ever would have expected in a circumstance such as this.

And the reason for her state of mind seemed to elude her

completely.

She wandered in the silent hallways of her home searching for the rationale behind her condition. Perhaps she was still in shock. Perhaps she'd finally been won over by 'good English manners'. After all, no one she knew on this side of the Atlantic ever became emotional over anything, save her mother, and even that presented itself on the rarest of occasions. Perhaps it was because she didn't love Miles at all — she loved Bradley.

Jillian came to an abrupt halt. "I love Bradley!" she shouted to no one in particular, then quickly covered her mouth with her hands, never having realized it — let alone vocalized it.

"Impossible!" she said, though it came out rather muffled. *More like improbable*, her mind echoed. But hadn't she always listened to her head and not her heart and much to her regret? *My greatest folly.*

She dropped her hands to her sides. "Then why, when?" she whispered in wonder.

On this, her sporadically intrusive mind remained silent, as if it was a moot point and she should have already known the answer.

A distant clamor, which alerted her to the fact that the household staff were about to begin their work day, echoed down the hall to her.

It was as if dawn had brought with it a new light to which the land adjusted and reflected it back to the sky with sparkling brilliance. And miraculously, along with the dawning of this new age, sprouted from her mind a fresh stratagem like flowers in the spring.

Next on her list if things to do — she thought for a moment.

"Bradley," she breathed, "the man who has stolen my heart without me even knowing it" — Jillian gasped — "has an entire night's head start back to America!"

With a squeak of protest, Jillian ran for her rooms and woke Anne for assistance. *Fool! Imbecile! So book-smart and yet so ignorant of my own heart!*

The second she bathed and dressed, Jillian had Anne call for a carriage then went to her mother in the breakfast room.

"Good morning, Mama."

"Good morning. I'm afraid you missed the departure of the Honorable Miss Mary Eberhardt and Mr. Bassett. He was kind enough to drop her home. Wasn't that thoughtful of him?"

Jillian quelled a nasty retort that would surely have done harm to Miles' and Mary's reputations, but in retrospect, would have reflected badly on her. Instead, she took a different route. "A true humanitarian if I ever saw one. Mama?" she asked, hoping the abrupt change of subject wouldn't raise an alarm. "I'd like your permission to take a day trip to Liverpool. There is some pressing…shopping I wish to attend to and I'd like to leave immediately."

Her mother considered her for a moment, and Jillian steeled herself for questions or, at the very least, a full description of her shopping tour. Or both. "I don't see why not. Your guests have all departed and our social calendar has nothing on it until the little season. I daresay, aside from the minor fiasco last night, your party was enjoyed by all attendees. And now that you've abandoned your more offensive wardrobe habits, I feel you deserve the respite."

Quelling a bark of laughter at the fact that her mother hadn't an inkling as to what had actually gone on, Jillian miraculously kept the outward appearance of a disciplined socialite.

Her mother continued, unaware as to what plans were on the verge of development in her daughter's mind. "Coincidently, Lady Bassett and I have planned a trip to London for some shopping. We should be gone the better part of a fortnight."

She could only blink at her mother who had not protested in the slightest about Jillian running off to chase after Bradley. Then again, her mother didn't really know the true reason. She promised herself that she would do all within her power to keep it that way.

"Thank you. I-I will be taking Anne with me, if that's all right with you." She hoped her mama would see her spontaneous spark of genius as forward-thinking and responsible.

"Certainly. I was about to suggest such, myself."

Jillian couldn't help but smile. Little did any of them know she was about to take charge of her life in an independent fashion she now held as her own.

"My dear, about the talk we had yesterday. I—"

"Really, Mama. I'm fine. I understand now. Honestly."

Her mother nodded. "That's my girl."

Jillian wasn't sure if she liked being talked to as if she was a child again, but she decided there were other, more pressing matters to attend to. She hurried through breakfast and headed upstairs to fetch Anne. Unsure as to what she would need, they each packed a valise. Following this whim was the single most irrational thing Jillian had ever done, but she refused to linger on her own chastisement. She'd have to take each moment as it came no matter the consequences.

Jillian walked over to her bed and pulled from underneath the mattress the reticule in which she'd stashed her excess funds. These were no 'rainy day' pound notes anymore, by God, it was time to subsidize a full-blown monsoon.

The worst thing was that she had no idea how long it would take to track down Bradley. Had he already purchased passage and even now sailed away from her?

Or, what if she found him still in Liverpool the same way she found Miles—but with some dockside strumpet? She'd— She'd what?

Well, first she'd scream her lungs out at him, threaten to tear the hair from the whore's head, then afterward, when the dust settled, she'd die of mortification, that was what.

Her heart would be shattered irreparably, but she would have left some sort of mark on the world.

Now, now. There is no cause to drive yourself into a dither, came the admonishment from somewhere deep in her subconscious. She'd just have to wait and see what the circumstances were before she began accusing Bradley of being a disloyal rat like Miles. She considered it a good thing she hadn't lived during the age of Jane Austen. Her imagination wouldn't have driven her insane with the waiting.

* * * *

"Miss Kelley, are you sure this is wise? I mean, chasin' after a man. Why, it just isn't done."

Jillian turned away to gaze out of the window of the carriage and grimaced. She'd somehow waylaid Anne's bellyaching on the trip across the Atlantic, which had been a miracle in itself. But now, having divulged the entire scheme to her impromptu companion, it may as well have been her mother sitting on the opposite bench, reprimanding her for going forward with the half-baked idea. "Come now, Anne. I've traveled before and completely alone for that matter. I'm surprised you're not lecturing me on what kind of strange characters we'll run into on this trip."

"That very thing is next on the list, my lady. The wharfs are not a place for well-born women to be prowlin' around in."

Jillian harrumphed. "My mother truly has influenced you, hasn't she, Anne?"

"But—"

"No. I'll have no more of it. Let us sit back and enjoy the scenery as it goes by." Jillian watched Anne out of the corner of her eye. The maid was obviously not comfortable with her plan. Perhaps she knew something Jillian didn't. She shifted upon the bench. Perhaps Anne had *the sight* and could see their future.

The sight, indeed. This time, Jillian had the wherewithal to admonish herself. It seemed her imagination had been running amuck ever since her argument with Bradley.

Thankfully, it wasn't long before they reached the docks

as the fourteen miles seemed to fly by while Jillian sat, deep in thought. She sent the carriage back to Fairfield Court, telling the driver they would hire a hack for the return ride.

A long avenue stretched out before them, bustling with sailors, travelers and a cornucopia of general commerce. Jillian thought there must have been a tavern every twelve steps and opposite each other from both sides of the street. Last time she'd come through Liverpool, she hadn't noticed so many places of questionable repute, but then again, she hadn't been looking for a man.

She needed to concentrate in order to locate Bradley. First, they'd have to find out if any ships had sailed to America between last evening and now, and remain composed as if she knew precisely what she was doing.

Because, to be perfectly honest, she had no idea what would come of this madness. Of course, she'd have to hide the fact from Anne unless she wanted her maid to make the biggest to-do since Queen Victoria's Golden Jubilee.

* * * *

After purchasing his steamship ticket back to America, the Salt House was the first tavern Bradley had entered upon his arrival into Liverpool and after his hasty retreat from St. Helens. He liked the name, Salt House. If there was one thing he required to make him forget this ill-fated holiday, it was for a couple of "cases" of salt to purify his wounds. Lucky for him this particular pub was well-stocked with fifty-year-old Scottish single malt whiskey. If one set out to obliterate the memory of a woman, that was the stuff with which to do it.

For over six hours, he'd held his own with sailors from all parts of the world — salty chaps who'd either taken to the seas because they wanted to or because they'd run from something, much like Bradley. The truth of it was that Bradley was haunted by a situation he couldn't escape from, at least, not mentally. For instance, Jilli's face floated intrusively before him at every opportunity—most especially whilst he paused between drinks. Which was another reason he felt obliged to continue with the demise of his sanity, not to mention his sobriety. Not that he'd ever indulged to such a great extent. Spirits had never been employed to fill a gap in his life, at least, not until the fated event at Fairfield Court had dislocated his heart.

"Mates," an Aussie had said. "We are mates, don't you know? And if mates is what we are then we drink like mates—drink like there's no tomorrow—and we forget everything and everyone else." Of course, the Aussie had been there longer than Bradley, and had drunken his weight in beer, or so said the others. But for whatever reason, Bradley had accepted his new friend's invitation to drink himself into oblivion.

They'd sung bawdy songs until the sun had risen, some of which Bradley had never heard before, ones he couldn't wait to share with his brother, Danny, who had the same ribald sense of humor he did, behind closed doors and certainly not in mixed company, of course.

"But low, my glass is dry!" Bradley exclaimed to his cohorts, slurring just a touch.

"And tis a cryin' shame, too," an Irishman named McGinnis retorted. He waved a hand at a passing server. "Another for Mr. Townsend—quick now, before he sobers up and recalls his troubles!"

Everyone laughed—everyone but Bradley.

Chapter Eighteen

With an air of nonchalance, Jillian slowly passed by each pub along the street and poked her head in the door. Various ill-smelling scents assaulted her nose and brought tears to her eyes. The one attribute, which the various taverns wore like a mourning veil, were the dreadful body odors of sailors who apparently went straight from their ships to drink and do whatever unsavory things sailors did, before having the decency to bathe. The crowd that had just come from a fishing boat won the loving cup for the worst smell she'd encountered. Jillian held her breath as she passed by that particular public house. She even considered crossing the street to do so, but the cart traffic proved to be far too thick and exceedingly chaotic.

Ahead of her, and most unfortunately, across the street, were the shipping offices where she had purchased her tickets to America all those years ago. Perhaps they could be of some help.

Bobbing and weaving between wagons, people and carts filled with fish and such, they finally made it to the door. Jillian reached out to enter, however, a man on the other side flipped a hanging 'closed' sign so that it faced out.

"Oh, sir!" She waved to gain his attention. "I must speak with you."

"No, I'm sorry, you'll have to come back during business hours."

"But I have a very important question which—"

"I'm sorry, miss. I can't help you." And he spun on his heel as if desperately desirous of taking his leave from a perfectly dreadful neighbor.

"But, sir!" Jillian banged on the glass with her gloved fist. "It is imperative that I speak with someone regarding ship schedules!"

Jillian's heart soared as the man turned back to her. "The gentleman who processes passages has already left for the evening."

He reached out and grasped the cord attached to the shade and Jillian's spirit plummeted. However, he must have taken pity on her at the last possible moment. "You can find him at The Salt House Inn." He jabbed his thumb in an ambiguous easterly direction.

Good God, not another tavern.

The man seemed to interpret her thoughts. "Not to worry, miss. The Salt House isn't as rough round the edges as most places. Good evening, then." And he pulled the shade closed.

* * * *

Jillian's previously installed optimism dwindled to almost nothing as she and Anne came to the end of Waterloo Street.

"Did we miss it, do you think?" Anne asked, sounding even more distressed than Jillian felt.

"Impossible. I was very thorough. I observed each shingle which hung before us with the shrewdness of a mother hen." Although the streets were all but empty and the sun had just set, Jillian's nerves were all a jangle.

"Did you observe the second story shingles?"

"Oh." Jillian swayed, needing to sit. But more than that, she wished to down a snifter of brandy to allay her worry. So far, this trip had gone nowhere.

"Miss Kelley," Anne whispered sharply.

"Yes, Anne?"

"Ever so cautiously, look over your right shoulder."

"At what?" Jillian hadn't heeded her maid's words and turned fully to where she had indicated. "I see nothing."

Anne's eyebrows drew together. "I thought there were

two men watchin' us from inside that tavern across the way."

"Oh, Anne. I don't have time to jump at every shadow which crosses our paths. Now bring your attention to the matter at hand. We need to find The Salt House as expeditiously as possible. We may miss the man who can help us if we stand here and deliberate over men who have the misfortune to look our way." It was one thing to have to navigate an unfamiliar city blindly, but now she had to mollycoddle her maid.

"But, Miss Kelley, one should, at all times, be aware of their surrounds."

Ignoring Anne's paranoid quirks and foreboding delirium, Jillian set her jaw. "I'm going to have to ask for directions."

Anne inhaled sharply. "Miss Kelley. I must insist. Don't be goin' thither and yon, lettin' folks hear that you don't know your way around!"

"I'm not a lost lamb. This is my country, for Heaven sakes. Now follow me, and in no time we will arrive at The Salt House conversing with a more friendly — and sane, I would imagine — person than we've encountered thus far."

Her maid still didn't look convinced.

"I promise." Jillian smiled to calm her — and her maid's fears.

Yet skeptical, Anne fell into step next to Jillian. They soon came across a man in a charcoal-gray sack suit. He was kind enough to point them in the correct direction and even provided a few landmarks to boot.

Two street crossings later, Jillian stood beneath the shingle, which annoyingly hung from the second floor, that in bold white script letters announced that they had in fact arrived at the sought-after establishment. "The Salt House. You see, Anne, not all strangers are kidnappers." She smiled in triumph.

Cautiously, Jillian stepped into the inn. The wide, L-shaped, richly decorated room was separated into two areas. The doorway through which they'd stepped gave one the option of going to the right or the left. On the right lay a lobby dedicated to checking guests into the rooms above stairs. To the left sat the tavern room, which, much to Jillian's happiness, didn't stink of unwashed sailors, as far as she could tell.

After leading Anne toward the desk, Jillian rang the brass bell.

A kind-looking old man came around the corner and smiled at Jillian. "May I help you?"

She smiled back. "Yes, that is, I hope you can. I am in search of the gentleman who schedules the steamship passages for—"

"Ah, you must be lookin' for Mr. Kendal. He'll be at his regular table, far side of the room." He indicated with a tilt of his head to the pub area.

Jillian thanked the man and turned for the tavern. Up until this moment, she hadn't actually entered a public house. It seemed clean enough and somewhat tame, save for the loud party of men near an upright piano at the far end of the room. Too bad they were merely setting their drinks upon the instrument and not playing. Jillian ignored them and headed for the opposite side of the room. There she saw a man at a table, all by himself and just starting on a full mug of beer.

"Excuse me, sir?"

He glanced up, his eyebrows raising high—either at the fact that before him stood a decently dressed woman in the tavern, or that an actual female had addressed him, she could not tell.

"Yes?"

She could barely hear his voice over the noise from the non-musical ones in the room, and leaned toward him to assist her cause. "The man at the front desk pointed you out to me. I do beg your forgiveness for the intrusion, but I was wondering if you could—"

Laughter erupted around the piano, interrupting her

question. And the man to which she was speaking shook his head as if to tell her he could not hear her. She began anew, louder than before. "I said, I was wondering if you would tell me when the next—" Yet another burst of noise from the revelers smothered the end of her query.

Jillian harbored no desire whatsoever to fight drunken men so that she could ask a simple question, but she was willing to go over and sock the leader of the liquefied fools in the eye to shut him up, if only for a moment.

She took a steadying breath and practically shouted, "When does the next steamship leave for America?"

"Oh!" Thank God, the man finally heard her. "Not until the dawn's tide. I'll be at the office first thing if you wish to purchase passage."

Damnation! She didn't want to purchase passage, she wanted to know if Bradley would be aboard. "Sir, if I give you the name of a passenger, would you be able to tell me if he's on a particular ship on not?"

"I'm sorry, miss. It is the Cunard Line's policy that only those who've purchased tickets can be privy to such information."

The news sunk into her belly like a well-placed fist. It seemed the simple information she sought was going to cost her quite dearly. She sighed and nodded. As long as she had passage, she may as well hop onto the damn ship, provided she even found Bradley.

"If you would come by the office tomorrow first thing and gain passage—"

The loud men around the piano half-groaned and half-laughed, as if they'd just been let in on someone else's dreadful news.

That did it. Jillian could barely hang on to the end of her rope and she needed at least six more feet to hang the instigator at the piano. She excused herself from the man with whom she'd tried to converse and began traversing the room toward the piano.

Part-way across the floor, Jillian froze in her tracks. In the middle of the drunken group stood Bradley, addressing the crowd, his arm around a sturdy post as if holding up both the building and his drunken self, a pint of drink in one hand, swaying forward and aft as if on a ship. He murmured something and his audience groaned again. His oration was obviously not jovial.

Her curiosity winning out over her annoyance, Jillian listened attentively.

"No, no, she was no harlot. She had given her virtue to me, akin to a gift from Heaven above, and I abused the privilege. She encompassed the very ideal of my perfect woman." His American accent slurred something awful, but the spectators didn't seem to notice.

"I've been around the world and back, as far as the east is from the west, as they say, and out of all the women I've met, she was the one for me. Sweet, feisty, intelligent, and yes, my friends, beautiful. Like a desert sunset after a satisfying rain."

Jillian slowly backed against a nearby wall but couldn't bring herself to leave the scene completely.

"I'd followed her here to her homeland. I had no plans as to what I would do or say when I found her again. However, when I did, I turned up as if I was an awestruck lad. And I fumbled about with trying to win her. I botched it, my dear brothers, I tell you. Completely botched it." He turned toward his cup and took a long draw.

One of the men spoke up. "You lost her then, mate? And for good?"

Bradley nodded forlornly and swallowed. "I did. All because she was under the spell of a milksop. A milksop who was, incidentally, bedding one of her other guests right under her nose.

Jillian's breath caught in her throat. *He knew!*

"Why didn't you just tell her, man?" an Irishman inquired of Bradley.

"Honestly, my friend? By the time I found out, my Jilli had already told me that she'd set her cap to marry him.

How could I break her heart like that?" He frowned into his newly emptied cup.

Jillian couldn't move for several seconds. She stood, dumfounded, staring at the scene before her. Abruptly brought back to the present by her maid, Anne stood next to her, tapping her on the arm. "Shall I go to Mr. Townsend and let him know we've arrived?"

Her wits gathered much quicker than she thought possible. "Certainly not. As you can see, he's in no position to entertain guests."

"No? He looks entirely entertainin' to me."

Jillian almost laughed aloud. She'd seen Bradley a bit drunk, and he did appear rather entertaining, however, not in the way that would facilitate more than one person— unless one were a woman—a woman hopelessly attracted to him. And they were alone. Completely alone. Her eyes closed for a moment as intimate memories flashed before her. Emerging from her girlish desires she squared her shoulders. "No. I think we should watch and see where he goes tonight in order to approach him, properly, in the morning."

"And where will we bed down tonight, then?"

Anne was right. Their lodgings for the night now took precedence over any plans she may have proposed. Jillian felt a pang of guilt at the irresponsibility she displayed. She had dragged Anne to Liverpool, the least she could do was provide a nice room for her. "Thank you, Anne. Let us go back to the lobby and hire a room."

When they returned to the registration desk of The Salt House, a sign lay upon the counter which hadn't been there ten minutes ago. 'No more rooms for tonight' it said.

Jillian's stomach lurched. *Now what am I going to do?* She was loath to go back to one of the other places they'd passed earlier in the day. But honestly, what other choice did they have?

"Come along, Anne. We'll have to go back to Waterloo Street and find lodgings there. Tomorrow we'll be first in line at the shipping office. Surely Mr. Townsend will be on the ship tomorrow."

"You're truly settin' our journey by the brim of your hat, aren't you?" Anne asked. The self-righteous horror in her voice spoke volumes of her attitude toward Jillian's independence.

"I am doing what is necessary — means to an end and all that. And besides, Mama has gone to London and won't be back for a fortnight. Now, please. I'm exhausted and I don't wish to speak on this further." She didn't have the energy to argue with Anne who was, after all, only doing what would've been expected of any decent lady's maid.

* * * *

Bradley had no idea where he was. He only knew that his head felt as if it had dynamite packed into it and was about to explode. In addition, his innards must have been stuffed full of gunpowder. The burning sensation in his throat, mouth and nose only worsened each time he retched.

It would also have been helpful if the room didn't toss from side to side so violently. At least that way he could more easily make it to the pot in which he unloaded the contents of his stomach.

Wasn't he just enjoying the company of a sympathetic group of sailors who'd bought him a drink or two? Hadn't they laughed and sang songs, patted each other on the back for the stout drinkers they were?

God, how his throat burned — dry as the Sahara, it was. He recalled his trip to the African continent not a year before…

"Hold everything," he mumbled and, with eyes that felt like dusty, hot rocks, he surmised his surroundings. "I'm on a bloody boat." The tossing about confirmed it.

Bradley lifted himself, as the ship tilted in the proper direction, onto his bunk. "Oh. That's right." He was on a steamship home to America — after botching his one and only chance to woo Miss Jillian Kelley.

"Blast." He gritted his teeth and suffered pain in his head because of it. *Jilli and her obsession with the milksop*. Perhaps he should have written her a note and left it with Fletcher. She had, after all, left a note for him with his valet, Bingham, on that fateful day she departed Bradley's bed, ever so stealthily, in America. If only he'd have been coherent enough to stop her—but he'd been so sated, so sexually satisfied, he'd slept right through her flight from his side.

And to think how she wanted to give that bastard, Miles, her beautiful body—

At once, the contents of his stomach erupted like a volcano.

Perhaps he'd stay the entirety of his five-day journey inside his cabin to sleep off his, er...*illness*.

* * * *

After Jillian paid for she and Anne's passage, the man at the shipping office said a Mr. J.B. Townsend was registered to sail with the line to America. She and Anne had searched the entire ship. Before they knew it, they were underway and they had seen no sign of Bradley. She should have wrung the man's neck to get him to tell her Bradley's cabin number, but she'd smiled and thanked him instead.

It had been a very frustrating voyage what with Anne paranoid about every little thing.

Finally portside in New York, Jillian raised her hand to shield her eyes from the sun. Peering across the street, she could have sworn the man now making his way toward the train station was Bradley. Her breath caught in her throat while her heart took a brief pause in its otherwise normal routine. Why hadn't they been able to find him before now? Readying herself for a very unladylike shout, she took a deep breath, and with his name on the tip of her tongue, someone interrupted her.

"Miss Kelley!"

Belayed by the holler, she glanced around. A woman had called her name, but who on earth knew she was here? She made to answer but then thought better of it. Her main concern was to locate Bradley before he melted into the crowd. Jillian automatically stepped forward, but not realizing until too late, that she'd placed her foot into a deep rut in the road and lost sight of him completely.

Damnation! She removed herself from the hole and stood on tiptoe in order to try to see over the tall hats or under the parasols which blocked her view.

"Miss Kelley!" came the voice once again.

Disregarding the call, Jillian forged ahead, miraculously crossing the street, without being separated from Anne, and looked in the direction in which Bradley had gone.

"Miss Kelley, it's me. Prudence Dearborne!"

Focusing on the young woman before her, Jillian tucked the thought of catching Bradley to the back of her mind for the moment.

"Miss Dearborne?" Not far behind stood Audrey. "Miss Van Amberg, what are you doing here?"

"Why, taking your advice, of course!" Audrey chirped happily.

"Yes. We've come to the United States, just as you prescribed."

"My goodness." Jillian shot a longing look toward the place she'd seen Bradley last. Too many things were presenting themselves at once and it made her feel overwhelmed for a moment. Gathering her wits, she refocused on the conversation. "How wonderful for you." She glanced toward the train station briefly, but again, no Bradley. "Have you no accompaniment?"

Audrey grinned at Prudence in a conspiratorial manner then turned back to Jillian. "No. Completely on a whim, and not a mile out from Fairfield Court, I had my man turn the carriage around and head straight for the docks at Liverpool. We hopped on the first ship to America and here we are."

One could have toppled Jillian over with the slightest of breezes. "What plans have you for your trip? I dare say your decision emerged so quickly, I can't imagine you have an itinerary already." A wave of guilt struck Jillian in the stomach. *And what plans do you have, hmm?* She shook off the nagging voice and again concentrated on Audrey. It was entirely her fault that the girls had set off from their homeland and ended up across an ocean, all alone. The guilt thickened in her abdomen like too much flour in a bubbling pot of gravy.

"We've decided to extemporize, you see."

Prudence nodded. "Yes, we shall rely upon the wind to take us thither and yon."

Audrey chimed in. "What about you, Miss Kelley? We had no idea you would be returning to the States so precipitously."

"Well," she said and glanced at Anne. "Our trip was rather of an impulsive nature as well."

"Oh, Miss Kelley!" Prudence's epiphany shone on her face. "We should travel together! Wouldn't that be a lark?"

"Er, how long do you plan on staying?" Jillian hoped they wouldn't turn around and ask her the same thing. She had no idea as to how extensive she and Anne's trip would be, considering how things were unfolding.

The girls looked at each other. "I say, we were so excited we hadn't talked about it." They giggled as if it were of no consequence.

Jillian knew from her own experience that, to the wealthy, funds were of no object on pleasure trips. Honestly, she couldn't think of a single reason the girls couldn't join her and her maid as travel companions, and besides, she had a responsibility toward Prudence and Audrey. After all, who put the idea in their head about going to America? And here they were, in a foreign country, with no connections — no itinerary whatsoever. Yes, it was best she keep them with her if only to watch over them.

"I'll tell you what. We can be companions until one or the other party decides to return to England."

Prudence smiled. "That sounds just fine."

"I agree completely," Audrey added.

Glancing toward the train station once again, Jillian indicated to everyone's bags while she picked up her own. "Well then, ladies. Let us see what America has for us, shall we?" With determined strides and Anne in tow sputtering protests, she headed in the direction of the train station.

Jillian noticed Audrey and Prudence followed her lead and took up their own bags. This short trip was turning in to a full-blown escapade.

* * * *

A resolution dwelt within her grasp, she could feel it. Bradley was but an arm's length away. However, along with that revelation came a sense of doubt, like clouds looming in the distance. Would he still want her after the way she had spoken to him at the stables, or would he be so upset with her that he wouldn't even look at her? The thought that they had no history together, no large amount of time spent in each other's company, continued to haunt her. No wonder she had a difficult time gauging what his reaction to her would be. She'd really lashed out at him, hurting his feelings, bruising his ego. He must have known she'd said those things because she'd been terribly upset. How could such a rational mind think otherwise? Regardless of what he thought, she wished to explain her actions and be forgiven by him — to be gathered up in his strong arms and kissed senseless. That single thought defined her goal and set it in stone. She needed to be with Bradley and feel his body against hers again. And by God she wouldn't be satisfied until he did so willingly.

Her search for Bradley inside the station turned out to be fruitless, but still her new resolve stayed put.

Depositing her traveling party onto a bench in the vicinity of the ticket window, she hurried over by herself, determined to garner information from whoever serviced the public at the station.

Thank Heavens, the man behind the counter told her, after she offered an extensive description of Bradley, that his ticket was good for Oberlin, Ohio. The tarnish which marred the new information, identical to her tainted luck of late, was that Bradley's train had already departed.

Jillian purchased passages for Prudence, Audrey, her maid and herself, and made certain they'd have access to a place to freshen up.

When she returned to the bench, all three girls looked up at her in anticipation. "Ladies, we are for Oberlin, Ohio."

"I say, isn't that where you went to university, Miss Kelley?" Audrey asked with mild curiosity showing in her deep violet eyes.

"It is. Now we need to get our things to the porter, the train departs in five minutes."

Prudence jumped up immediately. "Oh, I do so love to travel by train."

Audrey stood and extrapolated. "It's true. You should have seen the way she lamented the fact that there wasn't a train which traveled straight from Brighton to St. Helens."

They boarded their pre-arranged private carriage and settled into the first-class compartment in the nick of time. The whistle sounded and off they went.

Anne insisted Jillian use the lavatory first.

When Jillian returned to the group, Anne took her turn, but returned quickly as the washroom appeared to be occupied. She seated herself next to the window as if giving her mistress a sense of privacy.

"Tell me, Miss Kelley, merely out of curiosity, why have you chosen Oberlin as our destination?"

Jillian sighed. She supposed her scheme would be revealed at one point or another. Might as well get it out right now.

"Ladies, brace yourselves." She nearly laughed when Audrey and Prudence's eyes bugged out as if their corset strings were suddenly tightened to breaking point. "I am pursuing, with much zeal and determination, one J. Bradley

Townsend. I believe him to be in love with me — at least he may have been at one point, and I'm afraid I've been…less than hospitable to his advances. I have taken this journey to America to throw myself upon his mercy and beg his forgiveness."

Prudence wrinkled her nose and brow as if she understood how degrading such a thing could be and Audrey just stared, open-mouthed. Out of the corner of her eye, she saw Anne stiffen, but she refused acknowledge the reaction.

"W-what if he doesn't give in, Miss Kelley? What will you do then?" Prudence inquired.

Jillian smiled sheepishly and shrugged in a manner which conveyed uncertainty. "Throw myself from a moving train?"

Chapter Nineteen

Breaking the silence in the compartment, Audrey laughed at Jillian's declaration, however, Prudence stood as if she were about to give an ill-mannered congregation an oration they'd not soon forget.

"You will not have to do such, Miss Kelley. We" — she indicated to herself and Audrey — "will lend assistance wherever and however you need it. We won't allow defeat, not even a hint of it. And with us on your side" — she'd said the word 'your' as if Jillian had suddenly become some important political figure — "Mr. Townsend will be more than hard-pressed to deny you."

Prudence sat next to Jillian. "Now, what plans have you devised to snare said man?"

Jillian glanced at each of her traveling companions. Both Prudence and Audrey had very encouraging looks on their faces, however, Jillian was positive they were about to be disappointed in her.

"I hadn't really thought about it. I'm sort of playing it by ear, as they say."

Audrey chimed in. "But, Miss Kelley, one should always have a plan of attack."

Interlacing her fingers, Jillian stood. "Listen to us, we sound like a traveling cliché chorus." She chuckled, hoping to ease the tension she felt at the prospect of trying to win Bradley. "Believe me, when it comes to Mr. Townsend, any sort of plan is useless. Each time I've been around him, any, *every* rational thought, rule or preparation had proved to be completely futile. Ergo, the time one has spent pondering a stratagem is guaranteed to be an entire waste of energy."

"But he seemed so friendly during your house party," Audrey said with a pout.

"Oh, make no mistake. He's friendly, all right. He...he just has his own way of doing things."

"It must be that he's had a different upbringing than we have," Audrey said putting forth an air of diplomacy.

Prudence thought for a moment. "Perhaps we can use this weakness to your advantage. To what sort of things do you refer?"

Jillian shifted in her seat. "His little impromptu game of charades, for instance."

Audrey and Prudence were suddenly unable to look Jillian in the eye.

"Oh," Audrey moaned under her breath.

"I see," Prudence murmured at the same time. "Quite problematic."

Anne, who seemed as though she were trying not to listen to her lady's conversation, looked to Jillian for an explanation. Jillian waved her hand, letting Anne know that none was forthcoming. As if she'd understood, Anne returned her attention to the passing scenery.

Prudence was the first to come to her senses. "A man who is both handsome and smart is a difficult thing to tame."

Audrey turned back to the party and added, "If one chooses to tame him."

Prudence smiled at her friend. "You may have a point, Audrey." She swiveled a sly gaze to Jillian. "Do you wish to tame the stallion, Miss Kelley?"

Heat washed over Jillian's face and she averted her eyes. *Tame J. Bradley Townsend? As if one could tame a tempest, or a meteor shower or the out-of-control libido of an over-confident, physically well-endowed, excessively attractive male.*

While Jillian searched for her answer, Prudence redefined the quest. "Perhaps it is that Miss Kelley wants to submit to him." Jillian's head came up and Prudence grinned. "A marvelous prospect, if I may say so."

A giggle escaped from between Audrey's lips, which sent

the entire compartment, save for Anne, into hysterics.

Anne turned to the group with a disapproving set of her jaw. "It seems very unladylike to pursue a man as though he were a game bird."

Jillian sobered and sighed. If she failed in her mission and they returned to England, Anne would likely report every incident, move and sentence which commenced on the trip to her mother. Losing nearly all of her bravado, Jillian stood. "Perhaps Anne is right—"

"No." Prudence also stood and looked at Anne. "Your maid is wrong, if you'll pardon me for saying so. These are indeed modern times, as has been brought to our attention of late. Out with the old and in with the new, as it were." She returned her attention to Jillian. "In case you didn't notice, Miss Kelley, you and Mr. Townsend are a perfect match. Audrey and I discussed it the very first night of your party. We wondered why—even *how* you could be attracted to Mr. Bassett when you had Mr. Townsend to compare him to."

How could she explain to the girls that she and Miles had a past together? Not a lurid past, but a solid history. Not only that, but their mothers were friends. Everyone who was sentimentally attached would have been quite content had things worked out with her and Miles. Jillian took a breath to defend her former fascination for Miles, but Prudence continued.

"You, my dear, have a chance to live happily ever after, which is more than most girls have received in the past."

Audrey stood and added her thoughts. "She's right, Miss Kelley, which is another reason Prudence and I wish to be of assistance."

Nodding, Prudence agreed. "The first motive being that Audrey and I must give you credit for opening our eyes to certain truths. Truths which before we came to Fairfield Court, we were blind to."

Audrey drew herself to her fullest height. "We moved from girls to women in a single weekend."

"And without losing our virtues, mind you," Prudence supplemented.

Jillian couldn't help but laugh at the contradicting observation. In one accord, they all returned to their seats. With her resolve growing once again, she sighed. "Were you aware that my mother and Mr. Bassett's mother conspired to find decent society to invite to my house party, only to help me relocate my seemingly misplaced manners?"

Prudence giggled. "Then they should have invited a gaggle of old dowagers to your party."

Audrey's eyes flashed with humor. "And a handful of ugly men."

"And Mary," Prudence added

There was no helping it. All three women burst into laughter.

When Jillian came up for air, she didn't care if she was unable to relinquish her smile. She hoped they couldn't read the elated emotion her eyes as so many had been able to before. It was a curse that she wore her heart upon her sleeve. Everything that had happened throughout the duration of her party ended up being a pivotal, life-altering instance for all. Even Mary.

"Look, Prudence, it seems Miss Kelley has something further to add."

"Go on, then, Miss Kelley. Say what you have to."

Her companions had found her out and there was nothing to be done about it. The girls needed to be informed, she supposed, so she forged on. "The Honorable Miss Mary Eberhardt wasn't all she presented herself to be."

"Oh, you mean because she was consorting with Mr. Bassett?"

Before Jillian could react, Anne sucked in a breath so hard it fairly echoed in the compartment.

Jillian reached out and placed a hand on Anne's shoulder but looked at Prudence and Audrey. "You knew, too?" They nodded in unison. "It seems, even though I should have been the first to know, here I sit, the very last."

"How could we not know?" Audrey grinned. "The first night when he came to her room, she wasn't exactly discreet about her bedroom habits."

Prudence nodded. "You'd think she'd never had a man touch her before, she bellowed so loud. But Audrey argued that some women are just that way."

Jillian felt her eyes widen. "You mean to tell me that Mary wasn't a virgin?"

Anne jumped up. "If you'll excuse me. The lavatory must be vacated by now."

As Anne shut the door behind her, Audrey ignored the maid and tilted her head to the side. "And therein lays the debate du jour. Was Mr. Bassett man enough to take Mary's virginity or had her path been trod upon before?"

Jillian felt a pang of embarrassment for Miles, but more so for herself for not being aware of his shortcomings. Even after knowing and admiring him for all those years. "You didn't think Miles man enough?"

"Heavens no! I've seen livelier tea cups than him before," Audrey said with no little amount of reproach.

Jillian pressed her lips together. Miles indeed lacked passion and numerous other things, particularly in contrast to Bradley. But how could these two young girls know the difference by just looking at the man? Even in her limited experience, which could be counted slightly more than Audrey and Prudence might boast of, she wasn't so discerning. "Miss Van Amberg, I'm surprised at you. In fact, I'm surprised at both of you. You say you were girls before you came to Fairfield Court. I think you were far more mature than you led me to believe."

Prudence and Audrey exchanged glances. Jillian was under the distinct impression, coupled by a visual confirmation, that she'd found them out.

With a shrug, Prudence grinned, causing her lips to curl up at the corners. "One…hears things one can hardly ignore from neighbors and such."

"And from the next room over," Audrey mumbled and

Prudence shot her friend a knowing look.

"And the servants," Prudence whispered.

Jillian shook her head at them and smiled. "I guess it is that we are kindred spirits, then, ladies, and it was indeed fate which brought us together."

Prudence patted Jillian on the hand. "I fully agree. And we shall triumph in our endeavor, Miss Kelley, you wait and see."

Miss Prudence Dearborne, the world's greatest motivator, made Jillian grateful to be part of her team.

Audrey leaned forward and similarly patted Jillian on the hand. "Both of us are indeed up for this adventure. Who knows what wonderful experiences will transpire?"

* * * *

"I'm so sorry, Miss Kelley, but Mr. Townsend ordered the town house closed up until the semester starts. Then he and Bingham left post haste for his estate in South Bend, Indiana."

The information rang in her ears as she returned to her traveling companions who had waited for her in a hired buggy. The sun dipped below the horizon after a particularly exhausting and unproductive day.

She lifted her eyes to the girls who, in the faint light of sunset, looked at her with eager anticipation. "I— I— He—"

Audrey was the first to understand. "Come." She helped Jillian up and sat her down on the seat. "Now, what did he say?"

Jillian swallowed and bravely pressed on. "He— He wasn't there."

"Well, then. I suppose we should return home, Miss Kelley," Anne chimed in, finality ringing in her voice.

Completely disregarding the maid's opinion, Prudence asked, "Where exactly has he gone to?"

"To his family's estate in South Bend," Jillian nearly whispered as she considered Anne's words.

"Is that all?" Audrey asked. "South Bend sounds like a perfectly delightful place to visit."

Prudence smiled at Jillian and patted her hand. "I agree. No need to fret, Miss Kelley. We're not so put off."

Finding her voice, Jillian protested ever so gently, "You two are just wonderful. However, South Bend is yet another six hours away by train. I can't possibly drag you halfway across the country —"

"Why not? Don't you want us to go with you?" Audrey pouted.

"That's not really the point. I'd love for you to go with me, but — but I'm not sure how long this is going to take. What if we arrive into South Bend and he's gone off somewhere else? I can't just keep insisting you escort me on this half-baked journey."

"Miss Kelley. You need to understand. It is our desire to accompany you."

Audrey nodded. "Yes. Who else can we find to take us on such an exciting escapade?"

Ignoring Anne's disgusted huff of air, Jillian nearly laughed. She loosened her gloved fist and revealed the slip of paper the housekeeper had given her with the South Bend estate's address. "Make me one promise, you two." When the girls nodded, she continued. "If at anytime you wish to quit this wild goose chase, do so, and I shan't be offended."

"We promise," they intoned simultaneously.

They settled back into the carriage after Jillian instructed the driver to take them back to the train station. Audrey sighed then grinned at Jillian. "I do so love wild goose for dinner."

Chapter Twenty

It was full dark when they arrived at the Townsend estate. Exhausted and anticipating yet another setback, Jillian used the large brass doorknocker to alert the house of her arrival.

She was more than pleased when Bingham, Bradley's personal butler, answered the door.

"Sir, I— Oh. I do beg your pardon, madam. I was expecting—"

"That's all right, Bingham. Do you remember me? I am—"

Even before she asked, she noted a subtle grin lifting the corners of his mouth. "Miss Kelley. Of course. Mr. Townsend didn't mention—"

"No, he couldn't have known of my arrival. I'm, well, sort of…a surprise, you see." She hadn't known how to justify her visit and hoped it didn't show.

"And what a pleasant one. Do, do come in." He opened the door wider and swept the six-tiered candelabra farther inside, indicating for her to enter.

"Thank you, however, I have a confession. It isn't just myself who has come for a short visit this time around."

Thin gray eyebrows rose above his accommodating blue gaze. "Oh?"

Jillian felt a sheepish heat creep up her neck. "Yes. I have my maid with me and also two friends of mine—and, I might add, acquaintances of Mr. Townsend's, Miss Audrey Van Amberg and Miss Prudence Dearborne. But I must ask you, Bingham—and please be as candid as possible. Do you suppose Mr. Townsend would be inclined to entertain guests on such short notice?"

The butler smiled at her in a very fatherly way. "Were it

anyone else but your party, Miss Kelley, I'd have to say no. And I am most positive Mr. Townsend would dismiss me were I to turn you out."

Jillian's insides twisted for a moment. She would wager right here and now that Bingham had no idea about her and Bradley's argument. "Thank you, Bingham. You are too kind." Jillian signaled the waiting carriage and as the girls descended upon the house, several liveried men came out and lit the parallel rows of amber-tinted lanterns which bordered the half-circle drive.

Once the door closed behind them, Jillian inquired about Bradley.

"I'm sure he would meet you himself, were he here, but I'm afraid he's out for the evening."

Jillian nearly sputtered. "Oh…well, then. Perhaps…if you would show us to our rooms—"

"Indeed. You must be exhausted." Bingham then turned on his heel and held the silver candelabra higher for them. "This way, please."

They wound up a wide, curved staircase padded with thick carpet and flanked with paintings on one side, and an elaborately carved oaken stair-railing on the other. The breezeway itself was as cavernous as a cathedral. One thing was for sure, Bradley's ancestral home was quite extensive.

Bingham promised a meal would be sent up as soon as possible. He then deposited Anne into a maid's room adjacent to Jillian's. Prudence and Audrey were offered adjoining rooms just across the hall.

A servant set a cheery blaze in the fireplace and lit lamps about the room. After requesting the laundering of her clothes, Jillian positioned herself—clad only in her chemise—in the center of a very large, very soft bed. A circular fan of pleated ivory velvet adorned the upholstered canopy. Matching bed curtains draped luxuriously on either side of the bed and were held back with brass knobs which protruded from the ornately carved maple wood headboard. Bookcases filled two of the walls, however, in addition to a few books of poetry, delicate china plates and porcelain figurines graced lacy doilies atop alternating shelves.

The feel of the room exuded a perfect mix of femininity and strength, decadence and warmth. She wondered if Prudence and Audrey had similarly decorated rooms.

Just then, a knock came at her door. "Who is it?" She was sure her heart had stopped beating while she waited for a reply, which came not moments after her inquiry.

"It's Mrs. Goodwin, Miss Kelley. Bingham sent me."

"Come."

Through the door entered an older woman — stiff, starched, yet jolly, with rosy cheeks and a ready smile. Her immaculate black and white maid's uniform wordlessly enlightened Jillian of Bradley's good taste and high standards.

"I beg your pardon, miss, but Bingham had a bath drawn for you. You can access the room through that door." She nodded toward a dark corner. "We have all modern plumbing and are preparing the house for electric light installation. It's all very exciting. Now, shall I call your maid to you?"

"No, thank you, Mrs. Goodwin. Let her be," she said, knowing full well Anne would benefit greatly from some extra rest. Her gaze followed Mrs. Goodwin's indication. Surprised, she would have never known a door existed there unless she was told. It blended in perfectly between the carved cherry wood paneling and book cases.

The floral-scented steam welcomed her, drawing her deeper into the room with its exotic scent. Again, she was awed. A selection of elegant soaps sat next to the tiled bath, and on the opposite side, a silver candelabra spiraled upward, the thick white candles presenting steadfast flames of yellow-orange, causing the mist around them to glow. A large, fluffy light blue bath sheet hung from what looked like white piping, which protruded a few inches from the wall and snaked its way to the floor. Jillian reached out and stroked her hand down the fabric. It felt warm to the touch. The pipes must have brought in the hot water, warming the towel at the same time. Jillian smiled. Bradley's house was indeed a wonder.

After a long relaxing soak, she found Prudence and Audrey within her bed chamber in their chemises, sitting at a small table near the fireplace. "Perfect timing. Mrs. Goodwin just brought up supper. I thought to send Audrey to fetch you from your bathing room, but here you are!"

"Miss Kelley," Audrey said with wide eyes. "This house —!"

Jillian smiled and took her seat at the table. "Truly, I don't even think Queen Victoria herself has such wonders at Windsor." The familiarity of gossiping with dear friends caused a coziness to sweep over her. The combination of the beautiful room and Audrey and Prudence had inspired the intimacy. She couldn't imagine it any other way.

"All three of us have our own bathing rooms, can you even fathom?" Audrey whispered exuberantly and passed Jillian a plate.

"I dismissed Mrs. Goodwin so we could talk," Prudence announced and poured everyone water from a frosted pitcher.

Audrey picked up a heavy silver cover of the main dish. "Oh, my. Here we have what looks like stuffed chicken breast and thick slabs of beef."

"Stop talking about it and pass it over here," Prudence admonished her friend lightheartedly. "I'm simply starving."

"Look! They've whipped the potatoes as if they were egg whites!" Jillian exclaimed as she dug a serving spoon into them. "Were they planning on feeding an army?"

"I think they were! If this is a late supper, what must a celebratory meal be like in this house?" Audrey observed.

Jillian smothered a grin. What she wouldn't give to experience Christmas in this fine mansion.

After they had eaten their fill, Mrs. Goodwin, followed by

her staff, came and cleared the plates. Not moments after, another bevy of servants brought in dessert. Peach pie with vanilla ice cream.

* * * *

Jillian sat back in her chair with her arms over her stomach. "If I didn't know any better, I'd say they were trying to fatten us up for the kill."

Audrey giggled. "Well I could die happily in a house such as this."

"Both your houses in Brighton are elegant, aren't they?" Jillian asked the girls.

"Oh, they are," Prudence replied. "But you know how it is. Food tastes better abroad, and all — at least, that's what I have found recently."

"Always," Jillian agreed, grinning.

Prudence yawned. "What time do you suppose it is?"

Jillian glanced at the clock next to the bed and frowned. "It's nearly midnight." *Where on earth is Bradley?* She felt a hand come to rest upon her shoulder.

"Don't worry," Audrey reassured her. "I'm positive we'll see him at breakfast tomorrow."

"Although I may only have room for a single cup of tea for the next week," Prudence murmured wryly.

Mrs. Goodwin tapped upon the door then popped her head into the room. "Can I get you ladies anything else?"

"Mrs. Goodwin. You have done so much already," Jillian said as she and the girls rose from the little table.

"Nonsense. It's my absolute pleasure," the woman replied.

"Miss Kelley." Audrey claimed Jillian's attention. "I'm so very tired. I feel as if I haven't slept since we left Fairfield Court."

"Oh, my dear, don't think you have to stay up and entertain me. You, either, Miss Dearborne. Go on to bed. I shall see you in the morning." Jillian hugged Prudence and Audrey goodnight and sent them on their way while two servants brought in a tray on which they took away the used dessert dishes.

Mrs. Goodwin added another log and stoked the fire while Jillian crawled between the covers. "Mrs. Goodwin, how long have you worked for the Townsends?"

"Since well before the Master, Mr. John B. Townsend, passed. The children were not quite out of their nappies yet when I come to the household."

In need of more information, Jillian forged ahead. "And when do you expect Mr. Bradley Townsend tonight?"

"Not sure, Miss Kelley. He's come and gone as it pleases him since he was a sapling."

Jillian nodded. "Thank you, Mrs. Goodwin. One more thing. When is breakfast usually served?"

"Ten o'clock, miss," she said and set the table's centerpiece to rights.

"Ten?" Jillian repeated, somewhat astonished. "It's nearly noon by then."

"Indeed. If you are peckish earlier than that, you may venture into the dining room. I'll have the kitchen staff set out fruit, bread and coffee—and tea o'course, for you."

Shaking her head, Jillian corrected herself. "I'm sorry. What I meant was…does Mr. Townsend usually sleep that late?" *Good Lord. That didn't sound appropriate at all.* "I mean—"

Mrs. Goodwin smiled in understanding. "There's no need to fret. These are the new rules, now that Mr. Townsend will be teaching at Oberlin in six weeks' time. He'll be taking advantage of the summer, winter and spring breaks to sleep in. He does enjoy his sleep, that one."

Feeling a bit more assured that she wasn't being terribly nosey, she snuggled down under the covers. "Thank you, Mrs. Goodwin. You, Bingham and the staff have made us feel very welcome."

"We'd have it no other way, my lady." She grinned and shut the door.

* * * *

Jillian had drifted in and out of sleep though she didn't understand why. She'd hardly had any sleep in the last two or was it three days? Regardless, her incessantly chattering mind produced a very blurry picture from where she sat.

Rolling onto her stomach, she thought she heard horse's hooves on the gravel drive below. She ignored it at first, until she heard a low voice, distinctly male, float up to her window.

Jumping from the bed, she peered out through the drawn cream organdy curtains.

It's him.

Bradley handed a footman his cloak and turned back to the open door of the carriage. A thoroughly feminine laugh tinkled and spilled out of the cab, then Bradley reached through the door. Two gloved, delicate hands encircled his neck and they embraced for longer than was decent.

Jillian began to shake.

She'd pined away for him for over a week now, and had come all the way across the country to find him, and Bradley probably not even as much as thought of her! And to top it off, he'd been out carousing with some floozy on the very night she'd come to beg his forgiveness!

The cad, Bradley Townsend — and she knew him to be such from the time he'd set foot in the west gazebo — was in for quite a tongue lashing tomorrow at breakfast, and she didn't care who was in attendance to hear it!

With one final glance into the courtyard, Jillian observed Bradley shut the door. He blew a kiss at the carriage window and waved like a smitten adolescent.

This sort of behavior is what her conscience had been warning her about all along. She didn't know him, not really. Who knew how many women he had stashed away in odd places?

Gritting her teeth until it hurt, Jillian spun away from the window and marched back to the bed, promising herself that tomorrow morning would mark the end of her fixation with the rat J. Bradley Townsend.

Chapter Twenty-One

With the exception of a bit of distant clamoring from the kitchen, the household had settled in for the night, thank God. After the evening he'd just had, not to mention the steam ship voyage where he'd nearly met his fate vomiting then fell into a seemingly endless death-sleep, he needed the peace. Tugging at his silk tie, he loosened the knot and pushed the door of his bedroom open with his elbow. Just before he shut the door, Bingham appeared in the hall with a stack of correspondence and an odd look on his face.

"What is it, Bingham? I'm seriously done in."

"I need to discuss a few items with you, sir. Matters which are of considerable import."

Bradley blew out a breath. It was just his luck lately that his weary self would get no rest. "Very well." He nodded. If Bingham thought it important enough to come to him at this hour, then perhaps it was. He'd never rung false alarms before.

"Shall we step into the library, Sir?"

"If you don't mind too terribly, I'll hear you out right here." Bradley turned away from the door and Bingham followed him inside.

* * * *

Jillian couldn't even begin to relax. It felt as if she'd been tossing and turning for hours. She needed to speak to Bradley this instant and allow her emotions to have their say. She tossed the covers from her legs and slipped from the room. Tiptoeing past Audrey's and Prudence's chambers, she then headed downstairs. He was probably having brandy in his study, just like her father used to when he'd come home late at night.

Reaching the bottom of the stairs, she heard a noise and flattened herself against the curved alcove which flanked the staircase. Mrs. Goodwin conveyed her goodnights at the doorway through which Jillian presumed lay Bradley's study.

Once the head housekeeper was out of sight, Jillian crept to the door and peeked in. It was dark. The curtains were only half-drawn, which provided not nearly enough light to do anything productive. The fireplace sat vacant of fire, which made her believe he didn't plan on staying very long in the room.

Then she saw it. *Just as I suspected. The brandy decanter.* Her eyes narrowed. How very predictable of him. Apparently, men were men whether British or American. The crystal container was nearly empty as it sat upon a small table next to a high, wingback chair which faced away from the entrance where she stood.

A masculine hand reached for the snifter next to the decanter. Seconds later it returned to the tabletop drained of its former contents.

If she didn't approach now, she'd never stir up the courage. Jillian steeled her resolve, stepped into the study and took a breath. Knowing she shouldn't even look upon his face lest she lose that resolve, she stood next to and just behind the large chair. "There will be no need for formalities, so don't stand just because I've entered the room. I'm sure your legs have endured quite enough sport for one evening," she added the latter with a dash of sarcasm, far less than she felt he deserved.

"Wha—?" a deep male voice began, but Jillian wasn't ready to hear his excuses.

"No, no. Don't speak. I have something to say and you will hear every word of it." Without pause she unleashed her fury. "First off, you need to know that I am now convinced of being entirely wrong about Miles. He's a cad and I don't care if I see his face ever again. Now to speak to the relevancy of why I journeyed to these shores, I want you to know it was all a mistake. All of it. From the first night we slept together, to the fact that I stand here now."

"Madam, I—"

"Weren't you listening? For a future professor, you are indeed lacking when it comes to following directions."

She thought she head a muffled laugh disguised by a cough, but she had too much to say to analyze the response. "I can profess responsibility for the first night in America we shared in your bed. But when you ventured forth to my home and seduced me, right there, out of doors, where anyone could have seen us, the entirety of the blame for that wretched episode—and the similar episodes which followed—rests upon your shoulders. You should not have bared my body and soul the way you did, use your lips, tongue and other appendages on me, bring me to magnificent heights, and then almost, but not quite, tell me you love me.

"You need to know that I saw you through my window tonight, embracing that…that woman! You do work fast, don't you? Did you do the same things to her you did to me or did you just flip up her skirts and have her right there in the carriage? Oh, how could you, Bradley Townsend!" Jillian's voice cracked, but she didn't care now if she cried or not.

"I really don't know what I was thinking when I left for Liverpool to find you. It seems I've sent myself upon a fool's errand." Her anger returned once again as she thought of this whole affair. "I'm sorry I ever felt anything other than an acquaintanceship for you, Mr. Townsend. I am finished with you, do you understand?" She turned for the door but whirled around again, not through yet. "All your claims of not being a seducer of women were nothing more than complete and utter denial!" She sniffed and held her chin a bit higher, proud that she hadn't broken down completely.

"I will be leaving in the morning. You once accused me of breaking your heart, however, now I find solid evidence that you are completely void of one. You disgust me, Bradley Townsend!"

And with that, she fled the study and hurriedly took the stairs to her room.

* * * *

"And in the last of the correspondence I found this. It seems it came here first, then the staff here had forwarded it to your townhouse in Oberlin, and finally, because you had gone abroad, they sent it back to you here in South Bend."

Bradley took the proffered envelope, flipped it over and set it atop of the median pile he held. "It's from the art department at Notre Dame," he murmured and broke the seal.

While scanning what obviously was an invitation of some sort, Bingham seemed uneasy as he stood shifting his weight. "Is there something else, Bingham?"

"Yes, sir." He took a deep breath. "It seems you have a bit of unexpected company."

He groaned at Bingham's words.

"Now, now…you will welcome the party when you hear who it is."

Bradley's gaze jumped from the stack of letters in his hand to Bingham's somewhat mischievous smirk. After wasting an entire evening in a hospital waiting room, his time suddenly felt more valuable than before. "Well, man, who is it?" He couldn't even begin to guess.

"You mean 'who are they?', don't you?"

"Bingham, this is no time for games."

Hiding his smile behind a scratchy clearing of his throat, he conceded. "Your unanticipated guests include a Miss Dearborne, a Miss Van Amberg and a maid by the name of Anne."

"Good God," Bradley murmured.

Bingham reached out for the door and pulled it open. "Oh, yes. And your Miss Jillian Kelley as well, whom I have installed in your sister's old rooms." And with that, Bingham shut the door behind him.

Bingham's chuckle practically rang in the hallway as Bradley's heart had completely stopped pumping blood past his eardrums.

How in the hell…?

Not two seconds later, a knock sounded at his door and Bradley jumped at least a foot off the floor.

"Bloody hell. What is it now?" Bradley barked.

The door opened just enough for his impish little brother to pop his head in. "Jeez, Johnny. No need to bite my head off."

It was all too much to hold on to. "How many times have I told you not to call me by our father's name?" It had been an immeasurable number of instances in the twenty-five years since Daniel had learned to talk, but Bradley had sworn at a very young age that he'd admonish the twit each and every time. "And what the devil are you doing home from the hospital?"

Dan pushed open the door and hobbled into Bradley's room using a stylish crystal-topped cane. He shrugged. "My ankle is merely sprained, not broken as they'd once thought, so they released me. Regardless, it is I who will play inquisitor tonight, Brad."

Sniffing in his younger brother's direction he commented, "You've been drinking."

Dan grinned wryly. "For the pain." He made his way over to the chairs set before the fireplace and lowered himself into one. He indicated the chair opposite him. "If you please?"

"What is it with the games around here tonight?" Bradley murmured.

"Oh, that's not the half of it," Dan said and set his foot carefully onto the ottoman which separated them.

"You are going to be the end of me if you keep up this

ridiculous charade." Bradley stalked over and threw himself into the proffered chair. "Now what the hell is this all about? I have other things to attend to—"

"Damn right, you do," his brother admonished as if he were the older sibling. "Allow me to tell you the tale of a saucy British gal who not ten minutes ago bared her soul—and yours—to me."

"Ah," Bradley murmured and sank a little further into the chair. "So you've met Jillian."

"Not as such."

"Wha—?"

"I'm pretty sure she thinks she just gave you the what-for, when it was in fact me whom she addressed."

"How is it possible that she mistook you for me? I'm at least a foot taller than you."

"A scant six inches, to be exact." Dan smirked.

"It's irrelevant how many inches—"

"Unless one is jealous of his younger, more handsome brother."

Bradley growled at his arrogant little brother, losing what shards of patience he'd had to begin with. "Just tell me why she spoke with you and not me."

"We were in the dark together."

"You what?" Bradley nearly came out of his seat.

"Calm yourself and just listen. I was taking a brandy in the library just after I arrived from the hospital when I heard a lovely, British-accented, feminine voice begin a scalding tirade from just inside the door."

"What did she say?"

"You mean after the part about some 'cad' named Miles she never wants to see again?"

Regardless of the bolt of relief that shot though him, Bradley issued his warning through clenched teeth. "Daniel…"

Dan smiled. "Let's just say I can accurately pinpoint precisely how skilled you are on an intimate level and in which areas you excel with the fairer sex."

"Dammit, Dan," he growled. "Why didn't you tell her you were not me? You could have saved her from embarrassment."

"It was too juicy a bit of gossip to even consider telling her I wasn't you," he teased.

"That wasn't very gentlemanly of you, Daniel Townsend."

"Gentlemanly? You were the one who seduced her, not I."

Bradley raked both hands down his face. "This is all some sort of twisted misunderstanding. I—"

"Come now, Brad, you have my word, your confession will go no further. Have you been trifling with her?" he asked, raising his eyebrows impertinently.

"It's not quite that simple. I—"

Dan didn't let him finish. "For shame. We weren't raised to drown butterflies. Were Father alive he would have you horsewhipped for treating a woman so."

Theoretically, his brother was only half-kidding about the horsewhipping. "It's not what you think, Dan. I'm in love with her."

"Well done." He nodded. "I'm afraid you've lost her."

Bradley felt his brother's sarcasm all the way to his bones and went silent while he absorbed Dan's last words.

"I'm sorry, Brad," Dan finally said.

"Have you any idea how many times I've lost her?" Bradley whispered, nearly chuckling at the irony.

"Well, then you have a tremendous amount of work to do. She claims to have seen you tonight embracing some woman—"

"Caroline."

"More likely than not—and is planning on leaving here in the morning."

Bradley jumped up from the chair. "Not if I stop her first." And he exited the room.

Just after he took off down the hallway, the thought crossed his mind that he should have warned his brother about the other house guests. But as he approached his sister's old rooms, his mind flooded with thoughts of nothing but Jilli and how much he wanted her.

Chapter Twenty-Two

Bradley didn't want to stop and think. He raised his hand and rapped his knuckles on the door.

No answer.

"Jill— Miss Kelley? May I please speak to you?"

Following a brief pause, a muffled voice answered, No."

Bradley sighed and leaned his head onto the ornately carved, oaken barrier. "Please?"

"No."

"There has been a misunderstanding—"

"Understatement."

"Please. Just listen to what I have to say and if you want me to leave, I will."

"I already want you to leave. Why don't we just move forward from there?

"Please?"

No answer.

Bradley bit back a smile, confident she was considering it.

He waited.

Nothing.

Becoming slightly more anxious, he lost what little mirthful ground he'd gained.

At once, the door opened. "You have thirty, no, twenty seconds."

Bradley took a breath and made to step forward, but she stopped him with the door.

"Ah-ah. You now have less than seventeen seconds." Her gaze lifted to the ceiling as if she couldn't look at him while she awaited his oration.

He blew out the breath. "I understand you made a

confession of sorts earlier this evening."

The door opened a few more inches. Her gaze fell upon him and narrowed. "You 'understand'? What does that mean?"

Shifting his weight, Bradley forged ahead. "It was not I who sat alone in the dark downstairs, but my brother Daniel."

The door shut all the way and he distinctly heard a, "Oh, God" from behind it. Her distress now confirmed, he took charge, slowly turned the knob and stepped into the room.

She stood near the fireplace with her head in her hands, the fading red-golden embers illuminating her nightgown. He could hardly believe she was here, but he couldn't dwell upon that revelation at the moment. Disallowing himself from going to her, he stopped a scant six feet or so away. "Don't worry about Dan. He's not one to spread gossip."

Jillian merely groaned.

"Will you sit for a moment?"

"You mean before I fall down?"

Bradley wanted to laugh but he didn't. He could only imagine her mortification. When she didn't move, he took the initiative and placed himself upon the narrow padded bench at the foot of the bed.

Reluctantly, she followed.

He watched her. She still refused to meet his gaze. He wanted so much to comfort her, he ached inside. "About this evening," he began.

"I wish I'd never come here," she murmured flatly. "I wish I would have not been so fanciful as to think you cared for me, when all you are is a scoundrel."

"If hugging my little sister Caroline makes me a scoundrel, then so be it."

Her gaze snapped to his. "You expect me to believe it was your sister whom you entertained this evening?"

"If one considers sitting in a hospital waiting room entertainment, then yes, I do."

"What? What happened?"

That's more like it. She does care. Bradley stuffed down the hope which had seeped into his chest and continued. "My brother—"

"Daniel."

"Yes. Took a fall from a spooked horse. My sister—"

"Caroline?"

"Yes, Mrs. Linus Webber—the first to receive the missive from the hospital about Dan. She then sent me a note to meet her there which I received just moments after I arrived from the train station. Her husband met us after court—Linus Webber is a lawyer, you see. An early diagnosis alleged Daniel's ankle to be broken, but apparently afterwards they ascertained it was only a sprain. Later, the hospital discharged Dan and they brought him here. He wished to have a nightcap before retiring—"

"And that's when he had the misfortune of being the recipient of my tirade."

Bradley nodded in lieu of a verbal answer as if it would lessen her embarrassment.

She rested her palm upon her forehead. "I've really botched it this time. There will be no recovering from what I've done."

"It's not as bad as all that—"

She chuckled and slid her hand from her face. "Had I not given intimate details of our liaison, the situation in which I find myself would not be so horrific."

"Jill—"

"No." She stood and moved toward the fireplace to look down into the smoldering embers. "There is no getting around this. I must leave. If I were to come face to face with your brother I'd die on the spot from shame."

"He doesn't need to be here. I'll send him away."

Jillian turned to him, frowning. "And him with a hurt ankle? You'll do no such thing!"

Bradley felt his lips quirk threatening to smile, but repressed it just in time. "Daniel Townsend, I'm most certain, is eager to meet you properly—and forget the little one-sided conversation you two had this evening." When she didn't reply, he added, "If not, I'll hurt his other ankle."

A bark of amusement came from Jillian. "You would, wouldn't you?"

Ever so briefly, her laughing eyes met his. It nearly took his breath away.

He grinned. "Of course not. Don't be silly." He watched her as she crossed the room. Her shoulders—in fact, her whole person—had loosened up a bit since he'd first entered, which served to offer him hope once again. Hope that she would perhaps warm up to him. Or at least allow him to warm up to her.

She placed both hands upon a table and hung her head in despair. "How can I possibly face him?" she mumbled forlornly.

"Try humor."

Looking at him as if he were insane, she scoffed. "What do you think this is, *Much Ado About Nothing*?"

"It is, when you think about it."

Jillian shook her head again, but this time she was chuckling. "You do have a knack for turning things around, don't you?"

Bradley shrugged.

Jillian watched him out of the corner of her eye. He was terribly handsome—and seemed quite easy to be around, especially when he wasn't frowning. "Which reminds me." She dropped her gaze to the floor and her voice fell just as low. "I never got the chance to ask your forgiveness for the way in which I spoke to you at the stables."

"There is no need," he replied quietly.

"But there is. I—"

He took a step toward her, halting her explanation, but she didn't protest. His presence felt so warm and comforting—so agreeable. She wanted him even closer, she admitted to herself.

"Please don't," he murmured and reached out a hand to

stroke it down her arm.

It was the first time he'd touched her so tenderly since they'd danced together. *Or was it at the gazebo? My mother's parlor? Oh, it just doesn't matter anymore.* His spiced scent surrounded her, filling her senses to the point of dizziness. At once, Jillian noticed she had turned to him, though she couldn't remember doing it. He slowly closed the rest of the meager distance between them when the warning bells went off in her head.

Her lips refused to form the words that would stop him from seducing her again. Here they were—on his home field, so to speak—and if she didn't send up even a tiny protest, she may as well surrender right now.

But that wouldn't do at all.

His mouth brushed her temple and she heard him inhale deeply. She closed her eyes and her world spun. She reached out a steadying hand and found herself encircled in his arms. Her body simply buzzed. He held such an extraordinary power of attraction.

"How can I make all this up to you, Jilli?" His words nearly hypnotized her. She tilted her head forward, until her brow rested upon his chest. His voice rumbled beneath her forehead. "I don't want you to leave. Stay here. Be my guest for a week or two."

Jillian imagined taking a holiday in his grand mansion. Hot, fragrant baths every night, sumptuous meals three times a day—a girl could become accustomed to such luxuries. *But at what price?*

"What, and be seduced by you at every turn?"

"Is that so bad?"

The fact that he didn't defend himself brought her out of her relaxed state. She gently pulled out of his arms. "Yes, quite frankly, it is." She stepped toward the door and turned to face him, her hand on the knob. "Regardless of what you may think of me, I am not some strumpet who would trade her body for room and board."

"I never said—"

"No, not outright," she interrupted. "But your actions continually confirm your expectations of me."

Bradley's gaze came to rest on the floor. "What if I asked to court you? Properly this time."

He tilted his head up just enough to look at her out of the corner of his eye. He was actually requesting permission. Well, if this wasn't more than she could ask for, then she didn't deserve him. She removed her hand from the doorknob to face him fully.

Jillian nodded. "Very well."

The cutest boyish grin settled across his face and Jillian's toes curled. He started toward her and her heart pounded. When he came to stand just inches from her, she found her breath trapped within her lungs.

"In that case, allow me to welcome you to my home."

His voice sounded rich and deep as it reverberated in her ears, and held wicked promises which she didn't trust herself to dwell upon. She had to get him out of her room now, before she turned the tables and seduced him. She nodded her acquiescence if only to expedite his departure.

At once, he took her in his arms and threaded one of his hands through her hair, tilting her head backward. He pulled her by the waist with his other arm until her body was flush against his. The heat she felt radiating from him through the thin cotton of her nightgown was acute, unsettling—and it tempted her almost beyond what she could endure.

In one fell swoop, his lips claimed hers.

* * * *

Closing the door behind him, Daniel then set his cane down and felt around in the top drawer of his old bureau. The matches and emergency candle were still there, thank goodness. It had only been four years since he'd moved to his own apartments closer to town, but this house, where he'd grown up, would always be his home.

With the newly lit candle in hand, he turned toward the bed but stopped short. There, in his bed, lay an angel. Her thick, dark hair cascaded over his pillow, leaving uncovered a pale shoulder which peeked out of the neck of her nightgown. Quietly, he hobbled forward to gaze down at her. Her steady breathing was testimony to her deep state of sleep.

Who is she?

A pity she wasn't a gift from above for his ever steadfast character. He shook his head at the thought. True, he wasn't a rogue, but finding a beautiful woman in his bed, he could easily be tempted to unleash his darker side.

Daniel gazed at her for a few more moments. "Sleep well, little angel," he whispered. "We shall meet in the morning and perhaps I will convince you to be mine."

He grinned and made for the door. Reaching for his cane, he hoped to find one of the other guest rooms vacant. How was he to sleep this night when an enigmatic beauty had taken over his bed?

Chapter Twenty-Three

"Miss Kelley, please be still."

Poor Anne. Jillian knew she was fidgety this morning, but it could hardly be helped. Once Mrs. Goodwin had brought in her freshly laundered clothes, Jillian had called for Anne. She couldn't wait to see Bradley again. Her fear of confronting his brother Daniel all but dissipated with the thought that Bradley would be there with her, acting as a comfort, a shield—at the very least, something to cushion the critical second encounter. Although first impressions were so hard to overcome, especially the negative ones, all she had to do was imagine his stirring kiss from the night before and even the tiniest reluctance to meet his brother face to face vanished.

A knock sounded at the door and Prudence and Audrey entered.

When Anne finished, Jillian sent her to breakfast and sat the girls down for a briefing.

"The good news is, I've already seen Mr. Townsend and all is progressing nicely between us."

Audrey and Prudence grinned first at Jillian then at each other.

"The bad news is, I've also met with Mr. Townsend's brother."

With wide eyes, Audrey asked, "He has a brother?"

Prudence shushed her. "But why is that bad? Doesn't he approve?"

"Well, I can't be certain. You see, upon entering the downstairs library late last night, I assumed it was Mr. B. Townsend who sat brooding in the dark. I found out later that it was his brother, Mr. D. Townsend, instead. I had railed at him, insulted him and divulged intimate secrets which would have been better left unsaid."

"Intimate secrets?"

"Shhh, Audrey." Prudence turned to Jillian. "Oh, my dear. What did he say to all this?"

"Nothing. I didn't allow him to speak."

"What is his name?"

"What did you do next?"

The girls had spoken at the same time. "Daniel," she said to Audrey, then to Prudence, "I came up to my room and went to bed, fully expecting to leave this morning."

"Then what happened?" Prudence encouraged with a nod.

"Now, promise me you won't think me fickle."

Both girls shook their heads.

"We talked and he reassured me about his brother. Then he convinced me to stay on for a week or two."

Prudence and Audrey both became giddy, clapping their hands and bouncing in their seats.

Jillian held up her hands, urging them to cease their celebrating. "But that's not the best part. He asked my permission to court me properly."

"How lovely," Prudence stated, grinning. "I knew it would all work out."

"Miss Kelley," Audrey interjected with an inquisitive eyebrow arched above twinkling eyes. "You seem to have kept some vital information from Prudence and me — for instance your relationship between yourself and Mr. Townsend and the aforementioned 'intimate secrets'."

While Prudence began to protest Audrey's assumption, Jillian's cheeks heated. The time had come to confess all. Daniel knew, she may as well inform her allies of her little indiscretion. *Indiscretions.* She groaned inwardly. "No, Miss Dearborne. Miss Van Amberg is correct. I haven't told you everything."

By the time Jillian had finished her story, leaving out the

more sordid details of her and Bradley's affair, the girls were speechless.

"I do hope you don't think less of me for everythir.g I've done. Though I wouldn't blame you if you thought I was a complete hussy."

Audrey placed her hand over Jillian's. "On the contrary, Miss Kelley. Why, I think you are the strongest woman I know!"

Prudence nodded in agreement.

A strange noise at the door caused all of them to turn toward it. A note lay on the floor with Jillian's name scrawled across the front in a bold but elegant hand.

Audrey scooped it up and brought it to Jillian.

Terribly excited, she snapped open the seal.

Dear Miss Kelley,
It would be my honor if you were to accompany me to a dinner party and art premiere to be held tonight at Notre Dame University. I shall meet you at the bottom of the stairs at eight p.m.
Yours, J. Bradley Townsend.

"Well if that isn't the sweetest thing." Audrey cooed.

"She's right, Miss Kelley. He's earned points in my book with this formal invitation."

Jillian smiled remembering the 'points' she'd given Bradley for various things when he'd first come to Fairfield Court. It had been then she'd realized that this was no longer a game. What if the only reason he showed any interest in her was because she couldn't resist a good tumble? To bind one to another for that reason only could spell disaster in the long run. Again the thought nagged at her that their acquaintance didn't even span a year's time.

Refolding the note, Jillian spoke. "I'm still not completely comfortable with this. As much as it seems like I do, I really don't know him all that well."

"Miss Kelley," Prudence announced. "I think that is your

head talking as opposed to your heart."

Audrey nodded.

"Perhaps." Jillian smiled wanly. "But if this scheme falls short, be ready to leave at the drop of a hat pin."

At that very moment, Anne entered and announced breakfast could be obtained in the formal dining room.

An unexpected wave of nausea swept over Jillian. The time had come to face Bradley's brother.

She stood and smoothed out her skirts. "Shall we?" she asked, her voice nearly betraying her trepidation.

At the top of the stairs, Prudence and Audrey each took one of her hands and gave them a reassuring squeeze. They started down together, and it reminded Jillian of Anne Boleyn being led to her execution. With each step she took, she realized she should have left this morning as planned. Her feet became heavy, her pace slowing slightly.

No. She couldn't do it. Couldn't face the strange man to whom she'd disclosed all those private things to. Her stomach threatened to turn inside out. She thought to bolt back up the stairs, but Audrey and Prudence likely wouldn't allow it.

All too soon they came to the bottom of the stairs in the cavernous breezeway. With her heart seemingly in her throat, her friends disentangled their hands and they all turned down the wide hallway to find the formal dining room.

Again, Jillian almost made a dash for it until a familiar face emerged from around a corner.

"I was just coming up to fetch you," Mrs. Goodwin said then gave all three girls that warm smile of hers. "This way."

The girls took Jillian's elbows as if they sensed her nervous anticipation. Her pulse pounded in her ears while they followed Mrs. Goodwin down the hallway.

A solitary man stood when they entered, and it wasn't Bradley.

Prudence and Audrey released Jillian when she stopped

short just inside the room, but flanked her like fellow combatants.

"Please. Do come in," Daniel said, leaning on his cane. He held out his free hand to Jillian. "Forgive me for my ill manners last night. I was under the influence of a rather expensive brandy."

She had to admit his smile was nearly as handsome as his brother's. However, Daniel's hair fell almost boyishly across his forehead in soft, feathery waves, quite a few shades darker than Bradley's. His eyes, she noted, were the same dark brown, and his knowing gaze just as unnerving. With her cheeks aflame, she stepped forward to the table and took his proffered hand. He then turned to Prudence and Audrey. "Ladies, I am Daniel Townsend." He introduced himself, Jillian suspected, to alleviate any uncomfortable feelings she may have harbored.

"Mr. Townsend, these are friends of mine, and acquaintances of your brother's from his recent trip to England, Miss Audrey Van Amberg and Miss Prudence Dearborne."

While Daniel greeted the girls, Jillian felt a sense of wonder wash over her that the younger brother seemed as easygoing as Bradley was.

"Please join me, ladies. Brad will be down—"

"Right now," Bradley announced and stepped into the room.

Over her shoulder, Jillian watched him come to a halt behind her. "Allow me?" he asked just before pushing in her chair. He bent to whisper discreetly into her ear. "I'm so sorry I wasn't here when you came down."

She turned her head and murmured back, "Your brother defused the situation with that irresistible Townsend charm."

"I hope you didn't find him too irresistible."

"Jealous?"

"Damn right."

"What are you two whispering about over there?" Daniel

teasingly insisted.

"Nothing you'd be interested in," Bradley assured him.

* * * *

The party chatted amicably throughout breakfast, and much to Jillian's relief, the details of certain moments from the recent past weren't revisited.

"I have a pile of correspondence on my desk upstairs to get through this afternoon, ladies. However, I want you to feel comfortable during your stay, so please visit the library, take tea in the atrium or on the second-floor balcony overlooking the apple orchard. Provided the weather holds, have one of the grooms take you for a ride in our landau — do any number of things which strikes your fancies."

"Brad, I shall be more than happy to entertain your guests while you toil away in your study," Daniel said with a mischievous twinkle in his eyes.

"Of that, I have no doubt, sir." One would have to be deaf not to have heard the sarcasm in Bradley's voice, but because of the way he'd spoken in loving jest about his brother last night, Jillian was positive he was only teasing Daniel.

They rose and Bradley led Jillian to the bottom of the stairs. "Shall I see you at eight, then?"

"It's not a formal affair, is it?" She failed to keep the worry from her voice.

"Not at all. I understand a new art professor is going to be introduced and he'll be showing a few of his own works tonight. It's mostly for the incoming students. I'm quite sure the department isn't expecting dressy attire."

Jillian smiled, relieved. "Good."

Bradley lifted her hand to his lips and lingeringly kissed the back of it. "Until then."

Jillian climbed the stairs and called for Anne. Within moments, Prudence and Audrey were begging entrance to her room.

"Come."

As preoccupied as Jillian was with the thought of going to the art showing with Bradley, she would have considered herself dead if she didn't recognize the look on both the girls' faces. The two cats had divided equally the canary and were about to sit down to the feast.

"Er, Miss Kelley, would you mind terribly if Audrey and I... Well, sort of kept Mr. D. Townsend out of your way?"

These two were cooking something up, and Jillian knew it. "And how, may I ask, would you do that?"

"Well," Audrey offered. "He can't exactly join us about the place, so perhaps — I know! I'll read aloud to him."

"Yes, and fetch things for him if he so desires."

"He is handsome, isn't he?" Jillian asked wryly, already knowing their imminent answer.

Prudence smiled. "He is rather passable."

Audrey turned to Prudence. "Passable? My word, if he isn't the most desirable man I've ever seen..."

Prudence's face softened. "Do you really feel that way, Audrey?" Prudence inquired quietly.

Audrey nodded. "I do indeed."

Prudence grinned like the Cheshire Cat from *Alice's Adventures in Wonderland*. "Then you shall have him."

Jillian had watched the exchange, silent up until now. "Now, ladies, I find the need arising to inform you that Bradley's brother is not a horse which is for sale."

"Miss Kelley, I'm sure you have read *Emma*, by the one and only Miss Jane Austen?"

Ah, here lay a subject Jillian knew very well. "Why, yes. In fact, I had composed many a paper on Miss Austen while at Oberlin. *Emma* is high up on my list of favorites."

"Then from here on out, you may refer to me as Miss Woodhouse." Prudence giggled.

Audrey turned to Jillian. "Really, Miss Kelley, it's what we've been playing at from the beginning when one thinks on it. We've been merely assisting Cupid with his work."

Jillian grinned at the mention of Eros and felt an

accompanying flush rise from her body's core.

"Nay, Miss Kelley," Prudence replied whimsically. "Mr. Daniel Townsend isn't a horse to be bought, but more like a wild stallion that needs to be caught."

Audrey chuckled. "And as we said to each other quoting Shakespeare, Prudence and I, when we set out to make certain you and Mr. Bradley Townsend mended the rift between you, 'If it proves so, then loving goes by haps'."

Prudence nodded. "Some, Cupid kills with arrows, some with traps."

Jillian could only shake her head at the girls. "Then I shall light a candle for the soul of Daniel Townsend."

Chapter Twenty-Four

Daniel swallowed the last bit of tea from the cup Miss Dearborne held for him. "You haven't allowed me to lift a finger all day long. I'm going to be so spoiled, I won't be able to don my own trousers come tomorrow."

The lovely Miss Van Amberg moved to sit in the spot Miss Dearborne had abandoned. "But, Mr. Townsend, you are injured and therefore, should have your every need seen to by those of us who are whole," she announced, her voice soft and melodic as she swept cake crumbs from his silk cravat and shirt front.

He grinned, catching the cherub's alluring violet gaze. "I haven't broken my back, you know. I can still walk, feed myself and do all manner of things for myself—and for you." He ended in a whisper, his smile too mischievous to quell.

He watched her glance up at Miss Dearborne who stood across the room at the tea cart. It was obvious the other girl hadn't heard his last declaration. Or perhaps she'd ignored it on purpose.

"And what sort of things could you do for me, Mr. Townsend, reclining against a pile of pillows as you are?" she whispered back.

Oh, she is a saucy one. "Would you honestly care to find out?" he murmured.

Her sweet tongue slid over her lips and Daniel's cock inched its head a fraction higher. Damn good thing a linen napkin lay across his lap.

"Perhaps—" She hesitated for the briefest of moments. "Later tonight?"

The invitation hung in her rapidly darkening eyes and he nearly groaned. "If I don't die from anticipation first."

"Well." Miss Dearborne joined them on the settee once again. "What sort of amusements shall we devise for poor Mr. Townsend after supper?"

The intriguing chameleon, Miss Van Amberg, exchanged her glowing cheeks for a near-bored look and echoed her friend's tone. "Tell us, Mr. Townsend. Have you anything in mind for tonight?"

Daniel dragged his gaze from the cherub's. "Oh, I don't know." He thought fast. "I wish I could play music or something. Do either of you play an instrument?"

"Ugh," Prudence groaned. "Audrey and I are both lacking when it comes to music. We used to tell each of our mothers we were taking lessons at the other's house, and meet up in the woods for more interesting adventures."

Would she ever cease to amaze me? "Well, well. Aren't we naughty?" His eyes fixed on Audrey, insinuating numerous other things. Dark things. *Wicked* things.

Audrey stood, successfully suppressing a sharp intake of breath. She made for the teacart and swept the crumbs from her hands above the empty cake dish. From the moment she'd met Mr. Daniel Townsend, she'd practically been on fire. It was worse when subjected to his knowing stare. She was in trouble and she knew it. If within his words and innuendos lay any truth whatsoever, she knew she would hand over her virtue to him were he to look at her sideways. What a pitiful soul she'd turned out to be. To think that she'd ruin herself with the first handsome face that came along—this sign of weakness would surely render her scarred throughout eternity.

The invitation she'd issued not moments ago to join him later had demanded to be heard. The excitement was too much to bear, however, she didn't wish to appear the harlot. She had tried to think of something else to say, but nothing came.

Glancing around the room she espied the mantle clock.

Turning back to the settee, she spoke directly to Prudence. "My goodness. It's nearing the hour of eight. I'm going to go up and see if Miss Kelley needs assistance before she and Mr. B. Townsend go forth tonight."

"That is a fine idea, Audrey. I'll just make sure Mr. D. Townsend is comfortable and be up to join you shortly."

* * * *

"I feel I haven't seen you all day, Miss Kelley."

Jillian smiled at Audrey's reflection in the mirror. Nearly finished with her hair, Anne had just a few more pins to place and Jillian would be ready. "I know. I do apologize for my social negligence. I really needed to rest this afternoon. The running about thither and yon this past week seems to have caught up with me."

"Perfectly understandable, dear. We'd rather you stayed healthy than run yourself ragged." Audrey nodded, her cherub-like cheeks dimpling in accompaniment to her prim, closed-mouth smile.

Eyeing her friend closely, Jillian tempered a grin. "Have you had enough of playing nursemaid to Mr. D. Townsend?"

Audrey blushed all the way to her hairline. "Well, he has some interesting ideas about touring with his polo team." She clasped and unclasped her hands, then tucked her forearms close to her waist. "And the orchestration of similar prestigious sporting events to entertain the public—" She stopped speaking and glanced at the floor. "I-I just needed a moment or two to myself." Audrey's reaction said it all— Jillian found no need to force the issue, especially in front of Anne, so she let the comment go. "Has Mr. B. Townsend been about at all today?"

"Not that I was aware of. We kept to the formal parlor because of the rain."

"Ah. So much for the weather holding out today, hmm?"

"Indeed." Audrey paused, as if searching for a topic.

"Thank goodness it stopped, though. Otherwise you would've had a time of it tonight. I'm positive tomorrow will be more pleasant."

It was quite obvious to Jillian that Audrey had something on her mind. Now that they knew each other better, the girl no longer chattered on about the weather where there lingered other more important topics to discuss. Watching Audrey's gaze flicker to Anne then back to the floor, Jillian held fast to the suspicion that Audrey held her tongue on purpose until the maid's departure. Jillian followed suit out of respect for her friend.

"I'm finished, Miss Kelley." Anne gave Jillian the hand mirror then retreated a step or two.

Jillian turned and raised the mirror to observe the back of her hair. Patting a couple of curls to check the security of her coiffure, she thanked and dismissed Anne.

The second the door closed, Audrey crumbled.

"Miss Kelley," she rasped. "I don't understand what is happening to me."

Standing, Jillian indicated that Audrey sit with her on the padded bench at the end of the bed. "Allow me to guess. You are confused. Everything you've been taught about being a proper lady just flies out the window when you look at Daniel. Am I close?"

"Close?" Audrey blurted and sat next to her. "You have described my thoughts precisely! What's wrong with me?"

Chuckling, Jillian patted the top of Audrey's hand. "Nothing at all is wrong with you. Did you think that love wouldn't be as forceful as any other emotion we women experience?"

"Love? Do you really think I'm in love with Daniel, and so soon?"

"It's possible."

"Well, how does one know, I mean *really* know?"

"I don't think there is a way." She thought for a moment. "Chemistry between two people is a tricky thing. There are circumstances to consider. Does he love you in return?

Is it the right time for both of you, are their other parties involved? What do your respective families think?" Jillian knew she should have been asking herself these questions about Bradley all along. Regardless, she noticed that Audrey had paled during Jillian's short oration.

"What is it, dear?"

Audrey took a shaky breath. "How on earth can you determine all that when he's standing before you and whispered flirtations are rolling off his tongue, heating the very air around you?"

"Ah. I understand." She nodded once. "It's happened fast and furious, has it?"

Leaning forward, Audrey seemed breathless. "Oh, Miss Kelley — like an unexpected tempest, like lightning, like… like an unseen rut in the road."

Jillian chuckled. "The Townsend brothers apparently are two of a kind."

"Did it happen this way for you, too?"

A knock at the door caused Jillian's pending answer to remain unspoken. Did she merely amuse Bradley? Did they have a future together? Or did their physical chemistry only put a scratch in the surface of what should be deep, soul-entwining love? Would he grow tired of her once their mutual adoration cooled?

Mentally shaking off the dread that had plagued her for most of the day, she answered the call at the door. "Come."

Prudence entered. "Mr. D. Townsend is tucked safely away in his rooms to dress for dinner. I understand Bingham had the staff fetch his clothes from his apartments in town. It's eight o'clock, Miss Kelley, and don't you look delightful?"

Jillian thanked her chatty friend and stood. "How are things progressing with Mr. D. Townsend, Miss Dearborne? Has he proposed to our enchanting Miss Van Amberg yet?"

Audrey half-laughed, half-choked at Jillian's jest.

"Not yet, but time will be the tattle-tale, I think."

Sighing, Jillian brushed the wrinkles from her skirt.

"If only the men would merely sit back and allow us to determine their futures," she remarked dryly.

After the giggles subsided, Prudence asked, "Are you nervous about your outing?"

Waving a hand in dismissal, Jillian added with a shrug, "As anxious as anyone would be, I suppose." There wasn't enough time in a week to dissect her feelings concerning the nerve-racking circumstances in which she found herself entangled.

"Then let's get to it," Prudence announced and held open the door. "We mustn't adhere to anxiety, especially if it's regarding an amusement. It will only serve to hinder the impending pleasure."

Jillian turned to Audrey. "So sayeth Miss Woodhouse."

Audrey's eyebrows drew together. "I don't recall that line in *Emma*," she said to Prudence.

Prudence lifted her chin. "It wasn't. I am taking literary license in this case."

Not trusting her voice, Jillian grinned at Prudence.

"Now don't disappoint us, Miss Kelley." Prudence winked and swept her hand indicating the hall.

* * * *

"So, you've taken to driving your own carriage, Mr. Townsend?"

After settling himself onto the bench of the two-seated, covered buggy, Bradley unfolded a blanket then handed it to Jillian. He then took up the reins. "You don't mind, do you? However, I could have Bingham fetch Anne, that way we'd have a chaperone."

Oh, what a thought! She nearly chuckled while she snuggled into the blanket. "Thank you, but I think I'll take my chances," she said wryly.

Grinning, he clicked the horse into motion. After passing down the long drive flanked by trees which seemed to look down on them with the approval of ancient elders, they turned onto the lane. The moon had come up over the horizon and illuminated the wispy clouds scattered about the sky. The air was crisp, the recent moisture from the rain lingering in the breeze.

"I have a little something for you."

"For me?"

Bradley reached under the seat from where he had pulled the blanket then handed her a brown paper package.

"What on earth...?" She turned to him and watched a slow smile brighten his face.

"Open it and find out."

Jillian slipped the string over the corners and separated the folds of paper. When she lifted the item from the wrapping she began to laugh.

"I thought you would find it amusing."

"I'm afraid I still have yours at Fairfield."

"Don't you worry about it. I have plenty more."

Running her hand over the fabric, she looked up at Bradley. "Odd. I had forgotten you still had my trousers."

He shook his head. "I didn't remember myself until Bingham pulled them from my trunk. Had you not visited, I probably would have kept them as a memento."

"And done what with them?"

Bradley shrugged. "Run them up a flag pole?"

She giggled. "Well, I am indeed grateful you gave them to me instead of airing my dirty laundry, so to speak."

"I would never." He took a breath as if weighing his next words. "However, I am curious."

"Curious? About what?"

"About just how grateful you are."

Jillian couldn't have stopped the bark of laughter if she'd wanted to. She knew exactly what he meant but decided to play coy with him nonetheless. "What would you like, a gold-leafed thank you note?"

He thought for a moment — or at least feigned to. "I think a kiss would do."

Quickly, Jillian reached up and placed a sisterly kiss upon

his cheek.

"That's not exactly what I had in mind."

"You didn't specify."

"Did I have a choice?"

"You may have, had you thought in advance and asked nicely. Besides, where else should I have kissed you?" The spontaneous query escaped before she could stop it, and she caught the beginnings of his grin before she turned away.

"I would have wanted you to kiss me on my—"

"That's quite enough, Mr. Townsend," she interrupted. "I don't think I like where this conversation is headed."

"What? And just where did you think it was going?"

"Somewhere in the vicinity of your trousers, sir." When he began to laugh, she blurted, "And don't try and deny it! I know how you think."

"Then you must know—you owe me a kiss—a proper kiss."

"Yes, well. If the opportune moment arises, then you shall have my thanks in the form of a kiss—at both the time and place of my choosing."

"That's no fair."

She scoffed at him. "The person in charge of doling out the gratitude makes the rules, in case you didn't know."

He chuckled and turned the buggy onto campus.

A pity it was that this romantic affair wouldn't outlast his untried attention span. Jillian's conscience needled at her for the thousandth time that day.

She glanced over at Bradley and observed his dimples as he smiled.

A pity indeed.

Chapter Twenty-Five

"My polo pony is never going to be able to carry me if you ladies insist on serving me a midnight snack on top of everything else you've fed me today."

Prudence giggled. "Is this the same pony which threw you recently?"

"The very same." He grinned.

"Then perhaps your pony deserves a little extra weight upon his back as punishment," Prudence joked. She served the spoonful of crème brûlée to Danny, set the empty utensil upon his dish then turned to Audrey. "You are looking a bit flushed tonight, are you unwell?"

She knew it would be impossible to keep anything whatsoever from her best friend. "I'm a bit tired, is all."

"And you hardly ate any dessert. Come here. Let me see if you have a fever."

Audrey deposited her napkin next to her plate, rose from her seat and rounded the far end of the table. Had she passed the head of the table where Danny sat, she probably would have burst into flame. He'd watched her all night, covertly though, as not to raise suspicion, she was sure. Little did he know that despite his possible interest in her, Prudence had been driving the entire election party in Audrey's favor like a runaway coach and six toward victory. Or so it seemed.

Victory, she harrumphed to herself. *And just which one of us would escape with the winnings? Danny would likely have another notch on his riding crop, but what will I end up with?*

On one hand, Audrey wanted to be alone with him — wanted to feel what a woman felt with a man she was hopelessly attracted to. But the situation frightened her. If he only wanted to use her, it would surely shatter her heart. So there it was. She'd have to make the choice between a brief affair and total heartbreak or never knowing, which could also mean heartbreak. Prudence set her palm upon Audrey's forehead. She sighed. "I can't tell. My hand is just as warm as you look."

"Why don't you let me try? I've sat idle for so long I'm sure my temperature is normal."

"Oh, now Mr. Townsend," Prudence scolded jokingly, "I know plenty of men who would love to be in your pampered shoes."

Smiling at her friend's quip as she approached Danny, his gaze captured hers and her breath caught in her chest. Taking the final two or three steps, she then stopped before him and waited as he scrutinized her.

"Miss Dearborne is correct. You do seem a bit heated."

Indicating her face, he waved her forward. Audrey leaned down to meet his raised hand.

"Hm," he said with drawn-together eyebrows. "Come closer." At once, his hands were on either side of her face and his lips came to rest upon her forehead. Taking great pleasure in the soft caress, she closed her eyes. She could smell his light cologne and how it mixed with his manly scent. She suddenly felt very heavy.

Subtly he moved, placing a muted kiss on her left eyebrow then her right. He turned her head and brushed his mouth over her temple. Her mind spun as he did so. She reached out and set a trembling hand upon his shoulder in case she toppled over.

"Well?" Prudence asked after several rather content seconds ticked by. "How is our patient?"

Danny released her face. "I'd say a bit of sleep would do her some good. Perhaps the same goes for all of us."

"I think so, too," Prudence affirmed. "A fine idea, that." She stood. "Once Mr. Townsend is tucked into bed, I'll assist you, Audrey. Run along to your room now, dear."

* * * *

It took at least a half an hour for Prudence to leave Audrey's side. Her friend meant well, but her attentions were all together unnecessary.

Not that she could tell her so. The fact was Audrey had hardly been able to say a word to her ever since she'd promised Danny a secret liaison later that night. Having known Prudence for as long as she had, her best friend would have been able to detect the apprehensive anticipation in her voice. Audrey peeled the well tucked-in covers from her person then paced the floor of her chamber waiting for just the right moment in which to slip unseen into Danny's room. At once a thought invaded her mind. She had no idea where Danny slept in the massive house of his brother's. And there was no way she would lower herself to go from door to door to inquire as to his whereabouts.

Huffing out a frustrated breath, she flopped down onto the foot of the bed. She'd been saved by her own ignorance. How ironic.

Just then, a soft rap sounded upon her door. Audrey jumped from the bed and took a few steps toward the sound. Halfway to the door it swung open. It was Danny.

Her heart leaped at the sight of him and at the same instant, nearly all of her misgivings melted away.

Still in his black dress breeches, he appeared barefoot, his injured appendage wrapped in thick cloth. His shirt tails dangled wide open and his cravat tie hung undone, reaching from either side of his neck to his upper thighs. He was terribly handsome.

Before she could speak, he held out his hand to her.

"Come with me."

"To where?"

"Anywhere but here."

"Why?"

Danny's gaze swept the room. "Because I grew up in this room and"—his voice dropped to a whisper—"I'd like to be with you somewhere else."

Without another word, she placed her hand in his and he drew her into the hallway. He hurried her along, limping as they went.

"Where is your cane?" she inquired softly.

"It made too much noise on the floor."

She almost giggled aloud. It seemed he'd thought of everything.

In moments he ushered her into a room at the end of the hall away from all the others. At first sight of the bed, her nerves danced along her arms and she spun on her heel to face the door—her last chance at keeping her reputation whole. Among other things. But it was too late. Danny had employed the key to lock them in. He set in on the table next to the door.

He faced her, smiled boyishly and shrugged. "My apologies for the hasty escort."

His grin caused her tummy to do a flip. He was party to the misbehavior just as much as she and suddenly, she didn't give a fig. Her decision settled heavily in her mind. Ruin and heartbreak it would be. "My apologies for the need to have done so."

Danny stepped forward. "There is no need for you to be contrite."

Audrey couldn't possibly disagree. She pressed her lips together and gave him a soft smile.

"Come, sit for a while." He held out his hand to her again.

How could she resist? His strong presence was so comforting. He'd secured the door and the room in which he had chosen to bring her seemed warm and inviting. She placed her hand in his and in moments she was seated on a settee before a friendly fire that winked at her from the hearth. He must have prepared the room for them ahead of time. *How thoughtful of him.*

Sweeping aside a decorative throw pillow from against the back of the seat, Danny then sat facing her. "Are you nervous?"

Her little head tilt was meant to be a carefree toss. She ignored it and gave up a quiet, "No."

"Then look at me."

She had to admit, she wasn't acting like a mature adult at the moment. Inhaling as if filling her lungs would chase away her cowardice, she turned to him. My word, but he was handsome. In the firelight, half of his face dwelt in shadow, but the intensity with which he held her gaze made her feel desirable—wanted, and Lord help her, she fancied his attentions.

He reached out and stroked his hand down her cheek. "May I kiss you?"

"Yes." She almost chastised herself aloud for such a precipitous answer. But before her reaction could be amended, he gently pulled her to him. His lips brushed back and forth over hers and she reveled in the feeling.

This is your first kiss, her brain reminded her. *Hush up*, she retorted. *I plan on having an abundance of firsts tonight.*

Dan felt her lean into him. She simply surrendered to him. Her lips parted easily at his prompting—it must have been her very first kiss. He ended their kiss and looked into her shining eyes. "Are you all right?"

She nodded in accompaniment with the cutest lop-sided smile he'd ever encountered—that dimple reappeared in her left cheek, making her terribly irresistible.

"Are you?"

He began to laugh but stopped himself. "I've never been better."

"Neither have I," she murmured, still smiling.

God, but she is sweet.

She took a hesitant breath. "Would you be put off if I told you that you just gave me my first kiss?"

Dan shook his head. "Not at all. In fact, I thought as much."

Her glistening lips formed a petite 'O' which she held for a long moment. "Was I that obvious?"

This time he did chuckle. He placed the pad of his index finger on her chin just under her ripe lips and studied them closely. "Miss Van Amberg, you have an innocence about you which tells all."

Her countenance turned serious. "And what would you say if I told you I am tired of being innocent?"

He opened his mouth, but nothing came out at first. What was she asking of him? He'd have to clarify if only to set their boundaries. "What can I do to help?"

"Anything you want," she whispered and lay back against the pillow behind her.

"Miss Van Amberg—"

"Please call me Audrey." She purred like a satisfied kitten.

The only other sound in the room was the crackling fire—intimate and cozy, and so right. It seemed the whole night was ideal, and the little angle before him, sweet perfection. He swallowed. "Very well, Audrey. What would you like to learn?"

The corners of her lips curled up. "Everything."

"Everything?" he repeated while his cock stood at attention, ready, willing and most definitely able.

She nodded.

He considered his situation for a moment. A beautiful young girl was requesting his tutelage in the sensual arts.

He should refuse. He was a gentleman, for pity's sake. He didn't use women—well, not unless they were the paying kind, and only once in a while. Said strumpets had schooled him in things that would most likely frighten the chaste cherub who held him captive with her eyes.

He recalled one in particular. She remained faceless in his mind, but he remembered the earth-shattering climax he'd had with her that night. It had taken several pleasurable hours to build. Strange how even the most torrid of pastimes could lend an educational experience that would, in the end, recommend a man.

Refocusing on the beauty before him, he was certain he could achieve the epitome of sexual heights once again—

and give Audrey the same regardless of her virginal status.

"Everything?" he asked once more just to be certain.

"The lot," she whispered.

He reached up and slowly slid his tie from around his neck. "Promise me one thing?"

"Yes?"

"If at any time you feel uncomfortable and wish for me to stop, just say so, and I will."

She tentatively moistened her lips with the tip of her tongue and nodded. Then Audrey's wide, inquisitive gaze fell upon the silk tie in his hand.

Chapter Twenty-Six

"I still can't believe you won the door prize." After her slurred statement rolled from her spirit-scented lips, Jillian's laughter sparkled in the cool night air.

Bradley grinned. They'd enjoyed a significant amount of champagne between the two of them and she was foxed. Again. Just like the fateful night they had met. And made love into the wee hours. His entire body flashed hotly at the thought. To be fair, he admitted he wasn't too far behind her in liquid giddiness, but there was no reason to admonish her for it. One of them had to take the slightly drier road after all, he thought wryly. In retrospect, he was glad his little English sparrow felt free enough to let her inhibitions go whilst in his presence. "What, do you suppose, am I to do with oil paints and the accompanying brushes I won?" He looked at her from the corner of his eye, watching for her reaction.

"Mmmm...?" Jillian tilted her head and gazed out into the starry night. "Perhaps you could paint a lan...scape and include that exquisite house of yours in the background."

Grinning at the way she'd turned the adjective into two words, Bradley repeated her. "Exquisite?" The time was ripe to tease his Jilli, perhaps get a rise out of her — watch the sparks in her eyes. Her feisty nature, when pricked, caused her normally pretty looks to simply smolder. "So, you only like me for my home, eh? You are just like Elizabeth Bennett, who showed no interest in Mr. Darcy until she saw Pemberley." He harrumphed mockingly.

A squeak of protest came from his bubbly companion. "Well, Mr. Townsend." She swallowed — most likely a hiccup. "It appears you never read *Pride and Pre...judice*. Had you bothered to, before making such an unschooled ob...servation, you would have known that 'Lizabeth Bennett was too prideful to admit her feelings for Darcy. Though she'd secretly had them from the first moment they'd met." She nodded once then smiled smugly. "Hence, the title of the book."

"Ah, yes. The literary major."

"That's right. And don't you forget it. If anyone is familiar with 'the great romance between ink and paper' 'tis I."

Bradley grinned, rather impressed that she'd remembered his coined phrase, as tipsy-caked as she was. "So because you are so well-versed in literary history, you shan't repeat it."

"Lit...erary history, no."

"And what of our history?"

Jillian pulled back and placed her hand above her chest. "Please, Mr. Townsend. Don't think I don't know what you're thinking."

"What am I thinking?"

"I think you're thinking exactly what I think you're thinking."

He began to laugh. "I think you're confusing everyone within earshot."

"Me?"

"Indeed."

"I can't imagine why," she said almost indignantly.

"Then, answer the question."

After a significant pause, Jillian turned to him. "There was a question?"

He grinned then sobered, feigning offended airs. "Well, if you're going to be forgetful—"

"I haven't forgotten!" she interrupted.

"All right. Go on then." He nodded once then waited, knowing full well she'd lost the train of thought long ago. Glancing at her, he observed her eyebrows drawn together in earnest thought.

"Well?" he taunted, watching the wheels in her head spin via the look upon her face.

"I-I."

"Yes?"

"I...owe you a kiss."

"You—" Good God, he had almost forgotten himself, what with all the teasing he'd been serving up to Jillian. He turned to her and smiled. "Correct again, my dear. My but you have a bright mind."

Bradley watched as her lips broke into a smile. She had no idea of just how alluring she was.

One more bend in the road and they would be at the drive to his home. He pulled the horses to a stop, set the reins down and turned to her. "All Right, I'm ready."

Still smiling, she shook her head. "You really are a scoundrel, aren't you?" Her question sounded more like a statement of fact to his ears.

"I, madam?"

"You are. You always get your way no matter the cir... cumstances."

He snaked his arm around her slim waist and pulled her closer. "I know what I want, there's no denying it."

"Neither is there any denying you of your desire."

Pulling her closer still, he murmured against her lips, "Primarily when it comes to you."

She made to move away but he wouldn't let her. "Your voice tickles my mouth."

"Then open up to me, Jilli." His lips touched hers gently but only for a moment. "And let me in." He'd ended in a whisper.

J. Bradley Townsend was at it again, but this time, she didn't care. She didn't want to think about their nonexistent history as acquaintances and the fact that she didn't know him very well. The one thing this trip showed her was that they had indubitable chemistry together.

But that was all. There was nothing beyond.

Jillian leaned in and kissed him back. He tasted utterly wonderful. His body was so warm against hers. She didn't want to think about what they didn't have. She just wanted this moment. And once she returned to England, she'd treasure it forever.

Their tongues began the familiar dance which was second nature to Jillian now. His hands pressed her to him harder, closer, and her world spun. All of a sudden, her lungs felt as if there wasn't enough air around the whole earth to fill them. She broke out of the kiss and inhaled deeply.

He gazed into her eyes, a question in his own.

Once more. Once more with this beautiful man before I leave for home. She'd cherish the memory of his lovemaking for the rest of her life. "I think you'd better take me home now," she murmured.

He nodded once and whispered, "Stay with me tonight, Jilli. In my room. In my bed."

She tutted at him. "Well, of course, silly. Why do you think I asked you to take me home?" *What did he think I meant?*

In seconds, he had the carriage tearing up the drive to the main house. She smiled. He was certainly in a hurry.

The carriage had barely come to a stop when he jumped out. In a blink of an eye he'd gone around the rear and, appearing at her side, extracted her from the seat. Even before a single groom appeared, he ran up the front steps with her still in his arms. She held fast to his broad shoulders while he practically kicked the door open.

He flew up the stairs as if she weighed no more than a feather, up a third curving flight of stairs to the master suites and in moments, he set her before the fire in his bed chamber. Bingham must have anticipated Bradley's arrival, she mused.

She watched their fingers twitch as they worked at each other's fastenings. They giggled and hissed as things seemed not to work nearly as fast as they would have liked.

Finally, after she kicked off the stockings he'd rolled

down her calves, they stood before each other, naked and heated. His seeking hands went to her aching breasts and, sucking in a breath at the exquisite feeling of his palms, she reached up and removed the pins from her hair. Letting them slide out of her hands, she didn't care where they fell. His skilled fingers seemed to be everywhere, skimming her nipples, her belly, her shoulders, her back. She reached for his shoulders and her insides trembled. His skin was on fire, matching the heat of her own and she could feel his erection pressing against her belly. She dipped her hands down, skimming his well-defined chest, then smoothed her fingers up to his neck and into his hair.

"Jilli," he groaned, his voice sending urgent shivers over her. "Perhaps we should talk first."

"You never wished to talk before—and you've taught me well."

He took a breath to reply but she wouldn't let him. "No talking. Just take me."

Without another word, Bradley caught her up again and carried her to his bed. Kneeling in the center he loosened his grip and let her slide down to the burgundy and gold, velvet and satin, down-filled coverlet.

There was no slow seduction this time. No play, no teasing of straining body parts. He helped her to recline back against the pillows and covered her with his body. They did fit so perfectly together. He entered her heated center easily and with an undeniable insistence.

She gasped when he began to ravish her. His breath came harsh as his tongue glided around the rim of her ear.

"Jilli. My Jilli," he whispered a few times in sync with his grinding lower body.

God, but she wanted the empty ache deep inside to be filled—and yet she never wanted Bradley to stop making love to her. She could sense the tension building, feel her insides turn molten and swell as if reaching for him, urging him to dive deeper. With his tongue and lips, he found her neck, his teeth scraping her sensitized skin in between kisses. "Don't stop —" she rasped.

He groaned deep within his throat. He had taken her, just like she'd told him to. And it was Heaven.

Bradley changed his angle of approach and in that instant, she lifted one of her legs. Her calf grazed the side of his arm and he paused. At once he sat back and maneuvered her knee so that it crossed her body, then began again, thrusting himself to her yielding flesh.

Her breaths were coming in gasps now. This new angle allowed him to go deep. Very deep. Her insides clutched at him and her end was coming hard and fast.

"Oh. God. Bradley!"

He pressed into her while her insides trembled and gripped at him, and the muscles over her entire body spasming and twitching. It was wild. Overwhelming. Delicious. And when she began to calm, he began anew, this time harder than before, seeking his own end.

So intense were the sensations, something halfway between a scream and a groan tore from her throat. His voice echoed hers as he poured into her.

Their pounding hearts beat out a cadence between them. Their heavy breathing and a faint crackling from the fire were the only sounds in the room. Lulled by the ambiance, their adoration cooled in tandem and sleep came to claim them.

The last thought that scuttled through her head before she allowed her awareness to slip away was the regret she felt for having to leave him in the morning. *This time, forever.*

Chapter Twenty-Seven

Jillian had managed to slip away without waking Bradley. She'd gathered her discarded garment pieces and proceeded straightaway for her rooms. Her head only mildly ached from the champagne the night before, deterring her from sitting down for a good, long cry. However, she anticipated the gushing arrival of her tears the very next time she found herself alone and unoccupied. On the train journey to New York she would give herself time to think about the fact that she was leaving Bradley and their torrid scenario behind. Steeling herself against her resolve, she reached the door to her room.

It just wasn't complete, what they had. It was only physical chemistry, nothing more. They had not a single thing to occupy their time together but bed games. And two people could not exist happily for the rest of their lives with only that between them.

This was not an Austen novel, nor was she Marianne Dashwood, nor was the lovely home she'd left behind in South Bend, Combe Magna. Nor should she desire them to be so. *Honestly, once the fires of the body go out in years to come, what would we have in common? What would we do, merely sit and stare at each other?*

The thought nearly made her stomach lurch. She entered her chamber and crossed to knock on Anne's door.

"Miss Kelley, are you unwell?" Anne answered, sleepy-looking but alert.

"I am well, but we are leaving as soon as possible. I can manage my few items. Once you pack your things, please wake Miss Van Amberg and Miss Dearborne and see if they require assistance. Then alert Mrs. Goodwin of our departure. Tell her I have requested that the rest of the house, including the master, are not, under any circumstances, to be disturbed."

The tiniest hint of a smile, which to Jillian seemed presumptuously smug, lifted the corner of the maid's lips. No doubt she was anxious to get back to Mrs. Kelley and give her report. Anne sobered, nodded then went again into her small room.

And she didn't give a fig as to what Anne told her mother, either. It was her mother, after all, who kept a gossiping maid in her employment, not Jillian.

She shrugged off the notion as unimportant and made to gather her garments from the armoire, but paused at the window. The light which crept across the sky displayed a soft gray-blue at this hour. If luck was on her side, they'd be on their way well before dawn broke.

* * * *

Audrey couldn't help but smile. Not moments ago, Danny had ushered her back to her room. He kissed her and said he wished they could have stayed snuggled in his bed until noon. However, he had expressed his concern about her being able to hold her head high in front of her friends. She'd assured him that she would do so regardless, but he insisted.

A tiny giggle escaped her lips. The things he'd done to her... Never, not even when she'd played that naughty game of charades with his brother, did she even imagine such wicked things existed.

And that she'd like them.

Upon his bed, he'd tied her hands above her head and stroked her body with a fan full of white ostrich plumes. Up and down, back and forth until she'd been frantic with sensation. Then he'd placed kisses all over her upper torso and belly, pausing just above the juncture her legs.

She smiled to herself when she remembered his reaction when she'd asked him if he was going to kiss her pussy.

His eyes had gone huge. "Where on earth did you learn that word?"

What was she to say, 'from your brother?' She'd shrugged a shoulder in hopes he'd let the answer lie, which he had. But then he'd asked her if she wanted him to. She had only one answer. "Yes," she'd replied tremulously, "and lick it, too."

He'd required not another word more. He'd nudged her legs apart and feasted upon her person. It had been, without a doubt, the most exquisite feeling in the world. Her — what was the word he'd used? Orgasm. Yes, that was it. Her orgasm had sent her to the stars and when she'd fallen back to Earth, he'd had more wicked things planned for her.

"Now let's make believe you've captured me to have your way with me. You can do anything you'd like to me."

Without question, she'd followed him back to the floor in front of the fire. She'd tied his hands above his head and explored every hard inch of him. Then he'd taught her to put her mouth on him the way he had on her. She'd obviously done it right — his reactions had encouraged her to explore and use her own imagination with his body.

When it had seemed he could no longer stand it, he'd told her he was going to break free of his bindings and take his revenge.

She'd ignored him, of course, until at once, he'd done exactly what he'd promised.

It seemed her maidenhead had merely moved aside. She'd heard there was pain when a woman gave up her virginity. But it was glaringly obvious to her that these women didn't have nearly as skilled a lover as she did.

Audrey covered her mouth so she wouldn't laugh aloud. There were things she wanted to tell Prudence about her adventurous evening, but she couldn't possibly divulge all. Some things should remain private between a man and a woman.

As for her future, who knew where this liaison would lead? One thing was for certain, if she did return to England, the woman she'd turned out to be wouldn't for a moment tolerate a lesser man, one who couldn't fill the shoes of Danny as a lover, to be her husband. With all her heart she wished that Danny could be that man, but they, quite literally, lived an ocean apart.

Whatever happened, she at least had a week, if not two, of nights that would be filled with the physical heights that Danny knew how to bring her to. She hoped it was true that he felt the same about her. He had said as much, after all.

Her breath caught in her throat when a knock came at her door. Was she really the siren Danny had claimed her to be, and even now he could not stay away?

She tiptoed over to the door and pressed her ear to it. "Who is it?"

"It's Anne, Miss Van Amberg."

Instantly, reality came rushing back and she opened the door for Anne.

"Miss Kelley has asked me to come and fetch you and your things. We are to leave for home immediately."

Audrey turned away from Anne's self-righteous tone. She sounded entirely happy they were quitting this beautiful house — and the equally beautiful men within its walls. "Have you awakened Miss Dearborne yet?" she asked over her shoulder.

"No, miss."

"Would you be so kind as to do so, then come back for me?"

"I shall." And the door shut with a soft click.

Audrey felt sick to her stomach. She thought she'd have at least a week with Danny. For Heaven sakes, she couldn't exactly tell her traveling companions that she wanted to stay behind, let alone expound upon the reasons! Panic overcame her and her lungs pulled in air as if desperate for it. She probably wouldn't even be able to say goodbye to Danny. Tears stung her eyes and spilled forth. She momentarily quelled the great sobs which loomed at the back of her throat and she turned to the bed to throw herself atop it. She beheld the writing desk cross the room and swallowed down the emotion. Perhaps if ink and paper were found within she could leave him a message.

Hurriedly circumventing the bed, she then stopped in front of the desk and opened the drawer. A bottle of ink, a blotter and a few sheets of stationery, her salvation, seemed to await her instructions as if in anticipation. She pulled out the stool and sat. Arranging the items, she then uncorked the ink and took up the pen.

Once the pen tip was sufficiently wet, she wrote an upper case "I" onto the page. She paused and spoke aloud.

"I am leaving for— No. I must— No."

As if her hand knew what was in her heart, it touched pen to paper and wrote the words, 'am sorry.'

With fresh tears in her eyes she jotted down her initials, "A.V.A."

Replacing the ink and extra paper, she then folded the note and stood, determined to slide it under his door — the door to the room in which they'd made love all night long. Swallowing a sob, she hurried down the hall.

* * * *

The house shrunk in the distance while they made their way down the drive in the Townsend carriage. Jillian thanked Mrs. Goodwin for honoring her request even though the woman had protested up and down about waking the master.

For the tenth time that morning, Jillian blinked back tears. It was for the best, she kept telling herself. She had no business giving herself to a man — repeatedly giving herself to a man, who would probably never marry her. Didn't they say, "Why buy the cow if you can get the cream for free?"

He hadn't declared his love nor his devotion. And with

that knowledge in her pocket, she would have waited until the twenty-first of never before he asked for her hand. Not only that, but they had nothing in common, and what justification could have prompted her to say yes were he to ask? She couldn't live like that, having no history whatsoever with him.

So, yes. It was for the best that she left for home.

It wasn't long until the train station came into sight. They gathered their meager belongings, and Jillian thanked the Townsend driver, dismissing him. She watched the carriage draw away from the curb. When the conveyance disappeared around a bend, her connection with the man she would always love was stretched thin like a thread, if not broken altogether. It was time to look to her future. A future without J. Bradley Townsend. And bleak it was.

Jillian purchased tickets for the end car. She thought to give her friends, who had been curiously silent all the way to the station, seats in the most luxurious car — the one just before the caboose, farthest from the noise of the engine. She put Anne in the car ahead of theirs. She could no longer stand to look at the smiling maid when she herself felt a long-term depression was about to make itself at home where her heart used to be.

They settled into the velvet seats of their compartment to await departure. They had but a half an hour until the train pulled away from South Bend, separating her from Bradley forever.

* * * *

Bradley smiled still half-asleep. His Jilli, his lady love, was in for a grand surprise when at supper tonight, in front of everyone, he would propose that they become husband and wife. He would go into the safe and choose one of his mother's rings and offer it and everything he owned, the name of Townsend, including his eternal devotion to her.

Wishing to take the yet sleeping bundle next to him in his

arms and hold her in the early morning light, he rolled over, stretching his arm high into the air to gather her soft, warm body to his. His hand curved to scoop her up, however, his digits met with a cold pillow. Bradley's breath caught and he pushed up onto his elbow to get a better view of what obviously had become misplaced at some point.

Jilli was gone.

He drew air into his lungs to launch a string of curses when a ruckus at his door stayed his tirade.

"Brad, wake the hell up!" Dan's voice bellowed from the hallway and a pounding fist, which Bradley recognized from years of deflecting blows, hammered on his bedroom door.

Other than the fact that Jilli was not in his bed where she belonged, something else must have happened for Dan to appear at his room at dawn, agitated as a wet cat.

During the beating of his door and more cursing from his brother, Bradley threw on his trousers and saved both the fist and the wood from further abuse.

He yanked open the door. "Dan, for God's sake, you'll wake the whole house."

"Said whole house has decided to evacuate, so there's no harm there," he sneered sardonically.

Bradley's heart gave one hard thump then plummeted to his stomach. "What?"

Dan leaned on the frame of the door fully clothed, his cane tucked underneath his arm like a riding crop. "Mrs. Goodwin, in her over-efficiency, decided to have the guest rooms cleaned once the girls departed before dawn this morning. She apparently employed the entire staff and the noise was as if an army decided to march through. I awoke and inquired as to the commotion and, just short of having to attach wild horses to one of her legs and dragging her around the front lawns, she confessed."

Despite his brother's vivid scenario, Bradley's anger accelerated at an alarming rate. He turned to gather clothing items in which to be seen out of doors in when he whirled back to face Dan. "Where did she say they were headed?"

"The train station. Hurry, dammit, or we'll miss them!" He shooed at Bradley, as if frantic about the departure of the ladies.

Bradley scooped up a clean shirt from his bureau drawer and slipped it over his head. His brother's near fit was certainly odd. Grabbing his waistcoat from the night before and thrusting his fists through the arm holes, he addressed Dan. "I can't help but notice your over-concern. Why are you in such a rush to catch Miss Kelley's party?"

While he tucked the tails of his shirt into his trousers, he watched Dan's mouth open and shut a few times like a koi fish. Then his brother cleared his throat and folded his arms across his chest. "I—" he began, but paused while Bradley buttoned his waistcoat and reached for his cravat.

"Well?"

Dan exhaled through his nose as if annoyed he was being asked to present an answer to the question.

"I—"

Bradley sat to slip on his boots. "Yes, that much we know."

Dan growled at him. "All right." Then he sobered. "I've suddenly developed a deep desire to sire many violet-eyed children."

Instead of the bark of laughter which became caught in his throat at the thought of Jilli's womb nurturing a baby of their own, Bradley stood and clapped Dan on the back. "Race you to the stables."

Chapter Twenty-Eight

It hadn't been very long, but Jillian woke with a start from a cat nap as they waited for the other train passengers to embark. She looked at Prudence and Audrey and found that their heads were together. Hushed whispers floated by Jillian's ears and it seemed they could hardly restrain their frantic hand gestures. Whatever it was they were talking about must have been simply riveting.

At once they glanced up at Jillian and their conversation came to a halt.

"Miss Kelley." Prudence smiled woodenly at her. "We thought you were asleep."

"I—" Jillian's explanation was cut short as a huge black shadow flew by the window, briefly cutting off the light.

"What on earth—?" Audrey leaned her head against the glass.

"What was that?" Prudence asked as Audrey reached for the latches to open the window.

"Do you see them?" Bradley yelled to Dan while he hung out of the two-seater he and Jillian had taken to the art show the night before. He looked hastily into each of the windows of the train as they passed by.

"You are going too bloody fast!" Dan hollered back. Just then, the whistle blew, announcing the train's departure.

"The train is leaving the depot! I have no choice!" Bradley pulled the carriage to a skidding stop well after passing the engine, which was now steaming its way toward them. "What the hell am I going to do?"

"We need to get their attention!" Dan offered, even

though it wasn't exactly helping.

Bradley froze. "Under the seat!"

"What?"

"Pull everything out from under the seat! The package and the paints."

Dan only eyed his brother for a second before doing as he asked.

All three girls poked their heads out of the window.

"It seems to be someone who has missed their departure time, I'm guessing." Jillian shrugged.

"Oh, yes. I see their carriage up ahead of the train, just to the right. There." Prudence indicated with a point of her finger.

Well, so much for that brief and unexciting distraction. Without further comment, they settled back onto the seats.

"I shall indeed miss South Bend," Prudence sighed, but when neither Jillian nor Audrey commented, the girl fell silent once again.

Jillian felt for her, but there was no way either of the girls would miss it as much as she would.

An odd noise, not unlike applause, floated to their compartment. The applause became louder, accompanied by unintelligible yet jovial shouts.

"Have the travelers lost their wits?" Audrey asked, half-joking most likely.

Prudence shook her head. Jillian glanced up at the window as did Prudence and Audrey.

Prudence, who was closest to the window, stood with an inhalation of breath. "Oh, my word. Look!"

Jillian and Audrey stood and popped their heads out of the window.

Standing at the head of the train there was a man holding a sign above his head.

"Marry Me, Jilli," Audrey read aloud.

"Good God! Those are my trousers he's painted on!" Jillian blurted before pulling her head inside.

Audrey turned to Jillian and took her by the shoulders. "Miss Kelley. I know you had your reasons for leaving so hastily this morning, but now you must be honest with yourself. Do you love Mr. Townsend?"

Jillian's heart pounded, gaining her attention—and her soul cried out for the man who had gone to great lengths to make his intentions known, regardless of the fact that it was in front of a trainload of people.

For once in her life, her heart screamed louder than her head. And it was about bloody time. There was no denying it now. History or no, she did love him. And she couldn't possibly survive without him by her side, seducing her, loving her, for the rest of her life.

"I— I do! I love him. Oh, God, how I love him!" Her voice broke but she didn't care.

All three girls looked toward the window at the same time the train passed Bradley holding the sign and Daniel standing next to him, frantically searching the passing windows.

Jillian couldn't move—couldn't speak. Barely breathed.

"What should we do?" Audrey said, rather alarmed. "We're leaving them behind!"

Bringing Jillian out of her frozen state, Audrey addressed her in a calm, motherly like voice. "Miss Kelley. It appears you have a decision to make."

She almost laughed. "What do you propose I do, jump from the train?"

A sly smile lifted the corners of Prudence's lips. She reached for the emergency stop cord, her fingers curled around it, but she paused, looking to Jillian for her acquiescence.

Jillian glanced at Audrey who looked back with wide eyes.

"I don't know, I don't know!" she said, more flustered than she'd ever been in her life.

"Miss Kelley, is he worth it?" Prudence asked.

Holding her breath for what seemed like an overly long few moments, Jillian finally gave Prudence a tiny nod.

Prudence grinned. "I've always wanted to do this." With much vigor, she pulled down hard on the emergency cord.

Bradley dropped his arms, unable to believe she'd slipped from his grasp again. It would be impossible to go after her now, what with the semester's beginning just around the corner. Jillian's trousers slid out of his hands and fell unceremoniously to the ground. The brothers stood there, staring at the caboose of the train which had past them moments before, picking up speed as it went.

Suddenly, there was a high-pitched sound like metal against metal.

The bloody train was screeching to a halt!

Bradley's soul soared.

Jillian stepped from the train and began running toward the brothers Townsend. Instantly, Bradley headed for her, meeting her halfway. He caught her up in his arms and hugged her tightly to his chest.

When her cheek touched his, it felt wet. He pulled away and looked into her red-rimmed eyes. Tears streamed down her beautiful face in rivulets.

"I'm sorry I ruined your trousers," he murmured.

Jillian choked on what sounded like laughter then recovered. "I've been so utterly stupid."

He shook his head. "No. You've been logical."

"Hang logic! When it comes to matters of the heart, I'm a complete buffoon!"

Bradley chuckled and hugged her tighter. "And I'm not?"

"Well," she murmured. "Perhaps you are, too."

"Then let us go through this life fumbling over one another."

She giggled.

He sobered. "Marry me, Jilli."

"Yes." She sniffed and nodded. "Yes, I will." At that precise moment, they pivoted to watch Audrey and Prudence approach. Without a word, Audrey stood next to Daniel. Right next to him. Not a glimmer of light shone between them.

Jillian turned in his arms and whispered, "I think Daniel and Audrey may have formed an attachment."

"It gets worse." Unable to hide the grin in his voice, he wiped away the tears left on her cheeks with the pads of his thumbs.

"What?"

"I think he's going to ask for her hand," he murmured then pulled her closer.

"Well, good for them," Jillian said, snuggling against him.

"Who is responsible for stopping my train?" A tall, broad-shouldered man in dirty overalls was nearly upon them, voice bellowing, eyes glaring. As big and angry as he was, he could have frightened a pack of guard dogs.

"Walter?" Dan asked as the man got closer. "Walter Oswald?"

The large man stopped when he reached Dan. "Oh, hello, Danny," he murmured then turned back to the girls and shouted, "Which one of you stopped my train?"

"So, you've become an engineer. I remember you talking about it a few years back."

Daniel was obviously trying to divert his attention from the girls, a good idea in Bradley's book.

He glanced back at Dan. "Yup. And this was my very first solo trip." He turned back to the girls and glowered. "I will find out who set my schedule back and have you in irons before you can write to your mother!" he bellowed again.

Before anyone else could react, Prudence stepped forward, sparks flying from her eyes. "I stopped your silly train." She then held her wrists out. "Are you as good as your word? Will you restrain me post-haste?"

Audrey coughed. Or was that a laugh? Jillian then observed Daniel give Audrey the oddest look — a quirked eyebrow indicating a silent inquiry. Audrey merely gave him a sly grin.

Jillian turned and whispered to Bradley, "So Daniel

knows this Oswald fellow?"

He nodded. "School chums from way back."

Mr. Oswald had stood there with his jaw hanging open while he stared at Prudence. "Well, Mr. Oswald? Do haul me away. I'm dreadfully anxious to get to the interrogation."

He was handsome in a rugged sort of way, but if Daniel had been friends with him for years, Jillian supposed Prudence would be safe with him. *The question is, will he be safe with Prudence?*

His arms crossed over his massive chest and the side of his mouth quirked up in a grin. "Are you, now?"

Reemphasizing her statement, Prudence lifted her wrists higher.

Bradley cleared his throat, interrupting the staring match between the little English girl and the burly engineer. "Take good care of her, Oswald. I'll hear about it if you don't."

Jillian stepped forward and placed in Prudence's palm a handful of paper money. "This is for Anne. Give her a choice. Tell her she can stay in the States with me or go home to my mother."

Prudence grinned. "I shall. However, if she decides to go back to England and admonishes me for my adventurous spirit, I shall send her to Greenland by accident."

Jillian laughed. "Fair enough." She glanced over at Audrey who was now cuddling with Daniel.

"Come here, my love." Bradley pulled her to him.

How ironic that the impulsiveness, in which proper English girls were taught by society to avoid, found its way into all three of their lives. *Sometimes the heart does know better than the head*, Jillian realized with astonishment.

Mr. Oswald offered his elbow to Prudence. She took it and they made for the train. Just as they reached the caboose, Prudence turned back to the party and shouted, "And to think, Miss Kelley. None of this would have happened if you hadn't let us borrow your trousers."

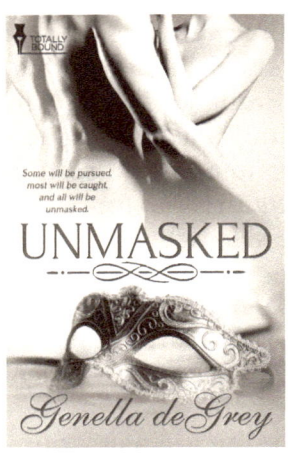

Unmasked

Excerpt

Chapter One

Venice, Italy, 1795

They call it 'carnal knowledge'. The tension melted from Weston's shoulders. It was nothing short of divine the way certain women just knew how to fulfill a man's desires, such as the one now sucking his cock. Somehow, she'd known every sweet spot, every pressure point on his torso and below that triggered the ultimate bliss in which he was now entrenched. It had taken little effort to lay down his money and body without so much as a few words.

"I wish a room with a bath and a proficient female companion, please," he'd respectfully requested in Italian and slipped a purse-full of silver *ducato* into the madam's palm. It was likely an overly generous sum, but he was on holiday. And wasn't the whole purpose of saving a hefty portion of one's income all winter long to indulge one's self in pleasures untold in lands far away?

He'd garnered the directions to this recommended establishment from a couple of his well-traveled peers back in London. And oh, how right they'd been to suggest this particular house.

The woman between his legs fondled his balls as her jaw went slack. She grazed the head of his penis against the roof of her mouth and down her throat.

His orgasm was building, but he was in no hurry. He *needed* this. He'd gone without for the longest time since he'd discovered the magic of being buried hilt-deep between a woman's lips — either the top or the bottom set. Either way, didn't matter to him just as long as she was accomplished in the baser arts. So he'd allow her free rein of his body for now. He drew a deep breath and exhaled a moan, sinking further into relaxation.

His sister and her entourage would arrive within mere hours, and he'd be obliged to spend at least one meal per day with them. While he loved his twin sister, he'd much rather spend his time in the luxurious brothels of Venice. Discretion was not foremost in his mind here as it was back at home. No one knew of him in this beautiful city, which would equate to no wagging tongues — save the one licking a circle around his anus at this very moment.

And with a companion who knew the lay of his land, why would he want to be anywhere else?

The woman stopped for a moment to enquire of him in Italian, "Can I do it differently for you?" In her eyes hung what could only be self-doubt.

"No, no. You are doing just fine, love. I'm taking my time not because of your skills — which are exquisite — but for reasons that have to do with my travels. I came directly to this room off the boat from England, you see, and it was an uncomfortable if not awkward crossing, to say the least. So, please continue."

"*Si,*" she replied with a grateful grin and licked the head of his cock, drawing it into her mouth once again.

* * * *

Smelling of French-milled soap, Weston waited at the end of the jetty, waving back at his sister as she stood upon the bow of the approaching Royal Navy ship. Slow was the going, but now that he'd been properly gratified by that achingly competent Venetian woman, he'd found a heavenly new patience.

"Weston!" She waved. "You look like you belong here," she shouted above the din of the sailors, scuttling hither and yon.

He smiled at her observation. Had he no other obligations for the rest of his life, he'd surely consider living here. But as it was...

He strode over to the gangplank and, once Gwen reached the bottom, he greeted his twin sister with a tight hug. "Is the Admiral's daughter properly wed, then?"

"Quite. The ceremony at sea was rather impressive. She is now on her honeymoon to her new husband's familial holdings in Austria. We are the last civilians to disembark after the wedding. Admiral Forbes was so accommodating. He lent us his cabin once all the other passengers had gone."

She seemed overly chatty at the moment — even for Gwen — but he ignored the girlish inclination. "And where is Miss Ellie?" His gaze landed at the top of the gangplank. Wherever his sister ventured, her best friend wasn't far behind. He quickly scanned the fore and aft of the portside deck but she was nowhere to be found.

A few sailors swept passed them. "Gwen, where is Ellie?"

Gwen made an unnecessary study of her gloved fingers.

The men who'd just disembarked laughed, drawing Weston's attention. There, just ahead of them, he spotted a young woman, scurrying towards the palazzo of Signore Bernardo, the host for their holiday, a leather valise in each hand. He took in the sight of the unmistakable bounce of her lush, chocolate brown curls from below her bonnet and the tiny waist set atop her fashionable, blue silk brocade-draped panniers. It was, without a doubt, Ellie Appleton.

He released his sister. "Gwen?" He'd be the first to admit that his tone was accusatory, but Gwendolyn Rawleigh wasn't exactly the type of girl whom anyone with a brain trusted implicitly.

"Well…"

He waited for her explanation, but when he realized that none was forthcoming, he began to feel the familiar tension creep up his neck.

"Sister, dear, would you be so kind as to enlighten me with the truth?"

Her gaze flickered to Ellie's retreating form and back. "Ellie went to enquire with *Signore* Bernardo about the rooms. Wasn't it kind of him, being an old friend of Father's, to have offered us a stay at his palazzo?"

Ah. She's chatty because she's done something. Good God, what now? "Don't lie to me, Gwen. Ellie wouldn't have gone ten steps without a chaperone." His gaze once again scanned the immediate area. "By the way, where is said faithful dog?" Weston had expected one, if not two elderly companions to disembark from the ship at any moment.

Apparently, Gwen's gloves required yet another inspection.

"You didn't."

At that moment, Gwen's and Ellie's trunks were brought down the gangplank.

"Oh, good. Please take them to Castello 4196, on the Riva degli Schiavoni, and ask for *Signore* Bernardo." She pointed in the general direction of where Ellie had, in her haste, disappeared to. "Come along, Weston."

She made to step around him but he wouldn't permit it. "I want answers, Gwen."

More books from
Genella DeGrey

The tale of widow Lady Melisande Dupree and Sir Devin Blackburn — a knight who isn't afraid to risk all, including his heart, to save the damsel.

*A proper lady would never steal or lie – nor would she
enjoy the sting of her lover's hand upon her posterior.*

In 1892, just outside Barbizon, France, Virginia Clark tucks away her scandalously wanton ways to become a chef, but her girlhood sweetheart turned assistant, Rory Hughson, has other plans.

In the American Wild West in the summer of 1880, a widow gets another chance at love with a handsome young wanderer.

About the Author

Genella DeGrey

Born and reared in Southern California, Genella DeGrey longed to be your typical blonde, tanned, surfer girl but failed miserably. Unable to sit idle without falling asleep, she embarked upon several artistic endeavours. Make-up and set dressing for the entertainment industry, Resort Enhancement for The Walt Disney Company and writing sexy historical romance top the list of her favourite activities. A consummate closet goth and amateur music and (red) wine enthusiast, she is also a hopeless romantic awaiting the arrival of her very own Mr Romance/Soul Mate with whom to share the rest of her life.

Genella DeGrey loves to hear from readers. You can find contact information, website details and an author profile page at https://www.totallybound.com/

TOTALLY
BOUND

Home of Erotic Romance